Second Chance

Second Chance

Evelyn Geisler

Second Chance

Published by
Lighthouse Christian Publishing
SAN 257-4330
5531 Dufferin Drive
Savage, Minnesota, 55378
United States of America

www.lighthousechristianpublishing.com

CHAPTER ONE

Christine woke up gasping—raw pain eating at her chest.

She struggled to prop herself up on her pillows as she reached toward the nightstand.

Pills! Where are my pills? The early morning light shone on a small brown glass bottle sitting by the lamp. Christine grabbed the container and twisted the lid. Pain seared down her left arm and into her back. She spasmed. The bottle slipped from her hand and rolled across the floor, small white tablets spilling out in a trail behind it.

"Oh, no!" She struggled for air. Desperate, she turned toward the side of the bed, arms reaching toward the floor. Her fingers clawed at the carpet's pile trying to inch their way to the pills.

Christine was too short of breath to make much of an effort. She hung over the side of the bed, panting, hoping the pain would let up so she could get a tablet under her tongue. Her teeth and jaws ached; sweat poured from her face and body.

I need help! What am I going to do?

She looked at the clock on the nightstand. Seven a.m.--too early for the volunteer from Telecare to make her daily check-up call on Christine. *Of course! The phone! Dial 911, Christine, and help will come.*

She grappled with the phone, knocking over a glass of water. As she grabbed at the glass to keep it from falling off the nightstand, she knocked the phone to the floor. She groaned as she heard first the dial tone, then a mechanical voice saying, "If you'd like to make a call...." Her head drooped over the side of the bed. Tears welled in her eyes. The pain surrounded her, all-enveloping, crushing her heart. She wondered how she'd get another breath into her lungs.

Then suddenly, miraculously, the agony was gone.

Christine lay quietly, enjoying relief from her suffering. After a few moments she tried to wipe the sweat out of her gray hair, but her hands felt different. In fact, her whole body seemed changed.

"I feel weightless like one of those astronauts. Did I have a stroke?" She spoke but heard the words only in her head. *What's going on? My body doesn't feel right. Why can't I speak?* Then she noticed the room was getting darker.

"That's strange. I thought the sun was coming up. Maybe we'll have a storm today." Once again she heard the words only in her mind.

The room was very dark now, but there was a bright light in the corner. Christine advanced toward it, knowing instinctively that she would find some answers in the radiance.

As she reached the light, she heard a voice.

"Hello, Christine."

"Great. A light's talking to me. I must be crazy." She tried to compose herself then spoke. "Okay, Mr. Light, who are you?"

"I'm Carello the gatekeeper." The voice in her head was soothing.

"The gatekeeper! What are you doing in my house? How do you know my name?"   She was confused and frightened.

"It's all right, Christine. I'm here to help. Right now you're between heaven and earth."

"Oh, please! Right now I'm hallucinating from the pain."

"Christine, you must believe me. I'm here to help."

"Fine, then help by handing me my pills."

"I'm here to help you in a different way."

Christine's fright turned to anger. "The only way you can help me is to call 911!"

"Please, Christine, listen to me."   Carello's voice quieted Christine.   "We're concerned about your unfulfilled promise. You haven't done what we thought you would."

"What do you mean—unfulfilled promise? I've always kept my promises."

"Yes, you've kept the promises you made to people, but I'm talking about the promise of your life. Let me show you something." Carello pointed to the light.

Christine looked to where he was pointing and saw pictures of her life flickering by rapidly.

"Look. There you are as a young girl. You had good parents. They took you to church and taught you to love and help others." Christine smiled as she saw her family again. "Time passes. You grow up and get married. Still reaching out trying to serve people, I see."

Christine saw herself teaching a Sunday school class. "I forgot all about that," she whispered, then looked back at her existence.

"What have we here?" Carello pointed to a picture. "A brand new baby! You and your husband look so happy at the baptism."

"Stop! Don't--don't show me any more," Christine choked. "I can't bear to see it again!"

"What's the matter?"

"If you know about my life then you know very well what the matter is! My son died when he was ten years old!"

"That's when you stopped believing, wasn't it?" Carello asked gently.

"What was there to believe in? I prayed and prayed to God in Jesus' name when Timmy got sick. He never did any harm to anyone, yet he died." Christine turned away from the pictures. "I decided then and there that Jesus was a myth like the tooth fairy or Santa Claus."

"Have you been happy with that decision?"

"I was never happy about anything again after Timmy died. I carry an ache in my heart all the time. Maybe that's where my heart trouble comes from."

"Again I ask; have you been happy with that decision?"

"The decision was easy. Maybe Jesus lived two thousand years ago, maybe not. Maybe he performed miracles, maybe not. I know he didn't perform any miracles in Timmy's case."

"You're still not answering the question."

"We're talking about a myth here. Why be happy or

unhappy about my decision?"

"Didn't you see other people who were happy in their faith even though they had problems?"

"You mean like Carol, the volunteer with Telecare? I know she's got a sick husband yet she calls me every day to see how I am. You know why she does that? Because it makes her feel good. It has nothing to do with me. She calls, punches her good deed card then goes on her merry way."

"You really think that's the reason Carol calls you?"

"I know it is." Christine looked defiantly at the light. "Seems to me you've been asking a lot of questions. Now I'm going to ask you one. How can you prove Jesus isn't a myth?"

The gatekeeper laughed. "You're not making this easy."

"You're the one who isn't making it easy. I'm tired of your questions," Christine snapped back. "Why can't you answer one of mine?"

"Fair enough," Carello agreed. "You do need an answer to your question, and I can take you to someone who would be happy to do that for you. Follow me." Carello drifted off through space. Christine, still used to the concept of arms and legs, hesitated, then cast off behind him.

"Wait! Where are we going? Who's going to answer my question? Are you trying to weasel out of this, Carello?" Christine was struggling to catch up.

"We're going to see The Father, Christine. Just be patient."

Christine was astonished at how she moved through space. She knew if she were back home, she would describe the feeling as flying. Her body now seemed to be lighter, and she didn't know how to manage her arms and legs in these new circumstances.

She and the gatekeeper entered a white mist. Christine occasionally caught sight of stars and their solar systems shining through the fog. She wanted to stop and look at the spectacular view before her, but Carello kept urging her onward. They entered a dazzling red cloud filled with bright white particles. It was impossible to see anything but Carello and the red haze.

Carello finally stopped at a place set apart from everything else--a block of bluish-white mist surrounded by the red cloud. He approached another being of light larger than himself floating in front of the mist.

"Does the Father have time to see us?"

The apparition stood aside from the entrance of the haze and motioned Christine and Carello inside. In the center of the fog sat a figure from which radiated a soft glowing light. The light warmed Christine. She felt she was being caressed by it.

"I understand you asked our gatekeeper a question, little one." The figure moved toward Christine. "I want to answer that question for you."

Carello went toward the entrance. "Shall I leave you now, Father?"

"Yes, you've plenty to do."

Christine was reluctant to see Carello go. He was the one familiar thing to her in this new universe. "It's all right, little one." The figure's voice was tender.

"Who – who are you?" The thought was barely out of Christine's mind when she flinched. Something about this glowing shape inspired respect and some fear in her.

"On your world I'm known as God in some circles, but I prefer the title 'Father'."

"Now I know I'm hallucinating." Christine longed to be back in her bedroom but felt, somehow that was impossible. "All right, I'll play along for a while. What did Carello mean by the unfulfilled promise of my life?"

"You started out well in life but got lost along the way. I'm trying to help you find your way back to me and my son."

"So we're talking about the fairy tale again, are we? Even if I believed Jesus came when he did and did the things he did, I think he had it pretty easy back then. I'd like to see him come today and try to handle the problems we face."

Father was silent for a moment. "You bring up an interesting proposition, Christine." He paused again. "I can make it happen for you. That's the beauty of being God. I know everything, and I can do anything. What would you say if my son did come back today and handled the problems you faced?

"You can't be serious." Christine wanted to laugh. "Sure, go right ahead. Send him down. Let's see how he does."

"All right. We'll have a look at how your world would be if Jesus came in your time; then you can see if you believe in him or not. Keep in mind, though; that this world may be different in some ways from the one you just left. This will be the first time my Son comes to this world. There is no two thousand year history of Christianity to influence the people you will see."

CHAPTER TWO

Father pointed toward the mist in the corner. Christine watched as Earth rapidly came into view. Then she was in a vortex. With lightning speed her vision was focused from planet, to continent, to city, to a tall building. As Christine's sight adjusted, she saw a floor of office cubicles, each containing a desk, chair and computer station. The color scheme was an unrelenting dull beige. The workers in some cubicles had attempted to bring warmth to their surroundings by decorating with fake flowers or pictures. Their attempts were futile.

Christine saw a well-built young man with fair complexion and curly hair working in one of the cubicles. He sat with tie slightly unknotted; shirtsleeves rolled up, staring at some papers. His suit coat hung over the back of his chair.

The phone rang. As the man reached for it, his hand brushed the paper coffee cup on his desk. The cup fell over. Brown liquid flowed over papers, pens and pencils. "Perfect!" The man sighed as he attempted to rescue his papers with one hand and reach for the phone with the other hand.

"Pete Stone, here. ... Yes, Mr. Halversen, everything's coming along fine. ... I'll check with Andy on that. ... Yes, Sir. We won't let you down."

Pete hung up the phone and rose to get some paper towels. Another young man with similar build and complexion approached his desk.

"Hey, Pete," the second man laughed, "you're supposed to drink coffee, not clean your furniture with it."

"Thank you, Andy, for your helpful comment." Pete started mopping up his desk. "Now please tell me you have some good news from the production line."

Andy's smile faded. "That's what I came to talk to you about. The foreman says the trial run on the Phaeton XL will be delayed."

Pete heaved the paper towels in the wastebasket. "That's great! I just got off the phone with Halversen. I promised him the Stone brothers wouldn't let him down." Pete picked up the soggy papers and waved them in Andy's face. "I've also been looking at these cost overruns. What's going on, Andy? Can't you keep up your end?"

Andy glared at his brother as he planted his hands on Pete's desk and leaned forward. "You're the one who wanted to make the big splash, Pete." Andy's voice went up a notch. "You wanted to get the Phaeton XL out faster than any other model car's ever been produced. I had to grab raw materials wherever I could find them. Now, I'm here to tell you the production line's jammed with cars we're actually selling. The foreman said he'd do his best to fit our run in, but he can't promise anything. I'd like to know what you're doing up here to help me!"

Pete felt the muscles in his neck tightening. "I'm up to my eyeballs trying to satisfy every regulator that has anything to do with this car. I'm also scrounging for money to keep the project alive."

"Well then, don't let me keep you from your important paperwork. I'll just go back down and see if I can actually make the car!" Andy turned on his heel and stomped toward the elevator.

"Andy, wait!" Pete called after him. He ran from his desk and grabbed Andy's arm. "I'm sorry I yelled at you. It's just that the Phaeton XL could be our ticket upstairs. Wouldn't you like to have an office and a secretary instead of a cubicle? A pay raise wouldn't be bad either."

"I know you have dreams, Pete." Andy shook off Pete's arm and continued walking. "Just don't let them take over your life."

Pete returned to his desk and persisted in his corporate battles throughout the morning using the phone, e-mail and memos as his weapons. After several hours, he glanced at his watch. It was time for lunch and a much-needed break. As he rose and put on his jacket, a woman came toward him.

"Mr. Stone," she called to Pete.

"Yes, Leslie, what is it? Do we have another brush fire to put out?"

Leslie smiled. "No emergencies, Mr. Stone. Mr. Halversen wants everyone to meet for a short presentation in the conference room. He promises it won't interfere with anyone's lunch."

Pete joined his co-workers in the conference room. Mr. Halversen, a stocky man with salt and pepper hair, stood beside a shorter man with red hair and mustache. When everyone was assembled, Mr. Halversen began to speak.

"Thank you for coming. You all know I like to give anyone who does good work a pat on the back, and that's why we're here today." He gestured toward the shorter man. "Phil Hiera here has come up with a design that prevents a hubcap from being stolen."

Pete's eyes widened. He watched carefully as Mr. Halversen presented the hubcap design. His jaw tightened, and his hands balled into fists as the blueprints he knew so well were shown on the overhead projector. *What's going on? How could Phil come up with the same invention I did? Nobody knows about it, not even Andy.* While people applauded Phil at the end of presentation, Pete edged past them and hurried back to his cubicle.

He opened his file cabinet and began thumbing through its contents. He stopped at a particular folder and examined it. All the paperwork seemed intact, but it was filed out of order.

"Pete, come on. It's time for lunch," Andy called as he strode toward Pete. "Get your head out of the file cabinet."

"Look at this." Pete handed the file to his brother.

Andy whistled. "How'd you get hold of this so fast? We just had a meeting on it."

"Because it's my design. That creep Hiera must have poked through my stuff while I wasn't around."

"What're you going to do about it?"

"Nothing. What can I do? Nobody's going to believe that I came up with the design first. Besides we've got our hands full with a bigger project right now." Pete turned toward the elevator. "Come on, let's go to lunch. After we eat, I'm going to stop by the hardware store and pick up a lock for my file cabinet."

After lunch Pete spent the afternoon on more paperwork. He watched his e-mails go through the upper levels of management like salmon swimming upstream. The replies trickled back down, filtered by layers of executives.

He was reading one of the messages when Andy came up to his desk. "Hey, Pete, time to go home. Let's pack it in for today."

"Wait a second. I just need to send a quick answer to this e-mail." Pete turned toward his computer.

"Okay, but hurry up. I want to go home when the big crowd leaves. You know Gordon got mugged in the parking garage last month because he worked late and left by himself."

"Yeah, I know." Pete's fingers flew over the keyboard. "That's it. I'm ready to go."

Pete dropped Andy off at his apartment, then drove home. He eased his sedan into the driveway and headed into the house.

"Connie, I'm home," he called.

A slim dark-haired young woman dressed in jeans and a casual top came out of the kitchen. "Am I glad to see you!" She brushed his cheek with her lips. "The garbage disposal is broken again."

"Yes, dear, my day was fine. Thanks for asking." Pete threw his briefcase on the couch.

"Pete, I'm sorry, but I worked all day, too. I don't want a problem with the disposal any more than you do, but it's got to be fixed." Connie headed back toward the kitchen.

"Can I at least wait 'til after dinner? I'm a little tired right now."

Connie stopped, then turned and smiled. "That's a

reasonable request, sir. Sorry I was so abrupt. I'm just tired of this thing breaking down." She patted his shoulder.

While they ate, Connie talked about her work at the pre-school. Pete tried to listen to her litany of the day's events, but his mind was elsewhere. He was still seething about Phil's deception. He was also worried about the trial run for the new car. What if he and Andy couldn't pull it off? Would they still have jobs?

"Pete!"

"What? I'm sorry, Connie. What were you saying?"

"I was telling you a story about one of the kids at the pre-school. You were a million miles away."

"I'm sorry. It's this new product. I'm worried that we won't make a deadline. Somebody pulled a dirty trick on me today, too."

Connie rose and began clearing the dishes. "You're always bringing home some problem from work. Sometimes I wish you'd quit that job, Pete! It's with you twenty-four hours a day!"

Pete shoved back from the table. "That job is keeping you well-fed and well-clothed. Now I'll see to the disposal."

That night, as Connie lay in bed beside him relaxed in sleep, Pete was wide awake. His mind kept churning as he went over and over the possibilities for solving his production problems. Exhausted, he finally fell asleep only to find his problems waiting for him in his dreams.

"That was certainly uplifting, Father." Christine's derisive laugh echoed in her head. "You show me a man who has a fight with his brother, has an idea stolen, is drowning in corporate paperwork and pays no attention to his wife. I don't exactly see Jesus at work here."

"Be patient, Christine. Your journey has just begun."

CHAPTER THREE

Christine looked back at the scene below. Once again she was at Pete's office. She heard shouting coming from the end of the cubicles.

"Piece a' junk copier!" Pete yelled at a large copier in the corner and kicked its side. Apparently it wasn't the first blow struck in frustration. The copier already had one shoe-sized dent in it.

Phil Hiera approached the copier. "Hey, Pete, what're you doing to that thing? I've got some work I need to run through it."

"Ah, my good friend, Phil." Pete's eyes were cold. "Can you help me out? I don't know what's wrong with this thing, and I'm under the gun to get this report out to the guys on the top floor."

Phil backed away. "Sorry, Pete. I've got my own problems; I've got a rush job, too.

I'll find another copier. Good luck." Phil rushed down the hall.

"Yeah, good luck. Thank you so very much," Pete muttered, then chuckled. "Wait 'til good ol' Phil finds out all the other copiers are busy. Serves him right!"

Pete continued kicking and yelling at the copier. "C'mon, machine! You're putting my job on the line! Let's get a few copies out, okay?"

A few other people approached the machine then backed off when they saw what was going on. Pete banged his fists on the copier. The blood pulsed in his temples. His forehead throbbed. The tension headache he was so familiar with was building.

He sighed, picked up his papers and turned toward the hall; his shoulders slumped. He straightened and smiled when he saw Andy coming toward him.

"Andy! Am I glad to see you! Can you give me a hand with this copier? I've got to get our report up to the top floor ASAP."

"Sorry, Pete. I've got to get down to the production line. We're still having some problems there."

"Hey, Andy, if I don't get these reports upstairs we'll be in a serious world of hurt. Remember we're both working on this project. I'd rather take my chances with the line than with the top brass."

Pete and Andy began shouting at each other about the importance of their respective duties. Two other men got off the elevator and joined them at the copier.

"What's up, you guys?" asked the frailer of the two. "We could hear you yelling from the elevator."

"My dear brother, Andy, says he's too busy to help me with this stupid copier even though both we're working on the same project." Pete's face was contorted with anger. "I've got a meeting with the big boys tomorrow; and if I don't get copies of this report up there today, they'll have my hide." Pete paused, wiped his forehead with a handkerchief, then asked the slight, dark-haired man, "John, are you any good with machines?"

"No, but my cousin, Jesse, is. He just started working here. Let him have a look."

The man John indicated stepped forward. He was dressed in corporate uniform--dark suit, white shirt and conservative tie. His weight and height were average, and his face was framed by coffee-colored hair.

"Hi, I'm Jesse Cartland." His warm brown eyes greeted Pete. "Let's see if I can do something to help. Got a flashlight?"

Pete fetched a flashlight from his desk as Jesse removed his coat and opened the copier. Jesse peered inside it for a moment, then said, "I see what the problem is." He reached in and touched something deep within the bowels of the mechanism. The copier hummed, ready for action.

"Go ahead and copy something, Pete." Jesse put his coat back on.

Pete put in his report and copies flew into the bin. "Wow, here they come!" Pete turned his back to the men and began gathering up copies. "Sorry I can't talk with you guys any more, but I've got this rush job. You know how it is."

Jesse moved to Pete's side. "My, my, not even a thank you."

"Okay, thank you." Pete waved an arm. "I told you I'm in a hurry. What more do you want me to do?" Pete turned back to finish collating his reports. Andy started to leave.

"I'd like you to join John and me this evening." Jesse replied quietly. "We're studying the Old Ways."

"Studying the Old Ways! Now there's a waste of time. Thanks, but no thanks." Pete snickered.

Andy turned toward Jesse. "I've always been interested in the Old Ways from a historical perspective. I didn't know anyone knew anything about them any more."

"Jesse does," said John. "He was considered a child prodigy. He knows everything about the Old Ways. Drop by Jesse's house about seven tonight if you're interested."

"Okay. Is it all right if I stay the night? You know how the streets get after dark.

I could bring a sleeping bag." Pete shook his head. Just like Andy to waste his time learning about the Old Ways.

"Sure. See you later." John and Jesse left to go back to work.

Pete stopped by his desk on the way to the upper floor. Phil was just getting off the elevator.

"Guess you're out of luck, Pete."

"What do you mean?"

"All the other copiers are busy, and one of the secretaries said the copier on our floor can't be fixed. They're carting it away tomorrow."

"Oh, yeah." Pete picked up the reports and fanned them in Phil's face. "I just got twenty copies out of our so-called broken copier a few minutes ago. Maybe they better hire that new guy, Cartland, to fix things around here."

"This is impossible." Phil stared at the reports. "From what they told me, there's no way that machine could work."

"Well, they're wrong, and I'm out of here. I'm

dropping these things off then heading home for a cold one."

# # #

The next morning Andy, whistling off-key, approached Pete's desk. Pete looked up from his work. "How was your exciting meeting about the Old Ways?"

Andy pulled up a chair. "You know, it was surprisingly interesting." He smiled. "Jesse has a way of explaining things that's unique. He really is an authority on the Old Ways. Makes them actually sound relevant to modern-day life. Kind of a pain, though, to go to the meetings. You know how the streets get after dark. He did let me stay over last night so I was safe."

"That's good. Anyway, our newly-elected regional attorney, Aaron Chapin, says he's going to clean up the streets and lower the crime rate right away." Pete started shuffling through his papers.

"Yeah, sure."

Andy watched for a moment as Pete started scribbling notes on a report, then said, "Hey, Pete, I've got an idea. Why don't you come to one of our meetings to see how Jesse teaches? We're going to have them earlier in the evening so no one's inconvenienced. I think you'd get a kick out of it."

"No thanks, Andy. I want to concentrate on this project. We've got a production deadline staring us in the face. You'd better be thinking about that, too. The boys upstairs are getting edgy. They want to see results. Need I remind you we're only as good as the last successful product we came up with?"

"Relax. I'm working things out with the foreman.

We'll be ready for a practice run on the Phaeton XL in a few days. I'll go down to the line right now if that'll make you happy." Andy chuckled. "Glad you're not ambitious or anything."

"I've got a wife and a mortgage. You don't. Besides I've always fancied myself behind a mahogany desk." Pete leaned back in his chair hands clasped behind his head, smiling, imagining the executive office for a moment; then sat up straight again. "Seriously, I'd appreciate it if you'd check up on things. I'll tidy up our paperwork."

# # #

For the next few days, Pete and Andy checked and re-checked the machinery on the assembly line to make sure everything was in order for their trial run. They held several meetings with the foreman rehearsing every step in the process. Finally the big day arrived. As Pete was leaving his desk to observe the run, John and Jesse walked up.

"Where are you off to, Pete?" John asked.

"Andy and I are doing a dry run on the Phaeton XL. Wish us luck." Pete turned to go, but paused in mid-step when his phone rang. He picked it up, then held it away from his ear. John and Jesse could hear shouting on the other end of the line. "Hold on, Andy. Calm down. I can't understand what you're saying. ... What? ... How did it happen? ...

This is terrible! I'll be right down!" Pete ran toward the elevator; Jesse and John trotting after him.

"What's wrong?" shouted John as he tried to catch up to Pete.

"The worst possible thing," Pete yelled over his shoulder. "They started the run, and everything looked great; then one of the guys got his hand stuck in the equipment. Andy says it looks like the man's badly injured."

"Mind if I tag along? I've had some experience with this kind of thing." Jesse was right on Pete's heels.

"You have? Sure, Jesse, I'd really appreciate it." All three men jumped in the elevator.

Pete banged his fist against the elevator's wall as it descended to the production floor. "I really didn't need this today. The accident paperwork alone will be horrendous. We'll probably have to cancel the run, too." Jesse and John rolled their eyes and shook their heads.

As the elevator door opened, Andy grabbed Pete's arm and pulled him toward the production line. "He's over here, Pete. The paramedics should be here shortly."

Pete saw a man leaning against a piece of machinery, his arm caught in a gear. He grimaced, eyes tightly shut, tears rolling down his cheeks. As the men got closer they could see blood on his forearm. He groaned.

"Is help coming, Mr. Stone? I can hardly take this any more."

"Yeah, Jeff." Andy put a hand on Jeff's shoulder. "They'll be here any minute."

"What am I gonna do without a hand? I won't be able to work any more." Jeff hung his head on Andy's arm.

Jesse studied the mechanism for a moment then rolled up his sleeves. "Let me see if I can help. I grew up with machinery on the farm."

"Do you think that's wise, Jesse?" asked Andy. "Maybe we should wait for the professionals."

"I won't do anything to hurt him. Give me a wrench so we can open the machine and free him. You!" Jesse pointed at the foreman. "Get a clean towel ready, too." With a few twists, Jesse was able to loosen the bolts and free Jeff's hand.

"Quick! Give me the towel!" Jesse wrapped Jeff's hand in the towel and placed his hands around it. He held on for a moment as he looked into Jeff's eyes. "How are you feeling now?"

"Fine. It doesn't hurt any more." Jeff's eyes were wide. "Did my hand go numb?"

"Let's take a look," Jesse unwrapped the towel.

Pete winced as the towel came off. The other men looked away then gasped as they looked back at Jeff's hand. It was in perfect shape. There was no sign of any blood or injury. Jeff stared at his hand and slowly raised it. He turned it around, all the time carefully examining it; then started wiggling his fingers. He hugged Jesse. "Mister, I don't know how you did this, but I sure am grateful. Wait 'til I tell the other guys in the plant."

"I'd just as soon you kept this quiet for now. I'm the new kid on the block. I don't need a lot of attention right now."

"Okay, mister. Thanks a lot. I'll never forget this." Jeff raced off waving his hand in the air.

"I don't believe what I just saw." Pete, wide-eyed, spoke to Jesse. "I saw blood on that guy's arm. I could have sworn he was going to lose his hand. Was Jeff injured or not?"

"I'll let you draw your own conclusions." Jesse smiled. "By the way, the invitation to my study group is still open if you'd like to attend."

"I'll definitely be there," declared Pete.

"Good. We'll start at six so you can get home safely. Andy knows where it is. Come on, John, we'd better get back to work." John and Jesse walked away.

Pete turned to Andy. "That guy's hand was injured, wasn't it?"

"Yeah, I'd swear to it."

"Then what happened? First the guy fixes a copier that is supposedly beyond repair, then he saves somebody's hand. What other tricks does he have up his sleeve?"

"I don't know, Pete, but I told you Jesse was special. Come on, let's do a product run."

# # #

The next night Andy and Pete parked in front of a yellow bungalow with a small, neat lawn and a few flowerbeds along the walk. "This is Jesse's house?" Pete asked. Andy nodded. Cars were tightly parked on both sides of the street. Pete looked around as he got out of the car. "More people here than I would have thought. Hey, isn't that Phil's car? He's coming, too?"

"Yeah, you'll know some of the people here. Let's get inside."

They entered the modest home. The furniture in the living room had been pushed back to accommodate several dozen people. Jesse came toward them, hand outstretched.

"Andy! Pete! You're just in time. Pete, since you're new to the group, I'll take you around and introduce you so you'll know everyone. You already know my cousin, John Thorson. This is his older brother Jim." Jim, thin and dark like his brother John, nodded at Pete. "Here's

Phil Hiera. I know you work with him. Phil, I thought you were bringing a guest."

"He couldn't make it this week. Maybe next time."

"Okay, well let's see who else is here. I don't think you know Si Cane and Thad LaBeau. They fix my car when it's ailing." Two muscular black men in jeans and T-shirts nodded at their introduction. "This is Jeb Kerry. He's an accountant." A blonde man with sallow complexion wearing white shirt and khaki slacks gave them a quick nod then looked away. "I've got some relatives over here." Jesse guided them to the other side of the room. "This is Tom Gems. He's a building contractor and a cousin." Tom in bib overalls and T-shirt, freckles peppering his face, said hi. The introductions continued until Jesse came to the last two men in the room. They were tall with ebony hair and dressed in business suits. "And last but certainly least, the two black sheep of the family, Matt and Jack Levy. They're lawyers." Everyone groaned at this introduction and shied away from the pair with mock disdain.

Matt, the heavier of the two, spoke. "Okay, let's get this over with. I'll tell one lawyer joke, then we can get to work. It's true that if Jack and I fall in the ocean, sharks won't eat us as a professional courtesy." Everyone laughed, then settled down as Jesse spoke.

"Okay, we're here to learn about the Old Ways. Anyone want to talk about what we learned last week?"

"Uh, Jesse?" Pete raised his hand timidly. "I'm afraid I've forgotten the Old Ways. I never was much good at history. What were they?"

"Interesting that you should put them in the past tense. They are a set of rules given to us so that we may live an orderly, peaceful life."

"Okay, what *are* they, then?"

"Andy, you want to answer that?"

"Sure. We're not supposed to sleep around if we're married, or lie, steal, or murder."

"Anything else?"

John Thorson raised his hand. "We're supposed to be good to our parents and not want to rip off our neighbors' possessions."

"You're leaving out some pretty important things," Jesse reminded them. "What about honoring God and setting aside one day a week for him?"

"I can see why they're called the Old Ways," Pete laughed. Doesn't seem like many people observe them nowadays."

"Why do you say that, Pete?" Jesse asked.

"Look at what we have to go through to get to one of these meetings. We have to come early and leave before dark so we won't get car-jacked on the way home. We have to install burglar alarms in our homes so our possessions won't get stolen." Pete stood and started pacing around the group. "There's something else. I have to watch my back at work so somebody won't stick a knife in it. There's a man sitting right in this room who got credit for something I did." Pete glared at Phil. Phil hung his head. "I think Aaron Chapin's got the right idea about an orderly, peaceful life. We start putting more police on the street. That'll straighten everything up better than the Old Ways." Pete returned to his seat.

"So a lot of police on the street will solve all our problems. They'll make everybody behave. Is that the way you want to live?"

"What choice do we have?"

"We have the choice of going back to the Old Ways

and looking carefully at their meaning, then re-shaping our lives. That's what I intend to do with this group."

"What happens then? Do we just learn how to be nice little boys and come to a feel-good meeting every week?" Pete smirked.

"That's a good question, Pete. Why don't you hang around for a while and see what tricks I have up my sleeve?" Jesse winked at Pete.

Pete looked open-mouthed at Jesse. It wasn't possible that he'd heard the remark Pete made to Andy at the plant. Or was it?

Jesse spent the rest of the meeting teaching the group about the Old Ways. Pete sat quietly watching as some eagerly raised their hands to answer Jesse's questions while others argued that the Old Ways wouldn't fit into their lives.

As Pete and Andy were driving home in the car, Andy said, "You really clammed up in there after your outburst. What were you thinking?"

"First of all, I'm amazed that a group of grown men can get that wrapped up in talking about the Old Ways."

Andy parked in front of Pete's house. "You said 'first of all'. Is there something else?"

Yeah, there's something I'm trying to remember that ties into the Old Ways. It's twisting around in the back of my brain. I'll have to check it out."

"Can you tell me what it is?"

"No, I'd rather wait."

"Are you planning to come next week?"

"If what I think I'm remembering is true, I'll certainly be there."

CHAPTER FOUR

Things hummed along for the Stone brothers the following week. Their practice run was a success, so Phaeton XLs began rolling off the assembly line and into dealerships. Pete was going over some paperwork when his intercom buzzed.

"Mr. Stone, your brother's on the line."

"Yeah, Andy."

"It's happened, Pete. The top floor folks want to see us on the double. Meet you there."

Pete's heart raced as he rode the elevator to the twenty-eighth floor. Maybe that big mahogany desk would finally be his! Or had they fouled up something? Andy met him at the elevator door. Pete wrapped an arm around his shoulder in a brief hug. "This is it, isn't it Andy? Our big break?"

"I think so, Pete. Things have been going well. I don't know what they'd have to complain about."

"Let's not ask them," Pete fidgeted. "How do I look? Is my tie straight?"

"Pete, you look fine," laughed Andy. "Let's not keep

the big guys waiting."

Together they strode into the conference room. The top executives were seated at a long, highly polished walnut table. Mr. Halversen was sitting at its head. He looked up from his papers and, with an air of command, gestured Pete and Andy to sit down.

"It seems the Stone boys have done it again." Mr. Halversen smiled. "You've added another valuable product to our line. We're already getting favorable comments from the dealerships. Looks like we'll be adding to our profits this year because of your efforts."

"That's great, Mr. Halversen." Pete was beaming.

"We think you and Andy should share in our good fortune since it was your hard work that paid off for everyone. You'll both be moving into an office suite with a support team suitable to your needs. You'll also get a raise and have increased research staff at your disposal to make those new and so nicely profitable products. Sound good, boys?"

"Yes – yes sir, Mr. Halversen," Andy stammered. "You won't regret this, sir. We'll work really hard."

"I know you will." Mr. Halversen was smiling. "Now use the rest of the day to pack up your offices and move upstairs."

"Yes, sir. Thank you, sir." Pete and Andy backed out of the room, bowing slightly as they left.

Once outside, they jumped up and down, embracing each other. "Can you believe it?" Pete asked. "We're on our way to the top! Like the man said, let's pack up. Oh, I've gotta call Connie, too. She'll flip over the news."

Pete and Andy spent the rest of the day moving and being congratulated by their co-workers. The following day Andy stopped at Pete's desk at quitting time.

"Hey, Pete. Get your head out of your paperwork. It's time to go to Jesse's for our meeting."

Pete made a face. "Oh boy, I forgot all about that. Don't know if I can make it. I've got a lot to do here." He gestured toward the pile of paperwork on his desk.

"I thought you were going to check something out for this meeting."

"That's right, I did find the time to do some research. On second thought, I am going to make the meeting. I have something I want to discuss with Mr. Jesse Cartland."

"Want to share what it is?"

"No, I'd rather not. I want this to be a surprise for everybody." Andy shrugged his shoulders as they left.

# # #

Andy and Pete were just about to enter Jesse's house when Phil and another man, bearded and wearing jeans, arrived. "Nate. How're you doing?" Andy asked. "Phil said you'd be coming tonight."

"I'm fine. Just thought I'd tag along and see what Phil finds so interesting."

Jesse opened the door. "Nate Bardo. How are you? And I see the rest of the gang is here.

"Have you met Nate before, Jesse?" asked Phil.

"No."

"Then how did you know his name? I never told you who he was."

"I saw Nate before you ever got here. He was standing by an elm tree in front of his house waiting for you to pick him up."

"That's amazing! How did you see me?" Nate asked.

"Don't worry about how I saw you, Nate. We're just getting started. You'll see many more things that will amaze you before we're through."

Pete thought, *So Jesse can see things as well as hear things when he's not around. What else can he do?*

"I'm certainly ready to listen to what you have to say, Jesse." Nate settled himself on the couch beside Phil.

"Okay, we're all here, so let's begin. We need to talk about what abandonment of the Old Ways has done to us and our society."

Pete rose from his chair. "Wait a minute, Jesse. I want to talk about a different kind of abandonment."

"And what would that be?" Jesse turned to face Pete.

"Something from my childhood days started rattling around in my head when you were talking about the Old Ways. I decided to look some things up. You know what else it says in the book that talks about these Ways?"

Jesse folded his arms across his chest. "What else does it say in the book, Pete?"

"It says that God will send a rescuer who will bring us peace and prosperity. That promise was made a long time ago." Pete looked at the rest of the group. "Where is that person? Why hasn't he been sent?"

"What's your point?" Jesse asked quietly.

"Most of us learned about God and the Ways at our havens when we were young. Later on maybe we did abandon some or most of what we learned. As far as I'm concerned though, God abandoned us first! He hasn't kept his promise! Why should we have to do anything special when God doesn't follow through?" Pete glared at Jesse as he flopped back into his chair.

"You know, Pete, I heard you got a promotion last week. Are you looking for another promotion now to being God's secretary?" The group laughed nervously. "Believe me, I know about those promises. God will keep them when it's the right time to do so. You must trust me when I tell you that. Meanwhile, we're taking the first baby steps here to understanding God and his purpose for us."

"Seeing is believing, Jesse," Pete said. Some of the group nodded in agreement.

"I understand that, and I promise you that you'll see things that will make everything clear to you. Just hang in there with me."

"You're asking a lot of us."

"Yes, I am. The door is over there for anyone who doesn't want to stay."

Pete started to get up. Andy grabbed his shoulder and whispered, "Remember the guy with his hand in the machinery." Pete sat back down.

"Pete makes a good point. Why should we follow the Old Ways? People usually like to see a pay-off for the things they do. The benefits are obvious if everyone would stop stealing and killing. What about lying?"

"I'd be in terrible trouble if I stopped lying!" Matt exclaimed.

"We all know you're a lawyer." John snickered. "You wouldn't be able to make a living."

"It has nothing to do with that. My wife buys the gaudiest outfits. She comes down every morning and asks me how she looks. I have to say 'fine, dear' or she'll kill me." The married men in the group gave knowing nods as everyone laughed.

"Matt does have a tricky situation. How can he get out of lying?" Jesse looked around the room. "Any suggestions?"

The men looked at each other with blank stares and shrugs; then Phil spoke. "I think your goose is cooked, man."

"Think about it, Matt." Jesse chuckled. "I bet you'll find a solution. Now let's talk about the big commandment -- putting God first." The group spent the rest of the evening arguing with Jesse about how family and jobs were more important to them.

At the end of the evening, Jesse appealed to the gathering. "You're having a hard time with the concept that God comes first, so I suggest we begin meeting several times a week until you understand. I also have two assignments for you. I want you to spend one day this week trying to follow all the Old Ways, and I want you to stop in at your havens this weekend."

Everyone groaned. "Come on, guys," Jesse implored. "This exercise will do you good. It'll be a real character-builder." The men chuckled as Jesse showed them to the door.

Pete and Andy got in the car and drove in silence for a while, then Pete spoke. "Jesse really asks a lot. I can't make that kind of commitment. Halversen will expect even more from us now that he's promoted us. I know I'm going to have to spend more time at work."

"I'll say it again. Remember the guy with the hand. Also, how did he know Nate was waiting under an elm tree for Phil? I tell you Jesse's something special."

"Maybe he knows where Nate lives."

"No way. Remember Phil never even told Jesse Nate's name. I'm going to start going to the extra meetings. I want to see what he does next."

"Okay, little brother. I'll go for the next couple of weeks just to keep you out of trouble. Besides maybe

Jesse'll pull another rabbit out of his hat. I have to admit the guy is a constant surprise."

# # #

Pete arrived home and unlocked the door. "Connie, I'm home."

"I'm in the living room, Pete."

The television set was on as Pete entered the room. "What're you watching?"

Connie looked up from her seat on the couch. "Aaron Chapin's talking about his plans to hire more police. He's going to double the coverage in cities our size."

"That'll be good." Pete sat down beside her.

"Hasn't said how he's going to pay for all those cops yet, though. He's also talking about having a curfew for a while 'til things shape up."

"Wow! Well, I'm all for it if we can feel safer."

"How was your meeting?"

"It was interesting. Oh, by the way, we're going to be meeting about three times a week for a while."

"Three times a week! You know I don't mind you being with the boys once a week, but three times! When will we have time for ourselves?"

"Andy's all caught up in the meetings. I just want to make sure he's not involved in something that's going to hurt him later on."

"Ever the big brother. You realize Andy's not married, and you are."

"Connie, I promise it'll just be for a few weeks. I think the whole thing's going to blow over eventually. I must admit Jesse's intriguing, though. I can see why

Andy and the rest want to go. Oh, by the way, I'm going to stop by the haven in my old neighborhood over the weekend. Want to come along?"

"Your old haven?   Let me feel your forehead." Connie placed her palm on Pete's forehead with mock seriousness. "Hm, no fever. You haven't talked about the haven since we've been married. What's gotten into you?"

"I did enjoy going when I was a kid. It was nice to hear about the Old Ways from my teacher. He was a sweet guy. I also want to see if any of the gang's still there, that's all. No big deal. Now come on. Let's curl up, and you tell me about your day."

CHAPTER FIVE

Christine took her eyes from the scene below her and looked skyward. "Okay, Father, God, whoever you are, I'm confused. So far I've seen a bunch of men getting together to talk about the Old Ways, which sound like the Ten Commandments to me. That I can follow, but what's this about havens and a rescuer?"

"First of all, remember I like to be called Father." Father's warm voice was in her mind. "Now what do you think of when you hear the word 'haven'?"

"A safe place," Christine answered.

"Right. Now think of other places you consider safe, and you'll figure out what a haven means to these people. As Jesse says, though, you'll have to wait for the right time to find out about the rescuer. Just keep watching these people's lives unfold."

"Okay, Father, I'll watch for a while longer." Christine looked down again at the scene below.

\# \# \#

Pete parked his car at the corner of Jesse's street. He hailed Andy as he crossed the street. "Hey, Andy! How'd your big assignment from Jesse go?"

"You'll find out when we get inside," replied Andy.

"You mean you actually tried to follow the Ways?" Pete shook his head. "Whatever. Anyway, I can't wait to get in there. I've got a story to tell I think is pretty funny. Should get a laugh from the guys. We'll see how Jesse handles it." They met the rest of the group and entered the house.

"Okay, who tried to follow the Old Ways for a day?" Everyone raised a hand. "And who visited their old haven?" Again all raised hands. "Great! Now who wants to tell me what happened?" Matt raised his hand. "Okay, Matt, you go first."

"It was the darnedest thing. You know how I told you about my wife's clothes last week. Well, she came down one morning, and sure enough, asked me how she looked. I took a deep breath and told her I didn't like the outfit. I got ready to duck then, but instead of being mad, she was relieved. Turns out she was wearing the clothes because she thought I liked them. She brought out some other clothes we both liked, so now I don't have to lie to her. I also know I didn't steal that day because I didn't send out any bills to my clients." Everyone stared at Matt. "That was a joke, folks." He laughed.

Si Cane spoke up. "We had a chance to steal from a guy. He thought he needed an expensive part for his car. Thad and I showed him he didn't need that part and fixed up his heap for a lot less money than he expected to pay. He was so pleased he sent us a couple of new customers.

We ended up making a lot more money by being honest."

Phil Hiera stood up and walked to Pete. "I went to my old haven. My teacher was still there and recognized me. It was good to talk with him. Then I sat there quietly and thought. Pete's right. I did take credit for something he'd done. I wanted to get ahead, but I realized last weekend that I was going about it in the wrong way." Phil extended his hand. "Pete, I hope you'll accept my apology. I'm truly sorry." Pete rose to shake Phil's hand then grasped Phil's shoulder. The rest of the men applauded.

"It's my turn," Pete said. "I'm proud to say I didn't kill anybody last week. I felt like it, but I didn't do it."

"What happened?" Jesse asked.

"Some jerk bumped into me in the cafeteria line and spilled his entire lunch tray on me. Can you imagine? I was standing there with soda and chili dripping off my suit, and I had to make a presentation to my boss right after lunch." Everyone started laughing. "I felt like wringing his neck, but I didn't."

"I can always count on Pete to help me bring out a point," Jesse smiled. "Tell me, do you automatically do things or do you usually think about them first?"

"I guess I usually think first."

"That's right, so I'm telling you that just thinking about wringing someone's neck is like actually doing it."

"That's ridiculous! How are we going to control our thoughts?" Pete stood, red-faced with hands on hips. "We'll never be able to live up to the Old Ways if you're going to count our thoughts against us!"

"There is a way to be forgiven for not living up to the Old Ways that you'll find out about eventually. For now it should be obvious that, most of the time, you don't act before you think. That's how important your thoughts are."

"It's always 'you'll find out later'. You're not giving us many answers right now, Jesse." Pete shook his head.

"I'm telling you what you're ready to hear. When you're ready to hear something new, I'll explain it to you. Now let's talk about putting God first."

"That's a hard one for me, Jesse," Phil said. "A lot of the guys here are single, but I've got a wife and four girls. My family has to come first."

"Tell me, when you were young, did your father care for you?"

"Yes, I had a good father."

"Did he give you everything you needed?"

"Yes, he did."

"Then think of God as your father. He provides for you. You put him first and everything else falls into line."

"Hey, did you hear that, guys. We can just sit around, and God'll do everything for us." Pete's sarcasm hung in the air.

"Would you be using your talents if you did that?"

"No."

"For the sake of argument, let's say God provides you with everything."

"Okay."

"So then where did your talents come from?"

"Following that argument, they would come from God."

"To be used, right?"

"Right."

"You're starting to understand, Pete." Jesse looked around the group. "By the way, I'm proud of you all.

You've made a good start. We're going to really buckle down for a while. I want you all to continue going back to your havens on the weekend." He turned to Phil. "Phil, you said it was quiet there and you could think. I want you fellows to think about your relationship to God. There's something big on the horizon for all of you. You need to be prepared." Jesse took his seat. "Now let's start studying."

John raised his hand. "I have a question before we start. I feel like we're following a laundry list of tasks with the Old Ways. We check off that we were good boys and didn't lie or steal or whatever on a particular day. Is there any simpler method of looking at the Ways?"

Jesse smiled. "Yes, there is. Just put God first and treat whoever you're dealing with the way you'd like to be treated. That's the Old Ways in a nutshell."

The group talked about how they'd like to treat some people then spent the rest of their time together listening to Jesse.

As Pete was heading to his car, Andy touched his sleeve. "Tell me something, Pete. Why do you come to these meetings if all you're going to do is argue with Jesse?"

"I told you. I wanted to make sure you weren't getting into something that might get you into trouble."

Andy's face was rigid. "In case you haven't noticed, I'm a grown man. I don't need a babysitter."

"Okay, okay," Pete raised his hands in a calming gesture. "Maybe I'm intrigued with Jesse and his ideas, but I'm not ready to swallow everything he has to say."

"Why don't you give some of his suggestions a try? Do it for a week to see if you notice a difference."

"Anything for you, Andy," Pete laughed.

Just then a burly man in a khaki uniform approached them. "Are you gentlemen on your way home? Curfew will begin pretty soon."

"Yes, officer," said Pete as he headed to his car. "We're on our way right now."

# # #

Pete decided to give the Old Ways a try with the men on the production line. He praised their work and helped patiently when they ran into problems. He soon noticed the foreman and men on the line gave the Stone boys' projects top priority. As the weekend approached, he felt a desire to visit his haven again.

He drove up to the old beige stucco building and pulled into the parking lot. Pete carefully crossed the lot, avoiding the potholes in the asphalt. He climbed the cracked cement steps, entered the haven, sat down and looked around. There was no one else occupying any of the other dozen or so chairs in the room. The old wood paneling on the walls was still in good shape. The heavy red velvet curtains at the windows muffled the street noise. Pete closed his eyes, enjoying the quiet.

A door creaked open at the end of the room. "Hello! Is anyone there?" Pete opened his eyes with a start. He could see a frail hand on the doorknob.

"It's just me, Mr. Brownley--Pete Stone."

An old man with sparse white hair entered the room. "Oh yes. I remember you. You were here a few weeks ago. How are you?"

"Fine. I felt like stopping here again. It's so peaceful. Not like at work with the phones ringing all the time."

Mr. Brownley took a seat opposite Pete. "You'd better enjoy the haven while you can. They're talking about closing this one down."

"What! Why?" Pete was surprised.

"Parents don't send their kids here any more to learn about the Old Ways. The government's looking for extra money to spend on police. If they close the havens, that'll free up more tax dollars."

"That's terrible, Mr. Brownley. There must be something we can do."

"Look at yourself, Pete. How often have you been back here?"

Pete hung his head. "You're right. I haven't done my part. Even a few weeks ago I wouldn't have cared if this haven closed, but now I find it's becoming important to me." Pete paused, then smiled. "You know what. I belong to a group that's interested in our old havens. Maybe we can do something."

"You better hurry up. This one's on the hit list." The two men shook hands. As Pete rose to leave, he heard the smash of glass. He ran out the door and saw two young men trying to get in his car.

"Hey! Get away from that car!" he yelled. The startled men ran away. Pete borrowed a broom and swept the glass off his car seat along with the rock the men had used to break the window. He shook his head as he climbed in his car. *Who's right—Jesse or Chapin? Do we need more police and curfews or will Jesse's way work?*

\# \# \#

Pete continued to meet with the other men several times weekly at Jesse's to study and discuss what the Ways meant. He found the meetings a welcome relief from the hectic pace of his work life. He was torn between getting ahead by any means possible and trying to follow the Ways. He found himself taking notice when he saw himself or others breaking the Old Ways.

One day as Pete was doing some paperwork, a co-worker, smiling broadly, walked into his office. Pete looked up and gestured toward a chair. "Have a seat, Hal. What's up?"

"I think you'll appreciate this, Pete. You know that guy, Jackson, who's always trying to one-up me on product designs?" Pete nodded. "The big bosses sent out an e-mail meant for him, but my address was on it by mistake. Seems they were looking to promote somebody. They listed the qualifications they were looking for, so I was able to get the jump on Jackson and apply for the position myself." Hal stood and spread his arms. "You're now looking at the new head of production for sports vehicles." Hal bowed slightly.

Pete felt shock and anger welling within him. "You mean you didn't even give Jackson a chance? You just went in and stole a job that might have been his? That's despicable!" Pete spat the words at Hal.

Hal stared openmouthed at Pete, then his eyes blazed. "That's rich coming from you, Mister Holier than Thou! I've seen you do a lot worse to get ahead, Pete, and you know it!" Hal slammed out of the office.

Pete went to the meeting that night and shared his experience with the rest of the men. After finishing the story, he said, "The worst part of it is that I knew Hal was right. It was like he held up a mirror, and I actually saw myself. A few months ago, I would have been the man bragging about getting the edge over someone for a promotion." With tears in his eyes, Pete looked at Jesse. "I don't want to live my life like that any more. I don't want to be like Hal. I don't want to step over other people to get ahead. Please help me."

Jesse embraced Pete. "You've taken the first steps, Pete. Your adventure is just beginning. Stay with me and learn."

From then on, Pete looked forward eagerly to each meeting of the group. Jesse was making a point one evening when Pete glanced at his watch.

"Wow, look at the time! Jesse, we've got to wrap this up. It's almost 8:30. Curfew starts at 9:00."

"Yeah, and I don't want those cops on the corner to have any excuse for stopping us," Si said. "Did you see the size of those guys? They're bigger than me and Thad, and that's saying something."

Jesse looked out into the soft spring night for a moment. "I just have one question for you before we close. Do you think following the Old Ways has made your lives better?"

Everyone nodded.

"Do you think the Ways could help other people?"

"I don't think there's any doubt of that," John said. "There would be no crime. Then we could get rid of the curfew and the high tax rate we have to pay for the extra cops. Maybe the havens could stay open, too."

"But how do we get the word out to other people about the Ways?" Pete faced Jesse "Do we publish them in the newspaper?"

"No, we go out and tell people about them and about the New Way of life that God wants them to lead."

"And what is that New Way?"

"You'll find out along with the people we talk to."

"Again with the 'you'll find out'." Pete shook his head; then paused. "I'm sorry, Jesse. If there's one thing I've found out in these studies, it's that you do eventually get around to what you say you'll teach us."

John interrupted. "How do we tell people, Jesse? Do we have weekend meetings or something?"

"My plan is that we go out full time, travel around and tell as many people as we can."

"Full time! You mean quit our jobs?" Jim Thorson yelled.

Jesse nodded. "That's what it will take. I need a commitment from each of you."

The men began to mutter to each other. Pete stood. "I'm probably the most ambitious man here. If you had told me when we began this that I would willingly quit my job; I would have told you you were crazy. But now I want to try traveling around, at least for a while. What I've learned here has made a difference in my life. Why not share this difference with other people and see what happens?" Pete looked at each of the men. "Maybe we can put in for a leave of absence from our work so we have jobs to come back to when the time comes. The thing that scares me is telling my wife."

Matt belly-laughed. "My wife would think it's a great idea. I'd be out from under foot. I'd have to figure out how to leave enough money for her to live on if I left, though. She'd never let me go otherwise."

Jesse stood by the door. "I promise you if you come with me, your families will be taken care of. Let me know by the next meeting whether you're in or out."

Andy drove in silence for a while after leaving

Jesse's then spoke. "That was a fine speech you made back there, Pete. Are you serious about taking a leave of absence?"

"Frankly, I surprised myself. Traveling with Jesse and telling people about the Ways does seem to be the right thing to do, though."

"I don't get it. You have pretty much everything you've always wanted at work, now you're ready to walk out on it all. You'd be making a big change in your life."

"I know. It's starting to hit me now." Pete shifted in his seat. "What are you going to do? Are you going with Jesse?"

"Yes, I am. It's not as big a deal for me, though. I don't have a wife, and I've never been as ambitious as you."

Pete looked out the window for a moment. "Maybe I'm finding out what's important in life. A mahogany desk isn't everything."

Andy pulled up at Pete's house. "Let's do it then. Let's talk to Halversen tomorrow." The brothers shook hands, then Pete got out of the car.

# # #

Pete and Andy squared their shoulders as they walked into Mr. Halversen's office the next morning. Halversen looked up from reading a file and smiled.

"Good morning. What do the Stone boys have up their sleeves for the firm this time?"

"Well, Mr. Halversen..." Andy stammered. "Something's come up…. We have to… that is, we may be…."

"Pete, what's Andy trying to say?"

"Sir, we've come to ask for some time off."

"Sure. How much to you need?"

"We're not exactly sure. We're going to be doing some traveling. We don't really know how long we'll be gone."

"We start the prototype run on your sedan in four weeks. Will you be back by then?"

"I don't know. I kind of doubt it." Pete lowered his eyes, afraid to face Halversen.

Mr. Halversen removed his reading glasses and stared at them. "We have to have you here for the run. You know that. Why can't you tell me when you're coming back?"

"We really don't know how long we'll be traveling."

"Is this about more money? I've already given you fellows what I thought was a generous raise."

Pete shook his head. "It's not the money. You've been very good to us."

"Have you been approached by another company?" Halversen's eyes narrowed. His hands gripped the file tightly.

"No, we haven't. It's just that we feel we need to do something else right now." Pete and Andy shifted from foot to foot as they stood before Mr. Halversen.

"And what is this 'something else'?"

Andy hung his head and spoke in a low voice. "We're going to travel around and tell people about the Old Ways and how they can live better lives."

Mr. Halversen laughed so hard tears came to his eyes. "You boys had me going for a minute. This is the best joke you've ever pulled. He wiped his eyes with a handkerchief. Okay, you got the old man. Now let me get back to work." Mr. Halversen put his glasses back on and returned to his file.

"This isn't a joke, sir," Pete said quietly. "We're serious."

Halversen's eyes widened as he looked at Pete and Andy. "You're serious?" His face grew stern. "Let me make something very clear to you two. I can't wait around wondering if you'll ever come back. I can give you a few weeks off to get this nonsense out of your systems, but that's all."

"I – I don't think that'll be enough time," stammered Pete.

"That's all you'll get from me."

"Then I guess we'll have to quit." Pete's voice was steady.

Mr. Halversen's mouth fell open. "I don't believe this!" he shouted. "I give you men money and staff, and this is how you treat me! I don't like ingrates! Don't expect to come back here for a job when you're finished with your little experiment!" He gestured toward the door. "Now get out of my office!"

Pete and Andy left hastily. "That went well." Andy's voice was shaking.

"That's nothing. Now I've got to talk with Connie. I may be sleeping at your pad tonight."

# # #

Pete turned off the engine and let the car coast into the driveway. He got out, quietly closed the door, stepped to the middle of the lawn, then stared at his house, willing his brain to become a photographic plate. He wanted to keep each detail of what he was leaving firmly in mind. His mental photo album recorded a perfect ranch-style house in a perfect suburban neighborhood. The carefully tended flowerbeds of pansies and petunias broke the monotony of the green shrubs. The spotless picture window looked in on a spacious living room with a fireplace.

Pete sighed, then went around the back of the house and opened the kitchen door.

"Pete, is that you?" Connie called.

"Yeah, it's me."

Connie, dressed in jeans and print blouse, entered the kitchen carrying a dirty dinner plate. "I'm surprised you're home this early. Thought you'd be out with Jesse and the boys again tonight. Need some supper?" She held out her plate. "As you can see, I've already eaten."

"Can I have a sandwich, please?"

While Connie prepared the sandwich, Pete went into the dining room. He sat with his head in his hands staring at the pattern on the lace tablecloth.

"What's the matter? Don't you feel well?" Connie placed the meal in front of Pete's elbows.

"Connie, we've got to talk. Something's come up." Pete looked up at Connie and took her hand.

She frowned. "Does it have anything to do with work? Is your boss being a jerk again?"

"No, it's nothing to do with work. Well, maybe it is. It's my new work."

"What do you mean? I didn't know you were getting a new assignment." Connie sat down and looked intently at Pete.

"This is hard to explain." He cleared his throat. "I guess I'll just say it. I'm leaving with Jesse and the guys. We're going to tour a lot of cities and tell people about the Old Ways and what they mean."

Connie sat for a moment, her eyes large, staring at Pete. "Are you serious?" He nodded. "You're actually leaving town?" She shook her head. "I can't believe this. When will you be back?"

"I don't know."

"What about work?"

"I quit my job." Pete stared at the pattern on the tablecloth again.

"You what?" Connie shouted.

Pete met Connie's eyes. "You heard me correctly. I quit my job. What we're going to do is more important than spending a lifetime at a desk pushing papers."

Connie pulled her hand from Pete's grasp. "Are you crazy? You're on the fast track at work! You've been promoted twice in the last couple of years!" She looked around the room and spread her arms. "You also insisted we buy the right house in the right neighborhood! We even put off having kids so we could afford this place! Now you want to throw all that away on some pipe dream Jesse's come up with?" Connie's eyes were blazing.

"It's not a pipe dream," Pete said quietly, but firmly.

"May I remind you, you don't know Mr. Cartland very well."

Pete took Connie's hand again. "I know Jesse well enough to know that going with him on this trip is the most important thing I'll ever do. If I don't go now, I'll never forgive myself."

Connie jerked free. "I see your mind's made up."

Pete nodded.

"And just how am I supposed to support myself while you're gone? A pre-school teacher's salary isn't going to cut it maintaining a big house plus all the other bills."

"Jesse says you and all the other families will be

taken care of."

"Jesse says … Jesse says. I'm sick of hearing 'Jesse says'." Connie turned to leave the room.

"Connie! Please try to understand," Pete called after her.

"The one thing I understand is that you'll be spending the night on the couch," Connie's voice broke as she went down the hall.

CHAPTER SIX

The next morning Pete and Connie fixed their breakfasts and ate in silence. Pete put his dishes in the sink, then returned to the table. He wanted to patch things up with Connie but didn't know how.

He sat on the edge of the chair and spoke quietly. "I'm taking care of some of our personal stuff today, then heading over to Jesse's." He tried to kiss Connie good-bye on the cheek. She brushed past him, turned on the faucet and began fiercely scrubbing a glass.

Pete left the house and leaned on the front door for a moment. Would Connie ever forgive him for leaving with Jesse? Head down, he walked toward his car. After a busy day of closing down his family affairs he met the rest of the group at Jesse's house.

Not everyone who had been attending the meetings was there. Matt and Jack Levy were pulling up as Pete arrived. They entered to find Nate Bardo, Phil Hiera, Tom Gems, Jim and John Thorson, Si Cane, Thad

LeBeau, Bill Stevens, and Andy already there.

Jesse looked up. "Hi Pete. How'd things go with you?"

"Just great. Halversen all but threw Andy and me out of his office, and Connie isn't speaking to me today." Pete fell into a chair, his face in his hands.

John spoke up. "You haven't heard the latest. Jesse, Phil, Jim, Nate and I went in to resign after Halversen saw you guys. He's really paranoid now. He thinks what we're actually going to do is form our own company. He said he'd sue us for every penny we had if he found out we stole any of the company's secrets."

"Guess we had it easier," Matt remarked. "Jack and I turned our workload over to some of the other partners in the firm. They weren't too happy with the extra work, but they'll be happy with the extra income."

"Thad and me got one of the mechanics to keep our business going," Si said.

Jesse looked around the group. "We haven't heard from Tom, Jeb or Bill yet. How did you all fare?"

"I don't have any building projects right now, so I have no problem with traveling," Tom replied.

"My company wanted to cut back on employees anyway," Jeb answered. "They were relieved that I wanted to leave."

"You guys all know I just graduated from college," Bill spoke up. "I don't have a job yet, so it's no problem. I am kind of worried about my dad, though. He hasn't been well lately."

"I'm glad you'll be coming with us, Jeb," Jesse placed a hand on Jeb's shoulder.

"We'll need an accountant to keep track of the funds while we're traveling."

"Speaking of funds," Pete piped up, "how are we going to finance this venture, Jesse?"

"Simple. We each pitch in some money to get us started, then ask for donations from each group we meet with."

"You think they'll actually give us money?"

"I'm sure of it. We have an important message. People will want to help get it out." Jesse took out a piece of paper containing some scribbled notes. "I'd like to leave tomorrow and get started by holding meetings in some of the smaller towns around here. John will set up the meeting places. Some of you have vans so let's travel in those.   Can everybody be back here day after tomorrow?"

Everyone agreed, then left.

As Pete pulled into his driveway, the living room light went out. The house was pitch black. He fumbled for a hall light, then went to the bedroom. Connie was already in bed with her back turned to the door. Pete sighed and decided to spend the night on the couch again.

The next morning he woke to sounds of slamming glassware and plates as Connie prepared breakfast. Pete bowed his head for a moment then took a deep breath and headed toward the kitchen.

"Honey, can we talk," he pleaded.

"What's there to talk about? You're leaving. You've made up your mind. You obviously don't care what I think." Connie turned toward the stove.

"But I do care. I know you don't believe it right now, but I do love you." Pete gently took her by the shoulders and led her to the kitchen table. They sat. He tried to hold her hand but she pulled away. "It's just that I have a feeling that the work I'm going to do with Jesse is the most important thing I'll ever do with my life. Haven't you noticed I've been more considerate since I started going to Jesse's meetings?"

"Yes, I've noticed that up 'til now."

Pete looked into Connie's eyes. "He's shown me a better way to live. I want to pass that way on to other people. Maybe we can make a difference in this messed-up world, maybe not. Anyway I'd like to try. We're leaving tomorrow, so I'll be packing today and making arrangements for you while I'm gone. I promise I'll keep in touch and see how you're doing while we're on the road."

"You do what you have to." Connie stood. "Meanwhile I'll do what I have to do. I'll even be considerate of you by making a suggestion. Why don't you pack now and spend the night at Andy's? That way you can leave even earlier. Won't that be nice for you?" Connie's sneering half-smile made Pete's heart ache.

"Connie, please..." Pete extended his arms toward her. She turned, grabbed a coat from the rack and left the house.

Pete packed while brushing some tears from his eyes, then sat on the bed. He was leaving everything he knew – a wonderful wife, a great job, financial security. Was this the right move? He looked around the room. Pete's brain was flooded with memories of Connie's laughter, her gentle touch, her lips on his. Then he thought about how his life had changed since he'd been attending Jesse's meetings. He shook his head to clear it. He had to follow Jesse. He squared his shoulders and left for Andy's.

\# \# \#

The next day he and Andy were the first to arrive at Jesse's. As they began to help Jesse sort through some clothing, Bill Stevens arrived.

Jesse looked up from his packing. "Hi, Bill. Ready to go?"

"I – I can't go right now. My dad died yesterday. We're in the midst of calling all our relatives and making the arrangements."

Pete moved to Bill's side and put an arm around his shoulders. "I'm so sorry, Bill. How's your mother doing?"

"She's holding up okay. We kind of expected it. It's still hard, though. Anyway, I can't leave with you guys right now."

Jesse cleared some luggage off a chair. "Sit down, and let's talk about this." Jesse sat facing Bill, looking into his eyes. "First of all, I'm sorry to hear about your father. You do realize, though, that we're going on a very important trip."

Bill nodded.

"You know our mission is to remind people what the Old Ways are and how they can live better lives. We're also going to talk about a New Way. It's vital that we leave now to start on that work. If you can't leave today, then I'm afraid you're out of the group."

Pete's mouth dropped open. His teeth clenched.

"But, Jesse," pleaded Bill, "just give me a chance to bury my father. I'll catch up to you guys later."

"I'm sorry, Bill. It's now or never."

Bill jumped up. "I can't believe you're serious! This is inhuman!"

"Now or never." Jesse's voice was quiet.

"Then it's never," Bill yelled over his shoulder as he walked to the door.

"Take it easy, buddy." Pete patted Bill on the back as he let him out.

Pete turned toward Jesse, his hands balled into fists. "What's the matter with you! That guy's father just died! Couldn't you cut him some slack?"

"You'd like to take a poke at me right now, wouldn't you?" Jesse asked with a half-smile.

"Yes, I would. I don't understand why you wouldn't let Bill catch up with us."

"As I told Bill, we have important work to do. That work must come before everything else, and I mean everything. It must be the top priority for everyone who joins me." Jesse motioned for Pete to sit next to him. "I'm sorry Bill's father died, but did it ever occur to you that Bill might find other excuses not to come with us? First it's burying his father; then it'll be settling his mother someplace. Finally it'll get to the point where he has to rake leaves in her yard before he can meet us."

"It still seems pretty harsh to me," Pete said, calming.

"People have to set priorities and decide what's important to them. If you want to come with me, then you must be dedicated to the work we will do."

The rest of the men gradually drifted into the house. When everything was ready, Jesse looked at the group and opened his arms to them. "Our first stop is a little farming community about twenty miles away. Let's go and make people's lives better!"

Pete climbed into a van with the others, wondering what lay ahead for them.

CHAPTER SEVEN

Christine snickered as she looked skyward. "You've got to be kidding, Father. These people left their jobs and families because of a few meetings and tricks Jesse pulled? I admit the thing with the worker's hand was slick, but fixing the copier and knowing who Nate Bardo was could easily be explained."

"Be patient, little one. I promise you'll be much more involved with the people you're watching very soon. Then things will become clearer."

"What? What do you mean, 'much more involved'?" Christine's voice quivered in her head. Why would she be more involved?

"Watch and wait, Christine." Father was gone. Christine sighed then looked down as the van engines started.

\# \# \#

Thad, his immense arm propped in the car window, was about to pull out when Pete shouted, "Hold it! I just thought of something. Jesse, where are we headed?"

"We're going to the little community of Mayville, about twenty miles from here. Why?"

"Is there more than one way to get there?"

"Just a minute. Let me look at the map." Jesse unfolded the map and studied it for a moment. "There's the main highway, and a couple of smaller roads that lead into Mayville. Why are you asking?"

"Look at the way we're set up. If we all leave right now, there'll be three vanloads of strange men driving into that town, one van following another. That might make a local cop look twice. I'm afraid we'll get some attention we don't want."

Jesse thought for a moment. "You're right, Pete. We want to get off on the right foot with these folks. Thad, honk the horn at the other vans, and we'll work out plans for meeting up at Mayville's haven."

The men worked out their strategy. Pete and Jesse's van left first taking the highway route. The other two pulled out at fifteen-minute intervals and went by different roads.

Pete rode in silence for a while. He thought about how his mornings usually started. He'd have a quick breakfast of toast and coffee, give Connie a kiss, then head to the office. Once there he'd load up on more coffee, read reports and start having product development meetings with the staff or Mr. Halversen.

Now, he was riding in a van with three other men going who-knows-where to do who-knows-what. Pete realized he missed Connie as they drove through mile after mile of flat landscape dotted with a few oak trees. Was he making a mistake?

"Not having second thoughts, are you Pete?" Jesse asked.

"What?" Pete started. "No--no, not at all Jesse. Just daydreaming. By the way, you said we were meeting at the town haven. How do we get people to come out so we can talk with them?"

"They'll come out, trust me. Oh, here we are." The van entered the city limits. "Turn right here, Thad. The haven's just a few blocks up."

The men waited until all the vans were parked at the haven. "Okay, Jesse, we're here, and no one's around. We can't even get in the building. What do we do now?" Pete was upset. Had they driven here for nothing?

"Ah, my dear practical friend, take it easy." Jesse turned to Andy. "Andy, if you'll be good enough to go to that house with the yellow wooden siding and ask for the key to the haven, I believe we'll be getting started soon."

Andy did as he was directed and soon returned with an elderly balding man. "I guess you're the folks I've been waitin' for," he said. "Name's Tom. I'll open the place up and let you all make yourselves comfortable."

The men filed in after Tom and set up chairs and a speaker's table for the meeting. Tom put a sign outside announcing the meeting, then made them all a light lunch. As they finished, people started coming in. The room filled up rapidly. A policeman, attracted by the crowd, entered and sat quietly in the back as Jesse rose to speak.

"Folks, I welcome you here today." Jesse's voice commanded attention as he stretched out his arms to the crowd. His warm brown eyes embraced each person there.

"I see fine folks before me. Folks who work hard for a living and provide the food we eat." Some in the crowd nodded. "Now you're probably wondering what a city slicker like me is doing here telling you what you already know." Scattered laughter came from the group. "I'm here to teach you about the Old Ways today and about a New Way.

Pete had been watching the crowd, now his head snapped toward Jesse. Jesse was going to talk about the New Ways! Some people in the group fidgeted in their chairs. Others looked puzzled.

"Oh, I know, you don't think any of the Ways are relevant to your lives today, but they are. Tell me, how many of you have been cheated on the prices paid for your crops?" Most of the crowd raised their hands. "How many have had something stolen from their farms?" Again most raised their hands. "The Old Ways tell us not to steal. You've just admitted most of you are victims of theft. Would those things have happened to you if everyone lived by the Old Ways? No!"

Jesse stepped closer to the audience. "Now you all know that, according to the Old Ways, you're not supposed to lie or murder anyone or run off with their husband or wife. I'm here to tell you that part of the New Ways is that you can't even think about lying, stealing or murdering anyone. If you think thoughts like that, it's like you've already done the deed."

The crowd started murmuring. Some rose to leave; then one man in faded overalls stood. "Well, I guess I'm guilty a' murder then, 'cause I been lookin' fer some hoboes who stole my pigs. I had my hatchet with me just in case I found 'em. I was gonna give 'em what-fer fer stealin' my livelihood. Now who's worse, them for actually stealin' the pigs or me for thinkin' about workin' 'em over?"

"Good question. You both broke the Ways. You both thought about actions that would be harmful to another person. God wants your thoughts and hearts to change so that you'll deal with other people in a loving way. It's just lucky for you that you didn't find those men. You might be in a heap of trouble with the law right now if you had."

The man stood rigidly glaring at Jesse. "Mister, you come up here in yer nice clean white shirt and tie and try to tell us how to live. You don't know what it's like here. Nobody cares about us. We got to take care of ourselves any way we can." The crowd nodded and murmured agreement.

Jesse brought the man to the speaker's table. "My friend, there is one who knows and cares about you. That's God. He knows your problems. He loves you."

"How's that gonna help me with my pigs?" The man thrust out his jaw at Jesse.

"Uh, Elmer," a man in the back wearing a weathered felt hat raised his hand. "I got me some extra pigs this year. You can have a couple if you need 'em."

Elmer left the speaker's table. Jesse looked at the crowd with a huge grin. "There you are, folks. People helping people out of love as God intended. Now let the hate for the hoboes go out of your heart, Elmer. It'll just upset your stomach anyway." Everyone laughed and clapped.

"Oh, Elmer," Jesse called after the man, "I'd like you to do me one favor. Say thanks to God for your new pigs sometime today if you will." Jesse turned back to the crowd. "You've just seen what God would like all you folks to do – help each other out. He wants you to talk to Him, too. Bring your problems to Him, and let Him carry some of your burdens."

"Okay, mister," a heavyset man in a plaid shirt and soiled jeans stood up. "I got a burden nobody can do anything about. This is bigger than somebody losin' some pigs."

Jesse gestured toward the man, "Come up, my friend. Tell us about your problem."

The man limped toward the table and sat down. "I got me a touch a' sugar in my blood. Now my foot's got a sore on it that ain't healin'." The man took off his shoe and held his foot toward Jesse. A bloodstained piece of gauze was taped to its sole. "I cain't work my land with this foot the way it is. Ain't nobody else here can take time off to help me. I'm about to lose my farm."

Jesse removed the gauze. The wound was an angry red pit surrounded by dead white skin. Jesse held the man's foot out to the crowd. They gasped, and many looked away. Jesse placed the gauze back on the wound, held his hand there and looked into the man's eyes. "God loves you and wants you to find your way back to him." Jesse removed the gauze.

The skin was a healthy pink with no sign of a wound. There was dead silence. People were open-mouthed, staring. Tears started falling from the man's eyes. "Mister, how can I ever thank you?"

"Don't thank me," Jesse replied. "Just remember what you learned today. It's important for folks to help each other because they care about each other, and it's important to talk to God about your problems and thank him for your blessings. Let's start right now to talk with God." As Jesse bowed his head, so did the crowd. "God,

I thank you for giving me the time to talk with these fine folks today. Help them remember what they learned here this afternoon. Let it be so."

As Jesse left the table, the crowd surrounded him. They were eager to touch him and talk with him. Pete, Andy and the others finally made a path up the aisle so Jesse could leave. The policeman lingered a while to make sure there would be no trouble at the gathering, then left.

# # #

At a local diner later, the men were animated as they talked with Jesse. "I just couldn't believe it when you healed that man's foot, Jesse! That was one ugly sore he had," Pete exclaimed. "Of course, it was also a nice coincidence that one farmer had extra pigs he could give to that other guy. Everybody went away happy."

Jesse turned toward Pete. "Was it coincidence, Pete, or did God want those two men to meet so that one man's problem could be solved?"

"Oh, come on, Jesse. We're talking about a couple of pigs here. God seems so distant to me. I think he's got more important things to worry about than a few pigs."

"Those few pigs were part of that farmer's livelihood," Jesse said firmly. "I think God's interested in that."

"When you put it like that, I guess you're right. Let's just say my remarks show I'm still learning."

"Okay, Pete," Jesse laughed. "You get an A minus for the class this afternoon." Jesse's expression grew serious as he looked at the men seated at the table. "Remember this. You'll see many things you'll wonder about as we travel. You won't understand all of them at first. Later you will. I'll explain them, so be patient."

"Jesse?" Thad half-raised his hand. "What are we doing tomorrow? If we're leaving town, I'd like to know where I'm headed."

"We are indeed leaving this town, Thad. I'll meet with you and the rest of the drivers back at our motel room. We'll work out the routes then." As they rose to leave, Jesse called back over his shoulder; "I can tell you it will be another small farm town like this."

Pete groaned as he walked with Andy. "Hope we get to a big city soon. I don't know if my stomach will survive these greasy hamburgers." Andy grinned then grew serious. "Are you going to call Connie tonight?"

"Sure am. I promised to check in with her. Just hope she doesn't hang up on me. At least she has my cell phone number in case of emergency. I'll call from our room."

Pete placed the call while Andy was freshening up in the bathroom. With a towel draped around his neck, Andy came out and sat on the bed. "Any news from home?" he asked.

Pete was glum. "No. I never realized Connie knew so many one-syllable words. I'm still shivering from her cold tone. I guess things are okay with her." He sat on the bed; looking down at his hands, shoulders slumped. "Sure hope I'm not making a mistake." He straightened slightly. "Oh well, let's get some sleep. On to the next town tomorrow!"

CHAPTER EIGHT

They drove through the countryside stopping in small towns where Jesse spoke about the New Ways, then healed people. They watched the seasons change from their van windows. The green velvet grass and wildflowers covering the hillsides turned to dry yellow brush as their journey continued. The crowds grew larger at each stop. Local television stations spread the word of Jesse's healing power. People wanted to see for themselves if it was true.

The men sat in Jesse's room one night poring over road maps. "Well, fellas," Jesse smiled, "I think it's time to spread our wings a little. Tomorrow we go to Middleton."

"Wow!" Matt Levy laughed. "Middleton's almost a city. We might be getting back to civilization, boys!" The group laughed then laid their usual driving plans. Each van would again arrive by a separate route. The men started to leave for their rooms.

"I need to talk with you, Jeb," Jesse motioned for Jeb to sit next to him. "We've outgrown the havens. The crowd will be too big tomorrow, so we'll need to rent a meeting hall."

"I don't know, Jesse. We've been getting by on the donations the folks have given us in each town, but it's tight. I don't think we have the money to rent a hall."

"Don't worry. The money will be there when we need it. Just trust me and try to remove your accountant's hat."

"Okay, you've been right so far. Maybe if we start hitting the bigger towns, we'll have a little more money in the treasury. That would make me feel better."

"As I said, the money will come. You realize money isn't the primary reason we're going to all these towns, don't you?"

"Of course. Guess I'd better get some shuteye now. See you tomorrow, Jesse."

# # #

They reached the meeting hall in Middleton a little behind schedule. The crowd had already formed. "Look," Thad pointed out his window. "There's police cars parked at the front entrance. Wonder what that's all about."

"Let's find out." Jesse slid open the van's side door. "Get Jeb for me just in case."

Several policemen got out of their cars as they saw Jesse and Jeb approach. "You folks the ones holding the meeting here?" The brawny officer stood with arms crossed, eyes invisible behind sunglasses.

"Yes, we are, officer." Jesse extended his hand to the policeman.

The policeman ignored his offer of a handshake. "We got new rules for meetings now. Mr. Chapin wants permits filed for any meeting where more than twenty-five people are gathered. You got way more than twenty-five people here waiting to get into the hall."

The policeman gestured toward the crowd. People on crutches and in wheelchairs waited by the doors with their families. Others stayed in their cars or lay on blankets in the grass by the hall. One woman was propping a man's head up as he drank from a water bottle.

"Course there'll be a fee that'll need to be paid along with the permit." The officer removed his sunglasses and looked intently at Jesse.

"Can our accountant fill out the paperwork now? I don't want to disappoint these folks."

"I don't want to either, mister. Just have your man step over here, and we'll take care of it. Remember though, that if you have any more meetings, you'll have to make arrangements ahead of time. We're just accommodating you today because it's a new rule."

"Dear sweet Aaron Chapin," Jeb grumbled. "I guess curfew wasn't enough for him. Now it's meeting permits."

The policeman turned to Jeb. "Had some trouble over in Hayward. Somebody tried to gyp people at a show, and there was a to-do. Mr. Chapin wants to make sure there's police presence at big meetings. Your permit fee'll help defray expenses."

Jeb looked at Jesse. "I hope you're right about money coming in. Meetings'll cost us a bundle from now on."

At last the paperwork was completed. Pete, Andy and the others pitched in to get the hall ready as people filed in. "Look at all the sick folks coming in," Pete groaned.

"What with the paperwork delay, we're going to be late getting out of here. Our whole schedule's shot."

Pete felt a hand on his shoulder. He turned to see Jesse staring stony-faced at him. "We'll talk later, Pete, about the schedule." Pete hung his head as Jesse went to the front of the hall and began speaking to the crowd. He knew Jesse always made time for everyone no matter how long it took. Pete was afraid his worry about the schedule had disappointed Jesse.

"Sorry about the delay, folks. Just some red tape. Seems like there's paperwork everywhere you go nowadays." The crowd nodded. "I think paperwork's a good thing, though." Jesse smiled. "I'm sure it's job security for somebody." The crowd laughed.

"I'm here to talk with you today about God, but before we get into that, let's assume something. Let's assume you've set sail on a big ocean liner without the captain on board. Can you imagine what might happen? How would you steer the ship? What would happen if a big storm came up? Who would you turn to? What would you do?" He paused, looking at the crowd. "Pretty scary, huh?"

"Well folks, your lives are like that ship. Your lives can be out of control or in control, and God's the one who can help you steer a good course. He can help you through the storms, but lots of you have forgotten about Him." He pointed his finger at the assemblage.

"You've left Him out of your lives. That makes everything harder. You've become separated from Him.

That makes Him sad. Just as you would need someone to rescue you from a storm at sea, so God will send a Rescuer to you to help you find your way back to Him." Pete had been counting the crowd, but now he listened carefully. Was Jesse going to tell them who the Rescuer was?

Jesse went on to tell the people about God's love. Some listened intently. Some tended to their sick charges, while others shifted in their seats. After Jesse finished speaking, he healed those who were ill. After the meeting, he turned to Pete. "Be sure you ride in my van. We need to talk."

"Okay, Jesse." Pete winced. He was in for a lecture. He went toward the van, his shoulders sagging.

As they drove to the next town, Jesse started speaking. "I don't think you really meant what you said about healing back there, did you, Pete?"

"No, of course not. Just chalk it up to seeing one too many hamburger joints."

"Do you know why it's important for me to heal people?"

"I guess to make us popular. People want to see us, and we're getting a good attendance at our meetings."

"It goes beyond that." Jesse paused for a moment. "If people are hurting, can they pay attention to anything else? Can they hear my message?"

"No, I guess they can't." Pete thought for a moment. "Now I understand! If you take care of people's physical needs then they listen to you better." Jesse nodded. "But if that's true, why don't you heal people first, then give your talk?"

Jesse smiled. "Because I want people to hang around and hear about God. You know some of those people today would've left immediately if they'd been healed first."

Pete laughed. "You've got it all figured out. I have to hand it to you, Jesse."

As the men ate that night, Pete made his usual call to Connie. He ran back into the restaurant, his face white. "Jesse, I've got to go home right away." Pete paused for breath.

"Why, what's the matter?" asked Jesse.

"It's Connie's mom. She's in the hospital with a high fever. The doctors can't get it down. If I don't go back now, Connie'll never forgive me. You guys go on without me. I'll catch up later."

Jesse stood and put his hands on Pete's shoulders. His face was full of concern. "We'll all go with you, Pete."

"I can't ask you to do that. What about the people who are expecting us?"

Jesse put his arm around Pete's shoulder as they started walking toward the vans. "The people will be there when we're done at your home. We'll only be a day or so late anyway."

"Thanks, Jesse." Pete was relieved. "I sure would appreciate it if you could take a look at Connie's mom."

They drove all night and reached the hospital about lunchtime the next day. The rest of the men decided to get a few hours rest at their homes. Pete and Jesse stopped at the reception desk, then made their way to Connie's mother's room.

Connie was seated in an easy chair, head back, eyes closed as she took a nap. Pete's heart ached. She looked so tired. Her mother was connected to monitors and intravenous tubing. Fluid dripped into her arm. Wavy lines on the monitor screen indicated her heart was beating. Her closed eyes had dark circles beneath them. Her cheeks were flushed, and her arms lay limp at her sides.

"What's your mother-in-law's name?" Jesse whispered as he approached the bed.

"Dora." Pete stood by Connie's chair. He longed to give her a big hug, but held back. He knew she needed her rest.

Jesse took Dora's hand in his. "Go ahead and shut the IV off. She won't need it any more."

As Pete reached for the tubing, he bumped into Connie's chair. She woke with a start and looked up at Pete. "Pete! When did you get here?" Then she noticed Jesse. "And who's this with you?"

Pete took Connie's hand. "Connie, I'd like you to meet Jesse Cartland."

Connie stood, removing her hand from Pete's grasp. "Well, well. The great Jesse Cartland. To what do we owe this honor?" Connie's words sliced through the air.

"Connie … honey…" Pete gestured toward Jesse. "Jesse came to help. We came as soon as we heard about Dora."

"How nice that you took time out of your busy schedule…" Connie's voice cracked. She began to cry. Pete folded her into his arms. As she calmed and dried her eyes, her voice still shook. "I'm at my wit's end, Pete. They can't get Mom's fever down. She's wasting away, even with the IV's. They've tried a bunch of different antibiotics. Nothing seems to work."

"Connie," Jesse's voice was soft. "Let me help."

Connie whirled around. "What can you do? All you've done so far is take my husband away from me!"

Her eyes blazed.

Pete gently turned her face toward him. "Honey, trust him. I've seen Jesse do wonderful things for people. I really think he can help Dora." Pete looked at Jesse. "Do you need me to do anything?"

"Yes, turn off the IV."

Pete reached for the tubing. Connie grappled with him. "Are you out of your minds? That IV is the only thing that's keeping my mother alive right now!"

Pete closed the clamp on the tubing. "Please, Connie, trust us. I'd never do anything to hurt Dora."

"You two are crazy! I'm getting a nurse!" Connie ran out of the room.

When she came back with the nurse a few minutes later, Dora was sitting up in bed. "Oh good, dear. I'm glad you brought the nurse. She can take all these contraptions off me. I don't think I need them any more." Connie and the nurse stared openmouthed at Dora.

"What's the matter, dear? You look like you've seen a ghost."

"Mom. You were so sick…" Connie clutched Pete's arm for support.

"But I'm fine now." Dora looked from Connie to Jesse. "Have you met this young man? We were just having the nicest conversation."

Pete helped Connie to the chair. She looked up at him. "What happened, Pete? What happened while I was out of the room?"

"Jesse took her hand and healed her. I told you he could help."

The nurse recovered her composure. "I'll call your doctor, Mrs. Anders. I have to check with him before I remove everything, but looks to me like you'll be going home soon."

Connie's eyes moistened as she looked at Jesse. "How can I ever thank you?"

"Just let God back into your life, and know that the work Pete helps me do is important."

Connie nodded as she wiped away tears with her handkerchief, then she turned to Pete. "I'll never question your work again." Pete embraced her.

Dora was well enough to go home that afternoon. She insisted on baking one of her special cakes for a celebration in honor of her recovery.

As the men and their families relaxed at Pete's house that evening, John asked, "What's next, Jesse? Are we going back on the road again?"

"Yes, we are. We'll rest up here for a few days; then you're in for a special treat.   We're going to my hometown."

The men laughed as Matt threatened to dig up any dirt he could on Jesse. "I'll bet the folks in your hometown could tell us a lot of stories about you growing up."

"I'll bet they could, too," Jesse smiled. "Get some rest while you can. You'll be glad you did."

He started out the door, but Pete caught his arm. "Jesse, in all the mess with Dora I forgot. You mentioned the Rescuer in Middleton. Are you going to tell us who or what the Rescuer is?"

"Soon, Pete. Very soon." Jesse walked across the porch.

"You're certainly teaching me the value of patience," laughed Pete as he closed the door. "Hope there aren't too many more secrets," he murmured as he joined the rest of the group.

CHAPTER NINE

Christine felt Father's presence. "I must say I'm impressed, Father. Jesse's helping people. He even got Connie on his side. Isn't it kind of cheating, though, to go to your hometown? Surely he'll get a hero's welcome."

"Maybe, maybe not. Watch and see."

"And what did you mean when you said I'd be much more involved?"

"Again I tell you patience, little one." Father admonished. "There's no such thing as time here. We don't have to rush." Father was gone again. Christine looked back as Pete, Jesse and the rest of the men drove off.

# # #

"There it is, Jesse," Thad pointed to a green sign by the road. "Cheviot, population 7,500. Thanks a lot!

We're back in the sticks, again! I thought we were headed to the big time after Middleton."

"Be patient." Jesse laughed. "I'd like to get a little family time in while I'm here. We'll go on to bigger and better places soon enough."

As soon as the vans met up, Jesse dispatched Jeb to take care of the paperwork. The desk sergeant looked up as Jeb entered the police station. "Good morning, sir. May I help you?"

Jeb leaned against the counter. "Yes. I'm here to fill out the paperwork for the meeting Jesse Cartland's having here."

"Oh, yeah. I heard Jesse was coming. He's a great guy. We grew up together. Can't wait to see him again." The sergeant turned to a stack of forms. "Here's the paperwork." He started to hand the forms to Jeb, then hesitated. "You know, Mister… what's your name?"

"Kerry."

"Mr. Kerry, I had an idea that might help Jesse. Why don't you step in the office with me." The sergeant gestured toward a door.

As the two men sat down, Jeb asked, "There isn't any trouble, is there officer?"

"No, not at all. I'm just thinking you're going to have to pay a pretty hefty fee for this meeting." Jeb winced. "I think the whole town'll probably turn out to see their fair-haired boy in action. Aaron Chapin's got this fee schedule set up so that it's tied to the size of the crowd that's expected. That helps cover our expenses. I think you're looking at two hundred and fifty dollars for this event."

"That much, huh?"

"Yeah, but I don't feel right about it. I know there's

not going to be any trouble, and I really hate to take advantage of Jesse like that."

"What can we do, though?"

"Well, I've been thinking, and this is strictly between you and me, you understand." Jeb nodded. "I'm the one who okays the paperwork and estimates the crowd. If I put down half the number of people I expect, that cuts your fee in half."

"That would be great!" Jeb grinned.

The officer moved his chair closer to Jeb's. "I would need a little consideration, though, since I'm taking a chance."

Jeb studied the man's face. "How much is 'a little consideration'?"

"Twenty-five dollars." The man spoke rapidly and looked hopefully at Jeb.

Jeb rose and extended his hand. "You've got a deal, officer. Thanks for your help."

Jeb decided to keep this arrangement to himself. He'd made a good bargain so he had a right to keep some of the cash he would have paid for the license fee. Besides it would be nice to have a little extra money for a rainy day. He knew if he told Jesse, Jesse would spend the money on something else.

After the formalities at the police station were complete, Jeb went to the meeting hall to help set up. Jesse looked up from arranging chairs. "How'd it go?"

"Everything's set. No problems." Jeb started to unfold chairs.

"How much did it cost us?"

Jeb looked at Jesse. "Seems the going rate for this size crowd is two hundred fifty dollars. Wish you weren't so popular, Jesse." Jeb laughed nervously. He was uneasy keeping the fee arrangement from Jesse.

Jesse stared into Jeb's eyes for a moment, then went back to arranging chairs. "Just make sure the buckets for donations get put at the doors. We're going to need them."

Later people started filing in. They hugged Jesse and shook his hand. There was much laughter and joking. As Jesse made his way to a table at the front of the hall, many friends and neighbors waved at him. His mother, sisters and brothers sat in the front row.

"My friends, it is indeed a pleasure to be here with you tonight." Jesse's broad smile warmed the room. "You've made a small town boy proud to call Cheviot his home." The crowd burst into applause. The few policemen at the back of the room smiled and clapped also.

Jesse picked up a well-worn book from the table and held it high. "Does this look familiar to any of you?" Some people frowned trying to figure out what the book was. Others shook their heads no. "This is the book all of us studied in our haven days, then many of us forgot. This book talks about the Old Ways and a promise of New Ways. Let me read a passage." Jesse flipped open the volume.

"I read 'and there will come someone to free you, to tell you of new ways, to heal you and bring you back to me.' Do you remember that ancient promise?" Some shook their heads; some nodded. Others were still frowning.

Jesse closed the book and stood very straight. He

spoke in a commanding voice. "God promised that He'd send someone to lead you back to Him. I came here today to tell you that I am that someone."

For a few minutes, there was complete silence. Pete, Andy and the rest had been lining the walls watching Jesse and the crowd. Now their jaws dropped and eyes widened. Jesse's family was shocked.

An older man in faded coveralls stood. "Jesse, you gotta be kiddin'. I knew your pa before you were born. He was just a poor workin' man like the rest of us. No offense to your family, but you come in here now sayin' you're fulfilling some old promise God made? I think you been drinkin' some happy juice, boy." The crowd murmured and nodded as the man sat down.

Someone else yelled, "Do you think you're better than us, Jesse!" Others took up that chant.

Jesse remained calm. He held up his hands to quiet the crowd. "Do you think promises are fulfilled, or did we all waste our time reading this book?" he asked them as he waved the book in front of them.

"I suppose they are," another man replied, "but, Jesse, we all knew you when you were buying ice cream cones at the local drugstore. I don't think anyone here can take what you just said seriously."

As Jesse started to answer the man, a woman marched down the aisle. "Wait a minute, Jesse. I got something I want to get off my chest that's got nothing to do with some fancy promise."

"Go ahead." Jesse stretched out a hand in her direction.

The woman's acid tone ate through the air. "I heard about these great healing miracles you've supposedly been doing. I want to know why you didn't heal my brother when that car ran over him and crushed his leg." Her voice rose. "You were right there with him. Why didn't you do something?"

"It wasn't my time," Jesse said quietly.

"It wasn't your time?" the woman yelled. "He spent months in the hospital, and it wasn't your time!" The woman's voice cracked as she started to cry. "Well, pardon me, but I don't have *time* to listen to anything you have to say."

The crowd's murmuring got louder as someone led the woman back to her seat. The policemen started watching the throng.

Jesse raised his hands to the assembly. "Folks, I know this is hard to understand, but God's schedule isn't always the same as ours."

"When were we ever on your schedule, Jesse?" someone else in the crowd asked. "I think that woman has a good point. If you're so powerful; seems like you could have done a lot for folks right here in your hometown. Why didn't you?"

Others in the audience stood and shouted, "Yeah, why didn't you." The crowd shook their fists at Jesse and started toward him. Some screamed about the favors Jesse could have done for them. Others shouted that he was a fraud.

Thad LaBeau was alarmed. He motioned for help from the other men lining the walls. One of the policemen ran outside to call for backup. Jesse's family sat frozen in their seats. As the crowd pressed in on Jesse, Thad and Si Cane pushed their muscular bulks through the throng to rescue Jesse. When they got to the front, people were yelling, "Where did he go? Where is that Cartland kid?"

Si and Thad made their way out the door and spotted Pete, Andy and the rest of the men.

"Where's Jesse?" Thad asked. "Anybody seen him?" The other men shook their heads no. Thad started toward the vans. "Let's get out of town now!" he shouted. "There's a diner called Mom's Kitchen about twenty miles from here. Let's all meet up there."

The men jumped in their vans and burned rubber getting out of the parking lot. They could hear sirens as extra police cars approached.

Pete, Andy, Thad and John rode in silence for a while. Finally Andy spoke. "I don't know about you guys, but I'm still shaking inside." The others nodded agreement. "What happened? What went wrong? We've been doing great up 'til now. Does this mean we're finished?"

Pete looked down for a moment then back at Andy. "I don't know, little brother, but I sure would like to know what happened to Jesse. I'm worried about him."

The men found the diner and sat at different tables. They drank coffee quietly and tried to remain as inconspicuous as possible. No telling how far out Jesse's neighbors might travel in their eagerness to vent their anger.

Suddenly, Jesse was in the room with them. "Come on, men. There's a table in the back. We won't be bothered there." He gestured for the waitress.

As they settled and ordered dinner, Pete asked, "What happened, Jesse? I thought we'd have a great time in Cheviot. Instead we almost got ridden out of town on a rail."

"You heard them. Some of the people in that crowd probably helped change my diapers. They couldn't accept the fact that someone they were so familiar with could have such an important mission."

"What is your mission, Jesse? You've talked in general about promises in the haven book. Now you say you're the Rescuer?"

Jesse cradled his head in his hands. "Not now, boys. I'm kind of tired. We'll get into that later."

Andy looked up from his coffee. "Did your family get out okay, Jesse?"

"Yes, they did. That's why it took me a while to catch up to you all. We talked for a bit. Seems they've decided it's best not to be seen with me right now."

"Jesse, I'm sorry." Pete put a hand on Jesse's shoulder.

"It's okay. The thing is--I came here to do a job, and I need your help. Can I count on you?" While Jeb sat staring at his coffee, the others at the table voiced their reassurances to Jesse.

Jesse smiled and looked at the group. "I guess you're my family now."

While they ate, Jesse and the men made plans to visit other towns scattered through the region and away from Cheviot.

Pete lay awake in his room that night. Things had been going so well. What had happened in Cheviot? Why did Jesse's friends and neighbors turn on him like that?

They acted like they wanted to kill him! What would happen in the next town they visited?

CHAPTER TEN

The men's travel became more complicated after Cheviot. Aaron Chapin set up checkpoints at the roads leading into each town so there would be no more riots. Jeb had to produce a set of paperwork and pay fees to the local officials, then the group was able to set up the meetings. Since the routine was always the same, the days were a blur for Pete. He hardly knew what the date was or what town they were visiting. Each time they pulled into a new town people in wheelchairs and on stretchers were waiting as they arrived at the hall. Umbrellas and crude canvas awnings protected the ill from the sun. Coolers and thermoses were close at hand. Those who attended the sick brought along camp chairs to rest in while they waited for Jesse and his group. Pete never got used to this sight of human suffering or the pleas for help that rose from the crowd when they saw Jesse and his men approaching.

One hot August afternoon Pete was guiding people

up to Jesse to be healed when a slender middle-aged woman approached him. "Please, mister, can you help me?"

"If you need healing, I'm afraid you'll have to wait your turn." Pete started wheeling a chair up toward Jesse.

"No sir, I don't need any help, but my mistress does."

"All right. Just wait in the back of the hall 'til we're finished."

Jesse continued healing with Si and Thad standing on either side of him. Pete and the others funneled the sick to Jesse for another hour. Shouts of joy and gratitude filled the hall. After they were finished with the meeting, Pete started to help the others clean up. He straightened for a moment to rub his back and noticed the woman sitting in the back, still waiting.

He hurried toward her. "I'm sorry. We were so busy. What did you need?"

"My mistress has been sick for a long time. Can you help her?"

"Why didn't you bring her here? We could have helped her by now."

"Mrs. Madsen never leaves the house." The woman tugged at Pete's arm. "Please, can you help her? I'm really worried about her."

"Come up front with me. We can talk to Jesse about this. By the way, what's your name?"

"Mary."

After Pete introduced Mary to Jesse, Jesse took her to the side of the room and talked with her for a while. After they were finished, Jesse approached Pete.

"Hey, Pete, can you get the van keys from Thad? Seems we're going to make a house call."

Mary led the way in her compact car. After about

twenty minutes, they arrived at a large two-story brick house. They drove into the circular driveway and passed one wing of the residence on their way to the main entrance. Rose bushes lined the small path to the front door. Pete glanced back at the huge lawn -- not a weed in sight.

Mary led them upstairs and knocked gently on a door.

"Come in."

They entered the bedroom. The heavy drapes were closed against the sun. A fan tried valiantly to stir the heavy August air. In the dim light, they saw a woman in a dressing gown; shoulders slumped, sitting on the side of the bed. Pete settled against a dresser. As Jesse started toward the woman, he bumped into an easy chair.

"Could we turn the lights on?"

"No lights." The woman spoke in flat tones. She remained with her back to Jesse.

"Mary asked me to come visit you, but it's hard to see you in the dark."

"I said 'no lights'. This is my house, and there will be no lights." The woman turned partially. "And what do you mean by bringing a stranger into my house, Mary?" Her cold, imperious voice cut at Mary.

"I … I was worried about you, Mrs. Madsen. I was trying to help." Mary shrank toward the door.

"Don't blame Mary, Mrs. Madsen. She cares about you. She asked me if I could come and help you." Jesse's voice was soothing.

"Thank you so much, Mister Fix-it." Her words biting the air, Mrs. Madsen turned to face Jesse. "By the way, who are you?"

"I'm Jesse Cartland."

"I've heard something about you. You're supposed to be some kind of healer?" Jesse nodded. "Okay, Mr. Healer, let's see what you can do with my little problems. My son died, and my husband ran off with another woman."

"I'm sorry." Jesse drew closer to the bed. "What's your first name?"

"Marika."

"You must feel very lonely, Marika. I can understand why you think no one cares." Jesse sat on the edge of the bed.

"I know nobody cares! When I needed my husband the most, he ran out on me!"

"And you feel alone in this big house."

"Wouldn't you? The house is so empty without my son." Her voice choked. She paused for a moment, then spoke, acid dripping from her words. "All it signifies now is my husband has a guilty conscience. He doesn't want people talking about how he cast his ex-wife aside when she was going through the worst loss of her life, so he supports me well."

"Wasn't your husband sad, too, when your son died?"

She sighed. "I suppose so. I wasn't noticing anything at the time. All I know is he wasn't there for me."

Jesse took Marika's hand. "Were you there for him?"

Marika's eyes widened as she looked into Jesse's eyes. She thought for a moment then began to cry. "No, I wasn't. I wasn't there for anybody." Mary handed her a handkerchief.

"Mary's been here for you."

"Mary's just worried about her job. If something happens to me, she'll be out on her ear."

"Mrs. Madsen…" Mary began. Jesse put up a hand to quiet her.

"There is someone you can count on to care even if you don't believe Mary does."

"Who?"

"God."

"You've got to be kidding! The same God who let my son die? I'm sure he's a big help."

"There is evil in the world, Marika. I won't deny that. Bad things happen, but God's there to help you pick up the pieces. Your heart is broken right now. Let him in to put the pieces back together."

"I … I don't know. I don't think anyone can help."

"Look at what you have in this room. You have three people who care about you, Mary and me and that fellow over there." Jesse gestured toward Pete. "Walk with me into the light outside this room. I promise you'll feel better." Jesse took Marika's arm and started to help her to her feet. She pulled her arm away.

"I don't know if I can leave this room. It's safe here."

"I know there are others who care about you. Please trust me and come out into the light. Let God and other people into your life." Jesse led her toward the door.

They all walked outside the room into the hall. Everyone squinted as their eyes adjusted to the light. Marika stopped and looked around. She walked toward the window and stared out for a while; first with a frown, then gradually her face relaxed, and she smiled.

"Mary, the garden's so beautiful! It's so full of lovely flowers! And the sunlight on the pond! It's so bright! Oh, and look at the ducks! They're eating! How cute! "

"Yes, ma'am." Mary smiled and mouthed a thank-you to Jesse.

Marika looked up and down the hall. "And the house. Mary, you've kept the house so well. I think I'd like to explore it later."

She turned toward Jesse. "I do feel better. How can I ever repay you?"

"You must let your heart answer that question for you," Jesse replied.

"Everything I have is yours." Marika reached for Jesse's hand and smiled.

Marika was as good as her word. She subsidized the group's travel and raised money from her friends. Her money allowed the men to make many more stops. When she wasn't fundraising, she traveled to the towns where Jesse was speaking to hear more of his talks.

CHAPTER ELEVEN

The young man sat in the reception room tapping his foot. His ill-fitting suit coat emphasized his skinny build. Periodically he glanced at his watch then flipped through a folder full of papers in his lap. A small stack of videotapes sat on the table next to him.

The receptionist answered her intercom, then motioned to the young man. "Mr. Chapin will see you now, Agent Vole."

As Artie Vole rose to enter the office, the folder slipped off his lap. Papers spewed out onto the floor. Blushing, he picked up the mess, then reached for the videotapes. He missed his mark, and the tapes also hit the floor. The receptionist sighed and helped him retrieve his things.

He straightened his tie then squared his shoulders and opened the office door. The office was sparsely furnished. Dark wooden bookshelves filled with legal volumes lined the walls. A television set hooked up to a VCR stood in one corner, but the dominant feature of the room was the massive walnut desk. The desktop was remarkably clear with only a few folders and pens carefully placed beside the phone and intercom. The desk appeared to dwarf the slight, fortyish, balding man who sat behind it until he raised his head. The cold flinty gaze from his gray eyes seemed to search out and record everything stored in Vole's brain cells. A shiver went down Artie's back.

"Well, Vole, what do you want?" Chapin shuffled papers on his desk indicating he had more important things to do than talk with an agent.

"It … uh … it seems that … uh." Artie blushed again.

"Have a seat, Vole, and spit it out. I've got a lot to do today."

Artie thankfully took a seat. His trembling legs needed a chance to steady themselves. He swallowed and began speaking. "It seems, sir, that Jesse Cartland's a blip on our radar screen."

"Jesse Cartland. Who's Jesse Cartland?" Chapin frowned. "Name sounds familiar."

"Remember the riot in Cheviot, sir."

Chapin creased his brow in thought. "Oh yes. Now I remember. Cartland was right in the middle of that, wasn't he? I thought we took care of him with the checkpoints I put in place."

"There's been no trouble with Cartland since the Cheviot incident, but he's held a lot of meetings in small towns. Look at all the applications that've been filed." Artie held up the folder. Some of the paperwork fell out.

"So what. If the meetings are lawful, and there's been no more trouble, why should we worry?"

Artie held up the videotapes. "You know it's my job to watch local news shows. Cartland's been gathering quite a following. He claims to be a healer."

"No kidding." Chapin gestured toward the tapes.

"Since you have the tapes there, let's have a look at them."

Artie popped a tape into the unit. It showed a local reporter interviewing a woman. She was laughing and crying at the same time, saying she was able to walk again after ten years of paralysis from a spinal injury. He fast-forwarded the tape showing Chapin snippets of various interviews much like the first. Each person interviewed stated Jesse had cured him or her of some horrific disease when no one else could help.

After Chapin finished viewing the tapes, he gave a dry laugh. "Well, I can see why the local medical profession might not be too happy with Mr. Cartland. He'll put 'em out of business." Chapin swiveled back to face Artie. "Any of the big talk shows get hold of this yet?"

"No sir, but, like you, I'm worried about that. Cartland and his crew are going to bigger cities now and larger crowds are coming to see him and hear him talk."

"He talks, too? What does he speak about?"

"Here's the unbelievable part. He talks about the Old Ways and about some New Way."

Chapin leaned back in his chair and howled with laughter. After a few minutes he grew serious again. "I can see now why you're suspicious of this Cartland. You mean people actually sit still and listen to that stuff?"

"I don't think everybody does. Some folks are just there to get healed and go on with their lives. Others do follow him from town to town, though. He also seems to be getting some pretty good financial backing."

"Really." Chapin thought for a moment. "I have trouble believing anybody's motive would just be to talk about the Old Ways, and if this guy's getting money from somewhere…." Chapin's voice trailed off as he cupped his chin in his hand. He thought for a moment, then looked up at Artie.

"Tell you what, Agent Vole. I think we should send someone in to infiltrate the group and see what's going on."

Artie nodded. "I agree completely, sir."

"How would you like to be that someone?"

"Me? But, sir, I'm a communications agent. My job is to watch the suspicious paperwork, computers, TV and such."

"You were trained in undercover methods, weren't you?"

"Sure, in the academy."

"Then spread your wings, boy. Make weekly reports on what this group is up to, or more often if you think something serious is going on. Remember, my number one goal is to maintain order in this region."

"Yes sir. If you think I'm ready, sir. Thank you, sir."

Chapin made a shooing motion with his hand.

Artie stumbled over the chair in his haste to get to the door.

Chapin watched him exit, then chuckled. "Nothing like sending a two-bit agent to watch a two-bit operation. This should blow over pretty quickly"

CHAPTER TWELVE

Artie whistled as he bustled around the apartment, packing his bags. He'd made the big time -- an undercover assignment! It was something he'd always dreamed of. He flipped on the television set to catch the news while he emptied out his bureau.

After he placed the last item in his suitcase, he headed toward the TV set to turn it off, then thought of something.

How am I going to find this guy, Cartland? Should I go down to the office and run through the tracking tapes to see if anybody's done surveillance on him? What would one of the experienced agents do?

He reached for the off switch on the television set, hesitated, then smiled. What luck! The talking heads were doing a story on Jesse Cartland. Artie sat down on the couch to listen.

A woman with carefully coifed dark hair was speaking to her news colleague. "Dan, what do you think of this Jesse Cartland? He certainly seems to be creating a stir in the small towns in the region."

"Yes he is, Lisa. I guess he's what you'd call in sports a phenom. I know folks claim he's cured them of all sorts of ailments. I think the jury's still out on that, though. Some doctors are checking to see if these people really have been cured."

"What do you think of all his talk about the Old Ways and a New Way?"

The anchorman's chiseled features fell into a frown for a moment, then he replied. "It's an odd platform. I don't know if he can maintain popularity for the long haul by talking about the Ways all the time. Folks may get tired of hearing about them. We'll have to wait and see. In the meantime, it sure is an interesting story."

The dark-haired woman turned to face the camera. "That it is, Dan. Mr. Cartland will be appearing in Fayetteville tomorrow evening. We'll keep you updated on this story and all the other news that's happening in this region."

Artie flipped off the TV set. *What a break! Now I can cruise over to Fayetteville and catch up with Mr. Jesse Cartland.* He reached for his bags, then hesitated. *Should I wear a disguise?* He pursed his lips for a moment weighing the options. *I know! I'll wear my glasses instead of contact lenses.*

After changing his lenses for glasses, Artie studied himself in the mirror. A thin face with spectacles perched on a long nose stared back at him. He smoothed back his blond unruly hair and karate-chopped at his reflection, then grabbed his bags and began whistling again as he closed the apartment door behind him. A moment later there was a thud as suitcases hit the floor in the hall. The door clicked open in response to the key. Artie reached in, sighed and pulled his coat free.

Artie was shocked when he reached the meeting hall in Fayetteville. He had, of course, watched tapes of

Jesse's meetings; but the tapes hadn't prepared him for what he saw now. Lines of people waiting to get into the hall extended for blocks in either direction. Police were roping off the street so that stretchers and wheelchairs could be accommodated. Some of the sick were moaning. Others were asking where Jesse was or when they could get into the hall. As Artie went to the back of the line, some of the crowd became impatient and started to yell rhythmically "Open the doors!" over and over.

Finally the doors opened. Artie was pushed and shoved as people jockeyed for good seats. He ended up against the wall and looked toward the front as people started clapping. A man stepped out to stand behind a spotlight-illuminated table.

Ah, there he is. Jesse Cartland. Vole started the tape-recorder he had hidden in his jacket pocket.

"My friends," Jesse spoke into the microphone, "it is indeed a pleasure to be here with you in Fayetteville." The crowd applauded. "I have a question for you. Have you ever lost something? Something that was precious to you?" People in the audience nodded. "Maybe you even said 'I'll put it right where I'll be sure to find it', then you can't remember where that sure-to-find-it place is." Light laughter came from the gathering. "Do you remember your happiness when you found that precious thing that was lost to you?" Some people nodded again.

"Well, folks, God's lost something. He's lost you! You're all very precious to Him, but you've stopped following the Ways. You've stopped letting God into your lives! I'm here to tell you, He wants you to come back to Him. And how do you do that?"

Jesse looked around at the crowd. "You love God with all your heart and remember to treat any person you deal with the way you'd like to be treated. Let God back into your hearts, and everything else will fall into place. Now let's pray together." Jesse bowed his head. "Dear Father, help these people open their hearts to you so that they may know you again. Let it be so."

He looked up at the crowd again. "I know there are many of you out there who are hurting. Please form lines in the aisle. My people will show you what to do. Let's get busy and use God's loving power to heal you." The crowd broke into applause then formed lines as Pete and the others instructed them. Si and Thad took their usual places on each side of Jesse.

Artie hung back by the wall. He watched Jesse touch a boy in a wheelchair. The boy jumped from the chair, and he and his parents danced in the aisle. A woman, arm hanging limp at her side, approached Jesse. After he touched her, she was able to raise her arm above her head and wave to the entire crowd. The miracles went on and on. There was much shouting, laughing, and crying in the auditorium as people rejoiced with their families.

At last the crowd thinned. Artie approached a muscular man with curly hair who seemed to be part of Jesse's group. "Excuse me, sir."

Pete turned toward Artie. "Can I help you?"

"Yes, I was wondering if I could meet Mr. Cartland."

"Gee, I don't know. Jesse's had a pretty big day. I'd like to see him get some rest."

"Please, Mr....."

"Call me Pete."

"Please, Pete. I've never seen anything like this. It was really inspiring. I was going to ask Mr. Cartland if I could help out in any way."

Pete looked at Jesse then back at Artie. "Well, we

could always use another hand. Come on up. I'll introduce you. By the way, what's your name?"

"Artie Vole." Artie gasped. *Should I have used an alias?*

"Are you all right?" Pete asked. "You seem to be having trouble breathing."

"Uh, yeah, I'm fine. Just a little muscle spasm. Happens every once in a while." *Quick thinking, Agent Vole!*

Artie followed Pete to the front. Jesse was wiping his forehead with a handkerchief.

"Jesse, I'd like you to meet Artie Vole." Pete looked toward Artie. "He's volunteered to help us."

"Has he? Well, Artie Vole, welcome aboard." Jesse extended his hand. "I'm sure Pete's told you we could always use an extra man."

"Yes, he has. When do you want me to start?"

Jesse laughed. "The most important question right now is where do we all want to eat."

"I've solved that problem for you," a female voice said from behind the table.

Jesse turned around and grinned. "Marika! You're here!" He extended his arms.

Marika gave him a quick hug. "I'd like you to meet my friend, Zach Abramson."

She gestured toward a short, middle-aged man with a beard. He stepped forward.

"Marika's told me many things about your work. From what she's told me and from what I saw tonight; I definitely want to help you. I think I have an interesting proposition for you, and I'd like to discuss it over dinner."

"Sounds great," said Jesse. "Did you have any place special in mind?"

"Yes, I've rented a private dining room at the hotel. I think you'll find the food satisfactory."

Pete whooped, "All right! No hamburgers tonight!"

Zach smiled. "I've also rented hotel rooms for everyone so you won't have to worry about the curfew. We'd better get moving though. The hotel chef's rather temperamental." Zach looked at his watch. "He wants to start serving in about fifteen minutes."

Artie turned to go. Jesse called after him. "You can come, too, Artie, if it's all right with Mr. Abramson."

Zach was halfway up the aisle. "Sure, the more the merrier."

Artie followed the others, congratulating himself on how easily he'd been accepted.

As the group left, a young woman came out of the shadows in the back of the hall. She was dressed in a tight red silk blouse and mini-skirt and wore heavy make-up. Her high-heeled boots made click-clacking sounds on the cement floor as she walked toward the door. She glanced furtively at the knot of people as she ran to her car, put it in gear, then followed Jesse and his men.

CHAPTER THIRTEEN

Jesse smiled as he watched his men gawk when they entered the hotel lobby. Soft upholstered chairs and sofas invited guests to sit down. The highly polished floor seemed never to have been walked on. They were ushered to a private dining room with dark paneled walls and tables set with sparkling silverware and gleaming china. Soft music played in the background.

"Sure doesn't look like Burger Boy, does it, Jesse?" Pete laughed as he sat down.

"No, it doesn't." Jesse turned to Zach. "How can we ever thank you for such luxury?"

"You haven't heard the half of it, Jesse." Marika smiled as Zach helped her into her chair. "Tell him about your idea, Zach."

"I guess now is as good a time as any since you're so excited, Marika." Zach sat next to Jesse. "Marika and I have been friends for years, but I couldn't believe what she was telling me until I saw it myself. What you're doing for people is wonderful, Jesse, and your organization is growing; but it's still small town stuff. Marika and I think you need to expand, to have a place where you can attract more people to hear your message."

"Your idea sounds good, Zach, but we have a lot of expenses. We have to pay for hall rentals and license fees for the meetings."

"I realize that. That's why I'm proposing that I furnish the stadium outside Parkersburg for your next meeting.   It holds between six and seven thousand people."

"That's wonderful!" Jesse's elation was palpable. "But how can you afford to do that?"

"Simple.   I own the stadium.   I also want to help sponsor your group."

Jesse, Zach and Marika continued their discussion, working out the logistics of the meeting.

# # #

The woman in red parked her car at the hotel and put on a long dark coat. She knew the hotel personnel would never let her in the lobby if they saw her dressed as she was.   She entered the lobby, scanned the schedule of activities for the day; then went down the hall to the dining room. She opened the service door slightly and squeezed through it.   When she saw Jesse at the head table, her heart started beating rapidly. Would he help her?

People were laughing and talking as waiters served coffee and dinner. She felt warm and dizzy. Was she doing the right thing? She took a deep breath, removed her coat and started toward Jesse.

Zach looked up as she approached. "Who are you?" He looked around the room. "Did anyone invite this woman?" Everyone looked surprised.

"Please, mister, I want to talk to that man for a minute." Her voice trembled as she pointed toward Jesse.

Zach gestured for a waiter.   "Throw that woman out!"

Jesse raised his hand. "Wait a minute.   Let her speak."

"Look at her. She's a common prostitute. I don't even know how she got in here." Zach gestured again for the waiter.

Jesse's voice was firm. "I would like to speak with her." He turned to the woman, his voice gentler, "What's your name?"

"Marie, sir."

"And why did you want to speak with me?"

"I – I'm in terrible trouble, sir. I didn't realize it 'til I heard you speak tonight." She began to cry. Mascara ran down her face. "That man's right." She gestured at Zach. "I've been with a lot of men." Marie hung her head, unable to look Jesse in the eye. "I've done a lot of things I'm ashamed of. I've lied, cheated people and stolen from them. I've been leading an awful life. I'm one of those lost people you talked about. I need help. What should I do?" Her legs gave way, and she went to her knees. She wept uncontrollably, her hands clasping her bowed head.

Jesse rose from his chair and went around the table to Marie. He placed his hands on her head. He said in a voice only she could hear, "The Father is so happy with you now, Marie. You're finding your way back to Him. He's forgiven you for everything you've done. Can you feel the forgiveness?"

Marie felt a great calm descending on her like a wave gently kissing the shore. Jesse removed his hands. She raised her head and looked into his eyes. He gave her a handkerchief. As she dabbed at her eyes, she said in a hushed voice, "Yes, I can feel it." She rose and spoke louder. "Yes, I can feel it! I can feel it!" She twirled around with arms outstretched, a big smile on her face. "Oh, thank you, sir! Thank you so much! I promise I'm going to live a better life." She turned to go.

"Wait a minute," Jesse called to her. "Why don't you join us for dinner?"

Zach raised his eyebrows, but had the waiter bring another chair to the table. Marie sat next to Jesse listening to everything he had to say.

Artie watched from the next table, smiling slightly. He thought how good this juicy incident would be for his report to Mr. Chapin. Jesse Cartland consorting with a prostitute!

CHAPTER FOURTEEN

The next morning as Jesse prepared to leave the hotel with his men, Marika and Zach; a young man and woman approached the group. "Pardon me," the man said, "can you tell me which of you is Jesse Cartland?"

"I am." Jesse extended his hand to the man.

The two men shook hands. "We'd like to introduce ourselves. I'm Gabe Oliver." Gabe brought the young woman closer. "This is my sister, Marta. We just wanted to thank you for what you did for our sister last night."

"You're very welcome," Jesse replied. "Was she someone I healed at the meeting?"

"You could say that. Our sister's name is Marie. She came home after your dinner last night and told us what you'd done for her."

Marta's eyes welled with tears. "We haven't seen her for months. We were terribly worried about her. What she was doing was so dangerous."

Gabe nodded. "Now she's home looking through

want ads for a job. I've never seen her so happy and satisfied. Anyway, Mr. Cartland, we thought we'd come over today and thank you. We also wanted to tell you that we'd like to contribute something to help your movement." Gabe pulled some cash from his pocket. "Please feel free to stop by our place any time. We'd be happy to put you and your men up for the night."

"It was my pleasure to help your sister. She's on the right track now." Jesse took the money without looking at it and handed it to Jeb. Jeb began counting. His eyes widened. His mouth fell open.

"We can see you're ready to leave. We just thought we'd stop by and say thanks." Gabe and Marta turned to go.

"Tell Marie I'll keep her in my prayers," Jesse called after them.

"Jesse, they gave us a thousand dollars!" Jeb could hardly contain his excitement.

"That's wonderful, Jesse. You're finally getting the support you deserve." Zach patted him on the back. "Say, Jeb, do you want me to help you with the permit paperwork for the stadium? I know the man personally who's in charge of that."

"No, that's okay, Mr. Abramson. I'd rather handle it myself. I'm really fussy with the books."

"Jeb always insists on taking care of the paperwork unpleasantness. You'd almost think he gets something out of all that red tape." Jesse fixed Jeb with a stare.

"Just trying to make your job easier, Jesse." Jeb escaped to the back of the group.

"Come on, folks. Let's hustle over to Parkersburg." Marika started toward the door. "I'm anxious to see what happens in that big stadium."

They arrived at the stadium several hours later. Zach was pleased to see that white banners with red letters proclaiming "Jesse Cartland appearing here today!" were hanging outside the stadium. People were already filing in. Zach entered the stadium with Jesse and his men, and started down the stairs toward the microphone. He could see that people on stretchers were being helped out onto the playing field. A man approached Zach, pulled him off to the side, and spoke to him for a few minutes. Zach began shouting and waving his arms, then with shoulders slumped walked back to the group.

"What's up, Zach?" Jesse asked.

"Terrible news, Jesse. We've been hit by a double whammy. The police have tightened up the curfew since the days are getting shorter. They've also shut down all the concession stands here because they were afraid we'd serve alcoholic beverages today. We assured them we wouldn't, but they don't believe us." He pointed to the back of the stadium.

"There are cops stationed at each stand to be sure we don't open up. If this meeting lasts any time at all, we're going to have some very hungry, thirsty folks on our hands. We've got a bunch of visitors here. They probably won't be able to get back to town soon enough to get something to eat, and they sure can't get anything here." His eyes pleaded with Jesse for understanding. "I'm so sorry, Jesse. I wanted to make this the best meeting you've had so far. Looks like it just might be the worst instead. What do you want to do?"

"Start the meeting. Don't worry,   Zach.   I've got a feeling things will work out just fine."

"Okay, Jesse. You're the boss." Zach walked away wondering if he should cross his fingers for luck.

The crowd saw Jesse as he strode to the microphone. They broke into applause, cheering, whistling, and shouting.

"Good afternoon, folks," he began. "Looks like you've got a nice stadium here. Do you like it so far?"

A thunderous "yes!" came from the crowd.

"I'll bet you like watching the sports here, but it wouldn't be much fun watching the games if they didn't have any rules. Everything would be chaos. The teams wouldn't know when it was their turn to have the ball. You wouldn't know if your side scored any points or not." Jesse started walking with the microphone.

"So it is with life. There are rules, and they're called the Old Ways. You know I've been talking about them. You know I've also been talking about a New Way. I haven't come here to do away with the Old Ways, but to expand on them." Jesse went on to explain about how people should live with love for their neighbors in their hearts.

When he finished speaking, he motioned for the men to start bringing the sick to him to be healed. After some time had passed, Pete came to Jesse. "Jesse, these people are really getting hungry and thirsty. They can't understand why they can't get anything to eat or drink here. I'm afraid we'll have a riot on our hands. Should we close down for today and come back tomorrow to finish up?"

A small red-haired boy stepped out of line and tugged at Jesse's sleeve. Jesse looked down into his freckled face. "Mister, I heard what that man just said." He pointed at Pete. "I got a lunch here my mom packed for me if that'll help." He held up a school lunchbox, and Jesse opened it. It contained juice, some sandwiches and some fruit. "See, Pete, our problem's solved."

"Yeah, right," Pete sneered. "Do you know what'll happen if I hold this lunchbox up in front of this crowd right now and tell them they're going to get fed? I might as well write out my will."

"I'm serious." Jesse turned back to the boy. "Do you mind if we use your lunch to feed everybody?" The boy agreed to give up his meal to feed the crowd. Jesse bowed his head and opened his hands over the lunchbox for a moment. He then held the container out to Pete. "Take this and split up everything among the men. Have them get ready to hand out food and juice to the people."

"Do you really think this is going to work?" Pete was fearful of the crowd.

Jesse's voice was stern. "Do it, Pete."

"Okay, Jesse, whatever you say." Pete sighed and took the lunchbox.

Jesse went to the microphone. "Folks, we know you're getting hungry and thirsty. Have a seat in the stands and food and drink will be given to you, so don't worry." A cheer went up from the crowd.

Jesse continued his work. The men ran up and down the stadium steps passing food and juice down each row. There was enough for everyone.

Pete ran up after the crowd had left. "How did you do that, Jesse? We had enough food for everybody! I still don't believe it!" Relief and joy radiated from his face.

Jesse smiled. "You have to learn to depend on God, Pete. He will provide the things you need. Now let's get to our rooms. I'm bushed."

"Sure, Jesse. Some of the guys would like to talk with you tomorrow before we leave, though. We've got some ideas that I think would really help our work, but they'll require a change in how we do things. We'd also like to get answers to some questions we have."

"Sounds fine. I'm always willing to listen to good ideas. Let's get going now, though. I'm really tired."

# # #

Artie Vole slipped into an alcove in the stadium and dialed a special number on his cell phone. He whispered into the receiver. "I must speak to you tomorrow. I'll contact you. I just saw something I can't believe."

CHAPTER FIFTEEN

The next morning, Pete, accompanied by Andy and John and Jim Thorson, knocked on Jesse's door. As he let the men into the room, Jesse wiped shaving cream from his face with the towel draped around his neck, then straddled the chair at the desk. "Hi, fellas. What's up?"

Pete sat on the bed with the rest of the men. "You remember last night how I said some of us had some ideas?"

"Sure. Let's hear them."

"I've been talking to Jim, John and Andy, and we think it's time to try some new ideas to reach more people. We've got computers, which, as you know, are great tools. We were thinking we could create a Web site. We also have great financial backing now so we think it's time to rent office space somewhere and have somebody permanent there to answer the phone and mail out information."

Pete rose and started pacing. "Of course we'd have

to develop brochures, a logo, things like that, but think how many more people we'd reach."

Jesse's arms were folded on the chair back; his chin rested on them. "I remember last night you also said you had some questions."

"Yes, they were organizational mostly. We'd probably have to form some sort of non-profit organization to do all this. Of course, Jesse, you'd be CEO. Since Andy, Jim, John and I have executive experience; we could step in as senior officers in any capacity you want."

"I see. You boys certainly have everything figured out." Pete and the rest of the men smiled. "How meaningful do you think our message would be in a cold brochure or on an impersonal Web site? How would we heal people?"

"We think the town meetings would still be important. We just think we need to get more organized now that we're growing."

Jesse rose from his chair. "And you're each volunteering to be at the head of that organization out of the goodness of your hearts, right? How do you think the other men would feel if they knew you were in here giving me ideas like this?"

Pete faced Jesse. "Wait a minute, Jesse. Part of the reason we're suggesting this is to take some of the load off you. I admit there are things we need to work out, but I also think we have more talent for this kind of operation than some of the other men."

"So you want to take part of the load off me, huh? I think it's time we had a little training session so you can see what my load really is. Tell the rest of the men we'll meet at that big table in back of the hotel restaurant to make some plans. Now scoot so I can finish shaving."

Pete and the rest of the men went down the hall grumbling about how Jesse was missing a big opportunity.

The entire group was seated at the table eating breakfast when Jesse entered the restaurant. He ordered coffee from the waitress, and then sat with them. "Men, someone gave me an idea this morning about how we can reach more people." Pete, Andy and the Thorsons looked at each other. "Now I have an idea I'd like you to try first. I want you to go out in pairs and tell people about the Ways and about the Rescuer who will bring them back to God."

Pete frowned. "Jesse, I don't think we're ready to go out by ourselves yet."

Jesse motioned them to be silent. "You've heard me talk about the Ways enough. Trust me that you'll know what to say when the time comes. You need to go out on your own so you don't have to depend on me. And guess what?" Jesse looked around the group. "You'll also be given the power to heal."

The men sat in silence for a moment, staring at each other.

Pete finally spoke. "What do we do? Where do we start? When do we leave? What do we need to pack?" He sputtered. "And the power to heal – that's a huge responsibility!"

Jesse laughed. "Take it easy. This is how you'll do it. First of all, packing is easy. You'll take nothing." The men started protesting. Jesse motioned for silence again. "If you have nothing, you'll have to depend completely on God. That alone will be a good lesson for you."

Pete leaned his forehead on his palm for a moment, the looked at Jesse. "Jesse, I'm used to planning operations in meticulous detail. If we plan carefully before we go charging off, we'll be much more successful. We'll have more control over the situation."

Jesse took a sip of coffee. "And what makes you think you have any control now? Do you have any control over what Connie does or what the man sitting next to you does?"

"No," said Pete, ducking his head, "but how can we communicate with God about our needs?" He looked again at Jesse. "It's easy with you. We can call or send a fax or an e-mail, but God seems so distant."

"God's not really distant. He wants you to talk to him and tell him your needs."

"How do we do that."?

"It's simple." Jesse looked at the whole group. "You've all seen me praying. All you have to do is praise God. Tell Him you'll set aside your will and follow His desires. Tell Him your needs and let Him decide what's best for you. Ask for forgiveness when you foul up in following the Ways and ask for the ability to forgive those who treat you badly. Lastly, ask for strength so you won't be tempted to wander from the Ways. I promise you, God will listen to you and provide for you."

Matt spoke up. "I hate to sound like a lawyer, Jesse, but I'm worried about the legal implications, especially if we start healing people. What if something goes wrong or somebody misunderstands what we say?"

Jesse's tone was sharp. "Did you hear what I just told you? Listen again. You will be given the right words to say when you need them. I also can't believe you'd be in legal trouble for curing someone of an illness.

Trust in God. He'll be there for you, I promise."

"Okay, Jesse," Pete said. "I think we're all nervous. We've never done anything like this before, but I know we're willing to give it a try. How do you want us to proceed?"

"You'll go to the small towns in the area and start meeting with groups. You're bound to find a place in each town that'll welcome you. If you don't, then leave that town and go somewhere else. I'm only asking you to do this for a week. It'll be good preparation for you."

"Preparation for what?" Pete asked.

"This is one of those times when I answer 'you'll find out later'." Jesse smiled as he got up from the table. "I'll meet you at my house in a week for a full report."

"Where will you be?"

"Think I'll spend some time with Gabe Oliver and his sisters then go over to see Zach and Marika. I'll get Artie to drive me there."

The men kidded him about taking time off while they had to work, then they drifted off for their assignments.

#

Artie paced around his room, phone to his ear. "Mr. Chapin? Thank goodness I finally got hold of you!"

"This better be good, Vole. I'm busy," Chapin growled in Artie's ear.

"Oh, believe me, it is! First of all, I saw Jesse Cartland eating dinner with a prostitute the other night."

"Was he trying to keep it a secret?"

"Not exactly. There were about twenty of us in the room at the time."

"It might come in handy as an add-on to smear him if

we need to but really, Vole, you'll have to do better than that."

"I saw him feed five or six thousand people yesterday."

"So what?"

"All he used was food from a kid's lunchbox. I helped pass some of it out myself. We only had some sandwiches, fruit and juice to start with; but the food kept appearing when we needed it."

"It must have been some kind of trick."

"No sir, I swear. He fed a bunch of people out of one kid's lunchbox. He also healed lots of people. I've seen that twice now. They seem to be authentic healings, but then I'm not a doctor. I don't know for sure."

"Well, maybe we should put him in charge of Health and Welfare. Sounds like he'd do a better job than the man we have in that position now. So far you're not giving me much, Vole."

"I'm sorry, sir. I'll keep trying." Artie moved to the window and drew back the curtain. He could see some of the men shaking hands then climbing into the vans.

"There's some movement, sir. They're getting ready to go." Just then there was a knock at his door. "Gotta go, sir," he whispered as he hung up the phone.

Artie was surprised when he looked through the peephole in his door. Jesse was knocking! Artie opened the door. "Jesse!" He gulped. "What can I do for you?"

"The rest of the men are going on a special assignment. I'd appreciate it if you could drive me over to the Olivers. I'd also like to see Mr. Abramson and Mrs. Madsen this week."

Artie loaded the van at Jesse's request. His suitcase fell from the back and spilled its contents on the hotel driveway. As he was scooping up his belongings, Jesse came out of the lobby. "You should take it easy, Artie. If I didn't know better, I'd think you had your mind on other things."

As they drove through the countryside, Artie pumped Jesse for information on his childhood. He was proud of the way he got Jesse to open up. He was becoming a good undercover agent.

Unfortunately the facts Jesse gave him were boring. Jesse had grown up on a farm where his father had also built furniture to supplement his income. Jesse had brothers and sisters, and his mother was still alive. He had worked with his cousin John Thorson for a while at Pete and Andy's firm before they'd started out on their mission.

Artie thought for a moment. Mr. Chapin was hard to impress. What kind of damaging information could he get on Jesse? Then he got an idea. "How do you get paid, Jesse?" he asked.

"You've seen how we exist. We cover all basic expenses with the donations people give us."

"You keep speaking about what you're doing as a mission. What do you hope to get out of it for yourself?"

Jesse smiled. "It may surprise you, but not everyone does something to get a personal payback. I'm here to show people they can't live up to the Old Ways, and they need to find their way back to God so He can help them."

Andy shook his head -- another dead-end. Would he ever get something on Jesse that would impress Aaron Chapin?

They pulled into the Olivers' driveway. Jesse and Artie stayed there a few days while Jesse taught Gabe, Marta and Marie about the Ways. Marie had gotten a job at a clothing store in the daytime and had gone back to night school to get a college degree.

When it was time to go, Gabe said, "Remember, our home is your home."

Jesse shook his hand. "And you remember that I care very much about you and your family."

After a few hours drive, they pulled into the driveway of Zach Abramson's spacious home. Marika was staying in the guesthouse. Artie went to a guestroom and left Jesse with Zack. They talked for a while; then Marika entered the room. She'd dressed carefully. Her V-neck chiffon dress caressed her body. Dark hair swept back, her olive-skinned oval face was fully revealed. Her heart beat faster as she came toward Jesse.

"Zach, you're monopolizing Jesse's time," she said with a light laugh. "I'd like to speak with him if I could." Zach asked to be excused as Marika sat on the couch next to Jesse. They passed some time in small talk; then Marika took a deep breath.

"Jesse, I don't quite know how to ask you this question. It may be none of my business."

"Ask away. I have no secrets from you."

"Okay, here goes. It seems you don't have much time for yourself right now. You're out on the road so much. Do you ever picture yourself settling down?" Marika paused. "Maybe -- maybe having a family?" Marika searched his face hopefully.

Jesse looked into Marika's eyes for a long moment before he answered. "Marika, this teaching and these meetings are my mission. They are the most important things in my life. You must understand that."

"I see." Marika looked at her hands folded in her lap, her spirits plummeting.

"That doesn't mean you're not important to me. Everyone who hears and believes my message is important to me."

"Not exactly what a girl wants to hear, Jesse," Marika said with a half-smile. "We don't like being lumped in with everybody else."

Jesse spoke gently. "I understand where you're coming from. What you must understand is that I won't be here much longer so this mission must take all my time."

Marika's eyes widened. "What do you mean you won't be here much longer? Where are you going? What will you be doing?"

"You'll understand in due course. I do hope that my dedication to this mission won't undermine your faith or interfere with the relationship we have now." Jesse clasped her shoulder briefly, then withdrew his hand.

Marika blinked back tears. "No, of course not, Jesse. You've already given me more than I dared hope for. Just chalk it up to a woman's daydreams." She cleared her throat and rose from the couch. "Now let's see if Zach has dinner ready." Her voice choked as she hastily left the room.

CHAPTER SIXTEEN

The vans began arriving at Jesse's house in mid-afternoon at the end of the week. Pete and the others were chattering and laughing as they entered the living room. They were a noisy bunch as they all tried to tell of their experiences at once.

Jesse was laughing, too, as he tried to quiet them. They ignored him for a while, as they were simply too excited to settle down. When they started sitting down, Jesse was finally able to get their attention.

He smiled as he looked around the group. "I gather this week was good for you." A chorus of "yes's" and "you bets" went up from the men. "I'd like to hear what each of you did. I'd also like to know how you felt about being out on the road. Pete, why don't you go first?"

"It was awesome. It was just like you said, Jesse. Andy and I went to a small town, and someone did take us in and provide for us. On our way to set up for our first meeting, we happened to pass by a schoolyard. We saw a little boy with a clubfoot limping around the playground. The other kids were making fun of him. Andy and I felt sorry for him and tried to think of a way to help the poor kid.

We decided to see if we really could heal someone. We went over to him and placed our hands on his foot. We asked God for power to restore his foot.

Right away, his foot straightened. He started jumping and running in circles. The other kids stood there for a minute then ran inside. I guess they told their parents when they got home, because we had quite an attendance at the meeting that night."

He paused and looked at the group. "I'll never forget that kid. He was so happy, so…." Pete choked up. He sat down, reached for a handkerchief and dabbed at his eyes.

Thad went next. "Si and me didn't have a great experience in the first town, so we left like you told us to. It was funny, though. The next town we went to was poorer than the first, but they welcomed us with open arms and couldn't do enough for us. We had a great time there, and they seemed to listen to our message."

John Thorson spoke up. "Jim and I started to hold our meeting. A mentally ill man kept disrupting it by shouting and running around. We healed him, and he quieted down right away. He even sat through the rest of the meeting to see what we had to say. His parents came by later to thank us. They said they hadn't been able to keep him at home for years. He was always running away. Now it looks like he'll be getting some job training and will be able to make it on his own."

Phil Hiera and Nate Bardo reported on their trip next. Tom Gems and Jeb Kerry followed them. Tom said, "I was surprised at how eager everyone seemed to be to hear our message about the Ways. I guess I underestimated the need for people to hear what we had to say."

Matt and Jack Levy spoke last. Matt said, "I knew God was on our side when they found out we were lawyers, and the folks in our town still welcomed us." Everyone laughed then listened as Matt and Jack told their story of a successful week. After Matt and Jack finished, everyone filed out to the dining room for supper.

Jesse sat next to Pete. "How did this experience compare with sitting behind a desk or mailing a brochure to someone?"

"You were right again, Jesse. You'd think by now I'd know not to question you. I wouldn't have traded this week for anything." Pete's eyes were bright.

At the end of the meal, Jesse saw the men to the door. "All of you should rest a few days and get re-acquainted with your families. Then we'll go back on the road. I'll give you a call when it's time to go."

Pete was the last to leave. "You know, the folks I met with really ate up the talk about the Rescuer. They figure if the Rescuer has power to bring us to God, then surely he's got the power to make our lives easier right now."

Jesse folded his arms across his chest. "And how would the Rescuer do that?"

"You know how oppressive things have gotten just from our experience with the meetings. License fees, permits, curfews – the list goes on and on. Our taxes are being raised again, all the name of maintaining order. I noticed in the small towns they're hiring anybody they can get to be a policeman because the need has grown and manpower is short there. Some of these guys are just looking for opportunities to extort money for their own gain. People are getting tired of having their freedoms taken away.

They're tired of having their pockets picked. They're looking for someone to set them on a better path. They think that someone just might be the Rescuer."

"Be careful what you teach them, Pete. The Rescuer may have a different mission."

"Sure, Jesse. You know best. By the way, I got a fee schedule for meetings from the town officials where I stayed. I didn't want to say anything in front of Jeb, but I don't think things are as they seem in that department. I'm going to check some figures out; then I'll get back to you. Right now, though, I want to go home and relax with Connie."

"Okay, Pete. Say hi for me." Jesse stood in the doorway as Pete drove off.

# # #

A few days later, everyone met at Jesse's house. They were eager to go out again. Jesse was on the phone as they entered. He motioned for them to sit down, talked a while longer, then hung up. "You won't believe what just happened! We were going to have to drive about ten hours to reach our next town meeting. Zach called me to chat, found out about our long drive and offered to charter a jet for us. Gentlemen, we're going to this meeting in style!"

Some of the men high-fived each other while Si said, "At least I won't have to worry about Thad's driving." Thad gave him a dirty look; then smiled broadly.

They piled in the vans and headed toward the airport. As they boarded the jet, the pilot conferred with Jesse.

Jesse took his seat last, next to Pete.

"What did the pilot have to say?" Pete asked.

"Seems there's a slight possibility of a storm right on the edge of our destination. He doesn't think it's anything to worry about, though."

Jesse turned in his seat and announced to the men, "Ridgeville in a few hours, guys. Sorry we don't have a flight attendant, but I guess we can't complain." He turned back to Pete. "Think I'll get some shuteye. It'll be nice to get a chance to rest before a meeting for a change." As he drifted off, some of the men pretended to be high-level executives flying in their own personal jets.

The plane taxied down the runway and took off into clear blue skies. The flight went smoothly for a while; then Pete noticed dark clouds forming on the horizon. He went up to the cockpit. "Hey, have you noticed the sky? Is it a problem?"

"Yeah, mister, it is. I've been in touch with the control tower. This storm's coming in faster and bigger than anybody expected. I'm going to try to fly around it. Now if you'll get back to your seat and let me do my job, I'd appreciate it. Tell everybody to strap in."

Pete told the others to strap in and fastened Jesse's seatbelt around him. The men talked quietly. After a while, Pete looked out the window. He noticed the clouds getting bigger and darker. The wind came up and started buffeting the jet about like a paper airplane. Every time the plane jerked, Pete grabbed his armrest. Jesse continued to sleep.

After about fifteen minutes, they hit a patch of calm. Pete and the others relaxed and began chatting again; then suddenly the plane was being flung about more violently than before.

Pete's heart started pounding when he heard the plane creak. He felt the blood pulsing in his ears. The seatbelt dug into his flesh. He fought a strong urge to vomit. Still Jesse slept. The plane went into a steep dive. Pete heard the others screaming. Alarms went off in the cockpit. The pilot called for help. Pete was too petrified to move. Thad rushed to the front to try to help him pull the nose up. They both tugged on the yoke with all their might, but the plane kept losing altitude.

Pete yanked at Jesse's arm. "Jesse, you've got to wake up! We're all going to die!"

Jesse awoke. He took a quick look around, removed his seatbelt, then stood and braced himself against the seat. He stretched out his arms and commanded, "Stop, wind! Plane, level out!"

At once, the skies cleared and the plane leveled. The pilot soon had the jet back up to its cruising altitude. The men sat silently in their seats, looks of wonderment on their faces.

"Who are you that you can command winds and planes?" Pete asked, his voice shaking, blood still pounding in his ears.

"Who do you think I am, Pete?" Jesse regained his seat.

"You – you're the Rescuer, aren't you?" Pete was amazed at his own words, yet he had just seen someone tame a storm by simply speaking to it. Jesse was no ordinary man!

"Yes, I am." After Jesse pronounced these words, the men all began talking at once. He motioned for them to be still. "You must not say anything to anyone about who I am.

It isn't the right time." He turned to Pete. "Your

wisdom in realizing who I am will be well-rewarded."

Pete smiled. He was to be rewarded! But what would that reward be?

The plane touched down at Ridgeville airport about fifteen minutes later. The men cheered as the jet coasted down the runway. Their legs still a little shaky, they gripped the handrail tightly as they descended the portable stairs. Pete kissed the ground. They gathered their baggage and entered the terminal.

Jesse looked around. "That's funny. Zach said he and Marika would meet us at the gate. He's providing transportation to the meeting." Everyone gathered together and waited a few moments. Jesse started walking toward the exit. "Let's go, guys. Maybe Zach and Marika got held up. We'll meet 'em outside."

As they approached the exit, they could see a line of angry people. A security guard was trying to calm the crowd. Jesse flagged down an airport employee. "What's the problem up ahead?"

The employee smiled wryly. "Aaron Chapin in his infinite wisdom now wants us to process people through security as they leave the airport."

"What on earth for?"

"He's afraid some airport employee will sneak something to a passenger or vice versa. Now we've got to put up with a bunch of people being upset because they want to get out of here, and this stupid security gate is delaying them. If you ask me, Chapin's paranoid."

Jesse and the men went through security without incident. They saw Zach and Marika waiting outside with vans and drivers. Marika stepped forward to greet them. "How was the flight?"

Jesse laughed. "I'll let the rest of the fellas tell you

how it went." He turned to the men as they boarded the vans. "We need to talk at the hotel before the meeting tonight, okay? I'll see you in my room."

Pete rode with Marika, Zach, and Jesse and gave an account of the flight on the way to the hotel. He was careful, however, not to mention that Jesse had confirmed that he was the Rescuer. After Marika and Zach expressed their relief about the flight landing safely, Marika grew serious.

"Jesse, I hope you know Zach and I are doing everything we can to finance you and your message."

"I have no doubt you are, Marika."

"You also realize that Zach and I are people of some means."

Jesse smiled. "I noticed that when Zach offered to fly us here in a jet."

Marika paused for a moment, then spoke. "Here's the deal, Jesse. My accountant called the other day. It seems Aaron Chapin has convinced the legislature to impose additional taxes for even more security measures. You saw how it was at the airport. He's managing to get the criminal element under control and wants to maintain absolute order at just about any cost. Chapin's the fair-haired boy right now with the lawmakers, because they can all go home and say crime statistics are dropping, so they give him whatever he wants."

Jesse looked at the passing scenery for a moment, then back at Marika. "What are you trying to say?"

"Zach and I don't know how much we can give you for your efforts any more. Of course we'll continue to support you, but we may not be able to do as much as in the past."

Jesse nodded in understanding. "I know you and

Zach will do the best you can. That's all anyone can ask. Whatever support you give will be appreciated."

Marika was relieved. "Thanks for being so understanding, Jesse. I can't wait to hear you speak again tonight."

CHAPTER SEVENTEEN

They checked into the hotel and freshened up. Pete was the first to arrive at Jesse's room for the meeting. He entered and looked around. "Good. Nobody else here yet. Jesse, we've got to talk about Jeb." Jesse motioned for him to take a seat. "You know how I said I'd check on meeting fees." Jesse nodded. "I got suspicious when the local guy in the town I went to said right away he'd lower the meeting fee if I'd pay him off. Seems word's gotten around that if the licensing official will co-operate with our representative on fees, that official will get a bribe. I checked with the other guys, and they had similar experiences in their towns."

Pete stood and grasped the back of the chair. "We all know that Jeb's the representative the official was talking about. I decided I'd better check with the accounting firm he worked for. They suspect he might have been embezzling from a client. They were only too happy to get rid of him when he offered to leave." Pete threw open his hands. "So what's he up to? I can tell you the figures I've seen don't add up. I'd like to know where's the rest of the money is."

Jesse took Pete's shoulders and gently seated him. "Would it surprise you to know that this isn't news to me?"

"After that plane flight, nothing would surprise to me. Surely we need to do something about this situation, though. I'm pretty certain Jeb's ripping us off. We can't have that!"

Jesse motioned for Pete to calm down. "Jeb has an important role to play in what will happen. Leave him to me and act as though everything's fine."

"Act as though everything's fine?" Pete's voice rose, and he frowned as he studied Jesse's face. "Are you sure, Jesse?"

"I'm sure." Jesse's reply was firm.

Pete shook his head and sighed. "Okay, Jesse. You know best."

The rest of the men gradually entered the room and took their seats. Jeb was the last to arrive. Artie was the only one who would make room for him to sit.

Jesse cleared his throat and began to speak. "Remember all those times when I said 'You'll find out later'?" The men smiled and nodded. "Well, this is a 'find out later' time. I'm going to tell you something important that I think you're ready to hear." The men grew still. Pete was excited. At last some questions would be answered!

Jesse's voice was quiet, but deliberate. "I won't be with you much longer."

The men all spoke at once. "Are you going on vacation? Are you going on a mission somewhere else?

Are you getting tired of traveling?"

Jesse motioned for the questions to stop. "This is much more permanent than taking a vacation. I will be dead soon."

Pete jumped up. "That's crazy, Jesse! You're still a young man!" He hesitated a moment. "You're not sick, are you?"

"No, I'm not sick. Here's what's going to happen. Soon we're going to travel to a large city where I'll be arrested, tried and sentenced to death."

Pete's mouth worked but no sound came out. He was suddenly dizzy.

Jesse continued. "But I will rise again from the dead after three days."

Everyone in the room was silent—each man taking in what Jesse had just said.

Images flashed through Pete's mind of all the adventures he'd had with Jesse. Jesse couldn't leave them now. They had too many important things to do. They needed Jesse too much for him to die. Besides he was the Rescuer. How could he die?

Then something Jesse'd said sparked a question Pete had to ask.

"How -- how can you be arrested when you've done nothing wrong?" Pete's voice shook.

"Believe me, they'll find a charge to pin on me."

Pete walked to the window and looked out, seeing nothing. He slammed his fists on the sill, then turned to Jesse. "Jesse, this can never happen! We need you! You know you have the power to stop this before it even gets started!"

"Enough!" Jesse's voice was harsh; startling Pete. "I must do this for you and everyone else. I'll explain more later. We need to get ready for the meeting now."

Artie and Jeb left without a word, as did the others. Jeb wondered what would become of him if Jesse died. The easy money would disappear. Jesse might not be as powerful as he'd hoped. Jeb couldn't go back to his old firm. What was he to do?

Artie interrupted his thoughts. "What'd you think about that bombshell back there?"

"I don't know. It really caught me by surprise. I'd like to talk to you about it later, though."

They decided to meet for coffee after the meeting.

#

Pete started preparing for the meeting along with the rest of the men. He moved like a robot; his thoughts still back in Jesse's hotel room. Life without Jesse? No! It couldn't be! He'd known Jesse only a short time, but Jesse was everything to him now. Pete again thought back to all the experiences he'd had with Jesse. Studying in Jesse's home, seeing healing miracles, watching Jesse bring the Old Ways to life, saving their lives in the storm. Suddenly his vision blurred. Tears fell wetting his cheeks. He wiped his eyes with the back of his sleeve; then hung his head, embarrassed. He looked out of the corner of his eye hoping no one had seen him cry and noticed some of the other men were crying, too.

Marika came in, tried to talk with some of the men; then looked for Jesse. She found him with head bowed, mouth moving. After a moment he looked up.

"What's going on, Jesse? The men look like they're going to a funeral instead of a meeting."

"In a way they are. I just told them something they

didn't want to hear."

"Is it something you can share with me?"

"Not right now. I need to prepare to speak to the crowd."

"That reminds me, you've got a great group tonight." Marika's acid tone hung in the air. "I overhead some of them wondering how much food they'd get at this meeting. Seems word of your ability to feed a crowd has traveled even this far."

"Oh, really. We'll have to address that tonight." Jesse turned away indicating he wanted to get back to his preparations. Marika left to find a seat in the front row.

The crowd started filing in. Some were carrying empty food containers. Others were laughing; saying that Jesse was going to help them with their food budgets this week. At the appointed time Jesse appeared on stage. Artie turned on his tape recorder.

"My friends," he began, "I see you've heard about the big crowd that got fed in Parkersburg. Maybe you'd like me to give you some food." The crowd whistled, waved their arms and shouted, "Yeah!" and "All right!"

"What would you say if I told you I'm prepared to offer you better food than I gave the folks in Parkersburg?" The crowd broke into thunderous applause and stamped their feet.

"What could be better than filling your stomach for free?" He eyed the audience. "Well, I'll tell you. I've come to give you food and drink that will last forever. You're separated from God now, but He's sent me to give you spiritual food and drink. If you eat this food and drink this drink that I offer, you'll have eternal life." People in the crowd starting looking at each other, puzzled. What food was Jesse talking about?

A man in the front row raised his hand. "Mister, are you talking about some kind of tonic – something that will make us live longer?"

"Yes I am, sir. I'm talking about the food and drink I can give you through sacrifices I'm prepared to make for you." Artie yawned. Jesse was launching into another one of his vague teachings. "You've been separated from God for a long time. I'm prepared to give my flesh and blood to save you. That's the food and drink I'm talking about."

"Mister," said the man, "you make it sound like we'd be cannibals to take what you're offering us." People started laughing.

"Not quite." Jesse smiled himself. "Look at your lives now. Curfews, security checkpoints, metal detectors, more police, heavier taxes to pay for these things – aren't you tired of all this?"

The crowd roared, "Yes!"

"Then you must have a revolution of the heart! Get back to the Ways and follow me! Take the food I offer you!" Artie had been daydreaming; now his head snapped around at the words Jesse spoke. Jesse had said the word 'revolution'! Finally he had something big to report to Mr. Chapin! He could hardly wait to get to a phone.

"We'd like to take food, mister. That's why we came prepared." The man in the audience held up a lunch pail. "But we don't know anything about any so-called spiritual food. Give us some real food."

The crowd took up the chant. "Give us food! Give us food!" they shouted repeatedly.

Si and Thad ran to the front. Thad was worried. "Jesse, should we start the healings? Maybe that'll quiet 'em down." Jesse shook his head and left the stage.

People started booing and yelling, "Fake! Cartland's a fake!" They threw their food containers at the stage. Some in the crowd started running toward the front screaming that they were going to get Cartland.

Si, Thad and the rest ran for the vans. Marika sat hunched in her seat, crying.

# # #

As the men climbed out of the vans at the hotel, Jeb looked at Artie and gave a quick jerk of his head toward the coffee shop. They slid into a booth and nursed their coffee in silence for a while, then Jeb spoke. "Just when I think I have Jesse figured out, he goes and pulls something strange like he did tonight. I don't get this spiritual food and flesh and blood stuff."

"Yeah, that was pretty wild, wasn't it?" Artie decided to probe. "What do you think of Jesse?"

Jeb shrugged. "Jesse's a great guy. He's done a lot of good, but he doesn't seem to be able to capitalize on his popularity. I thought after the meeting in Parkersburg we'd really be on our way. I thought we'd be a force in the region -- you know, have some power. Now it'll take weeks to repair the damage Jesse did tonight. I don't know if I can take this roller coaster ride any more."

"I know the group's finances have grown. About how much money's in the treasury right now?"

Jeb narrowed his eyes and studied Artie. He decided it wouldn't hurt to throw out a figure. "About ten thousand dollars."

Artie whistled. "And that's all due to you, Jeb. I can see how you'd hate to see your work ruined."

Jeb beamed, then tried to act modest. "I do have to give credit where credit's due. Marika, Zach and Gabe are generous givers."

"Yeah, but you're the one who's making the money grow. Maybe there's something I can do to help make sure you don't lose everything. I'll think about it then we'll talk again."

"Thanks, Artie. I'd appreciate it." The two men headed to their rooms.

Artie locked his door and grabbed his cell phone. His hands were shaking so badly that he bobbled the number the first few times he tried to dial it. Finally he could hear the phone ringing. The voice on the other end crackled in his ear.

"Whoever's on this line, it better be good. It's late."

"It is, Mr. Chapin. This is Agent Vole. I'm on to something big!"

"Go ahead, Vole," Chapin sighed, bored already.

"At the meeting tonight, Jesse Cartland talked about a revolution!"

"What! What did he say exactly?" Chapin's voice was crisp.

"Jesse talked to the people about how bad they had it now with higher taxes, curfews and everything. He said they needed to start a revolution."

"Oh, he did, did he? Did he talk about any specific plan?"

"No, he just spoke in general terms."

"This may be bigger than I thought. Do you need any help?"

"I don't think so, sir. I'm making headway with one of the men on the inside. I think he'll help us."

"What's his name?" Artie gave Chapin Jeb Kerry's

name. Aaron paused a moment. "Name doesn't mean anything to me but I'll check it out. I'm proud of you, Vole. You're really coming into your own." Artie smiled and sat a bit straighter. "Watch Cartland very carefully from now on and report everything he does to me. Don't be too proud to ask for help if you get in over your head. We don't want this character causing any trouble. Remember, the most important thing is to maintain order. That's what the people expect of me, and I intend to deliver. Anything else?"

"Do you have any plans to arrest Jesse now? He told us privately that he'd be arrested and tried."

"No, we don't have enough on him yet. Sounds like he's worried though. Keep up the good work and stay in contact."

"Yes sir. Thank you, sir," Artie gushed as he hung up the phone. He removed the tape of the meeting from the recorder and stashed it in his shaving kit. Gotta keep the evidence safe! Mr. Chapin actually said he was coming into his own! "I've sure done some good work tonight!"

# # #

Chapin slammed his fist into the reports on his desk. All the paperwork he'd been studying showed crime was way down in his region. He knew the big boys were beginning to look on him favorably for the National Attorney's position. Now this two-bit hustler, Cartland, might be trying to start real trouble.

"I won't have it!" Chapin shouted as he rose and started pacing. If Cartland dared try anything, Chapin would make sure he'd regret ever being born. No one was going to stop Aaron Chapin's rise to the top.

CHAPTER EIGHTEEN

Pete and Andy spotted Jesse sitting alone in the coffee shop the next morning. Pete began talking as he sat down. "Jesse, we're worried about what happened last night. We're going to get some bad publicity out of that meeting."

Jesse looked up from his coffee; eyes dull with fatigue. "So?"

"So!" Pete shouted then lowered his voice as he saw other patrons staring at him. "So maybe we'll lose some of our backing. You told us what Marika said about Zach's and her finances. They're already stretched. Probably Gabe's are, too. Do you think they'll want to back somebody who deliberately angers a crowd?"

Jesse took in a big breath and let it out slowly. "I'm trying to be patient with you men, but if you don't understand my mission, who will? I'm not here to win a popularity contest. I'm here to bring mankind back into a good relationship with God. Sometimes a sacrifice must be made in order to bring about something worthwhile.

Maybe loss of popularity will be the beginning of that sacrifice."

"You say that's the beginning. What's the rest of the sacrifice?"

Jesse smiled. "You know my favorite phrase."

"You'll find out later." All three men said the phrase together, and Jesse smiled.

"This is a hard one to wait on, Jesse," said Pete. "We're all worried about what you said was going to happen to you."

"I know, and I appreciate that, but I'm afraid you'll have to wait and see things unfold."

Pete pursed his lips then looked at Jesse. "Okay. We've come this far. We'll go the rest of the way with you." Jesse patted Pete on the shoulder, and the men finished eating.

As they were getting ready to leave, a waiter approached. "Excuse me. Are you the Cartland party?" Pete nodded as the waiter handed him a slip of paper.

He read the paper, then crumpled it and threw it to the floor. "That's just great! Our next meeting's been cancelled. What do we do now?"

"I have great faith that you and Andy will be able to find another meeting place for people who want to hear the message. Go ahead and see what you can do."

# # #

Pete and Andy got on the phone and managed to find a smaller venue where Jesse could speak, but the crowd was thin. Word had gotten around. Jesse wasn't passing out any more free lunches so people weren't interested in listening to him.

As Pete helped to prepare for the meeting, he noticed how tired Jesse looked. He watched while Jesse went off by himself and bowed his head. Jesse seemed to gather strength from his moment of solitude. He came out refreshed and ready to talk with the people.

Jesse began speaking to the small crowd. He again called for a revolution of the heart. Artie took note that another call was in order to Mr. Chapin. He caught Jeb's eye. They both nodded. They would be meeting again tonight.

As Jesse was talking, several men burst into the room. Artie tried to stop them, but they pushed past him. A woman turned, saw them and leaped from her chair. Her eyes wide with terror, she began slowly backing away from the men. The policeman on duty started to pull his gun from its holster. Jesse waved the lawman off and stood between the men and the woman.

"Friends," he said to the men, "we're in the midst of a meeting. What's all the fuss about?"

"Sorry to bother you, mister," said the tallest of the men, "but we're here to take that young lady with us." He gestured at the woman behind Jesse.

"You don't look like you're friends of hers. I don't think she wants to go with you." The trembling woman shook her head.

"We don't want any trouble with you, but that little whore slept with our sister's husband. Our sister's real upset so we're here to do something about it." The man drew a gun. The cold click of metal echoed through the room as he cocked it. People sat rigid in their seats, afraid even to breathe deeply. The policeman approached the group from behind. Jesse smiled slightly at the tall man.

He gestured toward the woman. "You know it's

interesting that you're upset about her. Didn't you find your next-door neighbor's wife attractive?" The man blushed.

Jesse pointed to a man standing next to the gunman. "Weren't you thinking about making a false insurance claim on your car?" The man's anger was replaced by a wide-eyed look of astonishment.

Jesse looked at the rest of the group. "Seems to me all you boys have done something wrong in some way or other. Can you say you're any better than this woman?" The tall man wavered, then lowered his gun.

The policeman stepped in front of the men. "Let's go." He motioned toward the exit. The men left quietly.

Jesse turned to the woman. "Doesn't look like anybody's after you any more."

"No sir. Thank you, sir." She seized Jesse's hand and held it to her cheek.

He took her to a chair. "Now I suggest you sit down and listen to what I have to say. That way you won't get into any more trouble."

# # #

Later that evening, Artie and Jeb met in a diner located away from the hotel. "Never a dull moment in one of Jesse's meetings, is there, Jeb?" Artie laughed.

"No, there sure isn't," Jeb agreed. "Did you notice the size of the crowd though? It was way down. I don't know what Jesse's thinking, not doing any more healing or anything. I'm wondering if I hitched my wagon to the wrong star."

"I can certainly understand why you're upset," Artie sympathized. "You spent a lot of time trying to build

Jesse up. You were so hoping you and your group could be a power in the region – really do good things for people. Now it looks like Jesse's not doing his part any more."

"I'm really glad you understand, Artie. For some reason, the rest of the guys won't talk to me any more. You're the only one I can share my concerns with."

"What would you say if I told you I know someone powerful who could help you realize your full potential?"

Jeb stared at Artie. "You? You know somebody powerful?" He started laughing, but stopped as Artie pouted. "Hey, I didn't mean…. It's just that you don't look like…. What I mean is--no offense, okay?"

"No offense taken." Artie was magnanimous. Jeb was too valuable a contact for him to lose. "Let me talk with this guy I know. I'll feel him out – see what he can do for you."

The two men stood and shook hands. "Thanks a lot, Artie. I really appreciate it," Jeb smiled. Maybe this little runt could actually help him!

After he returned to his hotel room, Artie waited for a few minutes then dialed Aaron Chapin. He didn't want anybody interrupting this phone call.

After the preliminaries, Aaron asked, "What have you got for me, Vole?"

Artie tried to adopt Chapin's clipped speech. "Cartland mentioned the word 'revolution' again tonight in his speech. I've got it on tape hidden in my shaving kit."

"Really! I didn't think the man was that stupid. Anything else?"

"Yes. I think we can count on Jeb Kerry to help out when we need him. He's money hungry and power hungry. He's talked to me about how he thought Jesse would someday have a lot of influence. Now he sees the meeting attendance going down, and he's getting worried."

"I looked up your man, Jeb Kerry. I know he's definitely interested in money. He'll be easy to buy off. Does he trust you?"

"Yeah, I think so, but I mentioned tonight I knew somebody powerful who could help him. I don't think he believed me."

Artie held the phone away from his ear as Chapin yelled, "You what? You didn't give him any names, did you?"

"No, of course not." Artie was irritated that Mr. Chapin would think he was that stupid. "Since the guy seems interested in power, I was trying to use that as a hook to reel him in."

Chapin calmed. "I'll give you that one, Vole. You're probably right. Tell you what. I'll give you some information so you can impress Kerry. Tell him you have it on good authority that the next time Jesse Cartland has a meeting, he'll have to provide metal detectors. I already heard what happened at your little soiree this evening, so metal detectors will be a must."

"Yes sir. Thank you, sir. That'll really help."

"Just remember, Vole, I've got a big apple cart that I don't want anybody to upset, especially some oddball who's talking about a revolution. Maintaining order is the most important thing."

Artie grimaced. How many times had he heard that? "Yes sir. I know maintaining order is your top priority." He hung up and got ready for bed. Artie drifted off to sleep that night with a broad smile on his face.

# # #

After dinner, Jesse went to his room. He unlocked the door and saw the blinking message light on the phone. He recognized the voice on the tape. "Jesse, please come right away." Marta was crying. "Gabe's very sick. We need you."

Jesse sighed as he dropped to the bed and slowly removed his tie. He was bone-tired. He would see to Gabe, but this wasn't the right time. He bowed his head for a moment, eyes closed, then got ready for bed.

# # #

The next morning, Pete and Andy scratched around until they found another meeting place. It was in a smaller town than they'd started out in. As they were leaving, Marika approached Jesse. "Jesse, I'm concerned that the message isn't getting out. I'm going home to try and convince some of my contacts to hold some larger meetings."

"Thanks for having faith, Marika. You will never be forgotten because of it." Jesse gave her a brief hug, then boarded the van.

As Thad pulled out, he muttered, "Here we go back to greasy Burgerville."

Pete eased into the seat next to Jesse. "You know, Jesse, I'm kind of relieved that we're going back to small towns. It's hard on us after hitting the big time, but you said you were going to go to a big city and be charged with a crime and killed. Where we're headed is definitely not a big city and we're not attracting big crowds. That means you'll be with us for a long time."

Jesse took Pete's hand. "Thanks, friend, for saying that, but the journey's about to get interesting."

# # #

After the meeting that night, Pete came to Jesse's room. "Jesse, I just got a message through Connie. Marta and Marie have been looking for you. Gabe's very sick. They'd like you to come at once. They left a message at the hotel last night, but for some reason, I guess you didn't get it."

"I got it,' Jesse said quietly.

"What? Well, let's go! I can load the van up right now." Pete turned to go make the arrangements. "We don't have anything definite planned, so we can get there to help right away."

Jesse grabbed his arm. "It isn't time to go yet, Pete."

"But, Jesse…."

"Trust me. Something good will happen if we wait."

"Okay, you're the boss. Do you want me to call Marta and Marie?"

"No. When this is all over, they'll understand. You're too upset now. Have Jeb arrange the next meeting."

On his way to talk with Jeb, Pete thought about what Jesse'd said. Jesse wasn't going to help Gabe. What was Jesse thinking?

Jeb arranged another small meeting in a town several days from their location. It was harder to find meeting places now since all the havens had been shut down. Chapin had his tax money. This time there would be no jet ride -- only a rough car journey over bad roads. He raised an eyebrow when the officials told him he'd need metal detectors at the meeting. The information Artie'd given him had been correct. Maybe he did know somebody powerful after all.

During the meeting Jesse seemed to make it a point to call for a revolution of the heart several times. Some people were interested and wanted a different life. Others drifted out of the hall before the meeting ended.

As the men were loading the vans, Pete ran toward Jesse, waving his cell phone. "Jesse, I just got a call! Gabe's dead! We waited too long!" He paused, catching his breath. "What can we do to help now? Those poor women – Gabe was all they had." He stood there clutching his cell phone, feeling helpless.

"Now it begins," Jesse whispered. He went to Pete and put his arm around him. Pete buried his head in Jesse's shoulder for a few moments; then Jesse lifted Pete's head. "Come on, Pete. Pack the vans and gather the men. We're going to Marie and Marta."

"Isn't it a little late?" Pete asked. "All we can do now is comfort those two women."

"You'll see. Let's get going!"

CHAPTER NINETEEN

Pete gathered the men and told them Gabe was dead. They all prayed for Marie and Marta; then Pete spread a map out on the table. "Jesse wants us all to go to the Olivers. Looks like it'll take us several days to get back there. Is everything packed?" The men nodded. Pete sighed. "Let's go then. This is one visit I'm not looking forward to. I'll never understand why Jesse didn't drop everything and go to Gabe while he was alive."

"What!" John turned in the doorway. "Jesse knew Gabe was sick and did nothing about it?"

"That's right. They called a couple of times, but Jesse told me it wasn't time to go." Pete shook his head. "I don't know what's going on in his mind."

"It doesn't sound like him. Let's give him the benefit of the doubt and see what happens when we get there." John motioned for the men to follow him to the vans.

They drove in silence for a while, then Pete spoke. "Jesse, why didn't we go to Gabe when you could help him? You know you could easily have healed him."

"How long have you been with me, Pete?"

"Gosh, I'm not sure. It's been quite a while."

"And still you question me. Gabe's death happened so that all you men will truly believe that I am the Rescuer. Now let's table the subject. There's no use talking about it further until we get there." Jesse closed his eyes, ready for a nap. Pete looked out the window but saw nothing. *How could Gabe's death be a good thing?*

#

The men spelled each other as they drove to the Olivers so they could make better time. They stopped only to eat and freshen up. Even so it took almost three days for them to reach Gabe's house.

#

At the sound of the vans, Marta came out the front door. As soon as she saw who it was, a wave of rage rose within her. How dare Jesse wait until now to show up! He came toward her ready to embrace her. She stood arms folded across her chest, eyes blazing. "My, my. Jesse Cartland's finally come to visit. So glad you could stop by. Guess you had nothing better to do." Her body was rigid. "You'll have to forgive Gabe for not greeting you. He happens to be dead!"

Her caustic words burned at Jesse. He came closer. Marta spat in his face. The spittle ran down his cheek and a tear formed in his eye. Marta stamped her foot. "You know you could have saved Gabe. Why didn't you?"

Fists raised, she tried to beat Jesse's chest as he gathered her in his arms. He gently embraced her. She broke down, sobbing uncontrollably. He whispered in her ear, "Marta, I'm sorry for your pain, but soon you'll understand."

"You'll have to excuse Marta, Jesse." Marie stood in the doorway staring coldly at Jesse. "We're both just a little upset since our brother died. Strange how you were the one who told Gabe that you cared about him and his family, then when the chips were down you did nothing. Guess all that caring stuff was just talk."

Jesse offered a handkerchief to Marta. "Marie, may I talk with you and Marta for just a moment?" His pleading tone angered Marie more.

"Sure you and the others can make your 'gee, I'm sure sorry Gabe's dead' speech, but do it quickly, then get out!"

"Marie, please." Jesse stretched out an arm to Marie. "I want you and Marta to come with us to the cemetery. I want to go to Gabe's grave. It's critically important to all of us that we go there now."

"Why now, Jesse? What difference can visiting Gabe's grave possibly make except to help you feel better?"

"Please, Marie. This is the most important thing I'll ever ask you to do."

Marie threw up her hands. "I give up. Sure, Jesse, anything for you. Let's all go admire Gabe's tombstone."

Jesse and the women climbed in the first van. Pete and the other men in the van tried to comfort them. Marie pulled away from Pete's arms. The men gave up trying to speak and all rode in silence to the cemetery.

Marta and Marie led the way to Gabe's grave. The small gray headstone stood in stark contrast to the brightly colored flowers surrounding it. "There it is," Marta gestured toward the stone, "Gabe Oliver, beloved brother of Marta and Marie Oliver." She began crying again.

Pete tried to hold her hand, but she pulled away. "Please, Marta, at least tell us how he died."

"We don't really know." Marta's voice shook as she tried to control her tears. "He got a strange infection the doctors couldn't control, then after a few days he passed away." Marie put her arms around her sister and tried to comfort her.

"It doesn't matter how he died," Jesse said. "We're here to help you and Marie, and we will." He turned toward the men. "Find shovels or any other equipment you can. We're going to dig up the coffin."

"Jesse, are you crazy?" Pete was scared. Had Jesse lost his senses? "What can digging up the coffin possibly accomplish?"

"I don't have time to explain. Do it!" Jesse's biting command sent them all scurrying to look for tools.

Pete found the caretaker. "Sir, is it possible for us or for you to dig up a grave?"

The elderly caretaker squinted at Pete. "You been out in the sun too much, mister? I can't just dig up a grave. There's regulations about that. I need an order from the police for that kind of thing." The caretaker grew uneasy as he watched the other men gathering around Pete. "Now you boys clear out or I'll call the cops." His voice quivered.

"I'm sorry, sir, but we're going to do this with or without your help." Pete walked to the tool shed. It was locked. As the men discussed how to get to the shovels, the caretaker ran to the phone in his office.

# # #

The phone rang at the local precinct. "Hello, Sergeant Miller speaking. ... What? ... Harry, take it easy. We'll be right there."

A stringer for one of the town's television stations looked up from his reading. "What's up, Miller? Anything I might be interested in?"

"Maybe, Bill. A group of idiots are out at the cemetery demanding to dig up a grave. There's a pretty big gang of them, so Harry's scared to death."

"Well, Harry's in the right place to be scared to death," said Bill with a chuckle. "Anyway, I'm on it." Both men sprang into action.

# # #

Pete and the others studied the padlock; then Thad took a tool out of his pocket. He expertly picked the lock. Pete laughed. "Your talents never cease to amaze me, Thad. Remind me to ask you sometime how you learned that skill."

"Never mind," said the big man. "Let's get busy. It'll take awhile to dig up the coffin if we only have shovels to use."

# # #

Harry, the caretaker, paced nervously in his office as Marie entered. "Sir, I'm with the men out there at the tool shed. Is there anything I can do to make this process easier? Is there some paper I can sign giving permission to have my brother's remains dug up?"

"Yes, there is. I'll need to see some identification first." Marie showed him her driver's license. "I have a form here somewhere." Harry started looking through his file cabinet. "I never expected a relative of the deceased to go along with this."

"I realize it's unusual, but I've been thinking. The man who's requesting this action helped me in the past. I'm sure he has some good reason for digging Gabe's coffin up."

As Harry was searching for the paperwork, Marie stared out the window. She saw the flashing lights of the police car as it approached. A van from a television station followed close behind. Marie stood in front of the window, blocking Harry's view. "Having any luck finding that form?" She tried to sound casual.

"Let's see. No, that's not it. Wait a minute. Here it is. Now if you'll sign on this line." Harry pointed to a space on the paper.

Marie quickly grabbed a pen from the desk and scribbled her signature on the form.

As she finished, there was a knock on the door. Harry opened it and saw the blue uniform. "Oh, officer, thanks for coming. I'm sorry to have troubled you. Seems like everything's been cleared up. One of the relatives signed a form so it's okay for the body to be dug up."

"You don't mind if we stay for a few minutes to make sure there's no trouble." The officer looked around the cemetery.

"No, of course not. Now if you'll excuse me I need to fire up some machinery to make the exhumation easier. Young lady, you can tell the men they might as well start digging. Sometimes Old Betsy gets temperamental, and it takes me awhile to get her going."

Marie raced back to the group.

#

Bill, the stringer, exited the van and talked with the

police officer. After finding out there was no problem, he started to leave, then thought better of it. "Guys, I don't know if we'll set up or not. Let me take a look at what's going on, and I'll let you know if there's anything here to report."

He trotted over and watched the group dig. He noticed one man who seemed to be giving directions. The man looked familiar. Who was he? Suddenly Bill's jaw dropped. He ran back to the van. "Guys, set up ASAP. Jesse Cartland's the one who's digging up this grave! I do believe we just might have a story!"

As the men set up, Bill notified the station and started gathering facts.   Terry Allen, the station's star anchorwoman, was pulled from another assignment to handle the story at the studio. Soon the station was receiving a signal from the cemetery. Pictures of men digging up a grave were televised to homes in the area. As soon as the big television stations learned what was happening, the program went national.

"Bill, can you tell us what's going on." Terry was poised and well coifed as her image went into millions of homes.

"Yes, Terry. It seems a relative has given permission for Jesse Cartland and his men to dig up the grave of a man named Gabe Oliver. We have no idea why Mr. Cartland's doing this."

"How long will it take?"

"Probably a while. The caretaker's trying to get his equipment going, but right now it's just some men with shovels and muscle who are doing the digging."

"Bill, we'll keep the picture on for the folks at home while they're exhuming the body and come back to you live when something breaks. Meanwhile I have Doctor

Kent Campbell here in the studio to discuss the so-called healing miracles that Jesse Cartland's been performing."

The picture shrank into the background over Terry Allen's shoulder as she began speaking with the physician.

# # #

As the other men dug, Artie said he needed a break. He slipped behind a tree and quickly dialed a number on his cell phone. "Hello. I need to speak to Mr. Chapin immediately. … I don't care if he's in a meeting. Get him now!" Artie was uncharacteristically firm. He watched the men work as he waited for Chapin to answer.

"What is it, Vole? You always pick the worst times to call." Chapin sounded irritated.

"Listen to me. Something's happening that might be important." Artie wasn't going to be intimidated by Mr. Chapin this time.

Chapin's voice softened. "Okay, Vole, let's have it."

"We're all in a cemetery with Jesse Cartland. He's having us dig up a grave."

"What! Why? Did he give any reason?"

"Not yet. All he said was that it was very important for us to do this. There's police here and a TV crew. You should be able to see what's happening on your TV."

"All right. Give me a second." Chapin turned on his television set and flipped through the channels. "Ah, yes. I see it. This man never ceases to amaze me. Never know what he's going to do next."

"I'd suggest you keep watching for a while, sir. The way Jesse's acting I think this is going to be something big. I've gotta get back now. The rest of the guys may get suspicious if I'm gone too long."

"Right, Vole. I'll keep watching for a bit. Thanks for the heads-up."

#

Bill kept the cameras trained on all action in the cemetery. Harry finally got Old Betsy to respond to his coaxing. He rode over on the backhoe and motioned the men out of his way. The machine chewed away at the earth until it reached the coffin. "Okay, fellas," Harry directed, "get some ropes under the box, then we can lift it up."

Si and Thad jumped into the hole and worked with the ropes until they were properly adjusted under and around the coffin. They climbed out, then together with Pete and Andy began pulling on the ropes. The coffin gradually came into view. The four men pulled until the casket was resting on the grass.

Jesse walked toward the casket. "Open it!" he ordered them.

Bill heard Jesse's command and called into the station. "Quick, get us back on the air. Something's about to happen!"

#

Aaron Chapin was pouring himself a cup of coffee when he heard Terry Allen's voice. "We're interrupting our conversation with Dr. Campbell to go back to the cemetery. Bill, can you tell us what's going on now?"

"Yes, Terry. Jesse Cartland has just asked that the coffin be opened. One of his men seems to be arguing with him about doing it."

Chapin settled into his large upholstered desk chair. What was Cartland up to now?

# # #

Pete couldn't believe what Jesse was asking them to do. "Jesse, do you realize what condition Gabe's body might be in? Why put Marta and Marie through this pain?"

"Pete, I said open the casket, and I expect you to do it." Jesse's stinging tone hurt Pete. He'd been through a lot with Jesse. Why was Jesse talking to him this way?

Pete, head down, walked back to the other men. "Jesse insists we open the casket. Anybody want to do it?" Si, Thad and Andy shook their heads no. "Okay, then I'll do it." Pete started to raise the lid slowly then averted his eyes as he gave it a final tug. The TV cameraman shifted positions as he tried to focus in on the coffin.

The crowd around the grave was completely quiet. Pete took shallow breaths, afraid to move, not knowing what to expect. "Gabe!" Jesse's voice cut through the silence. "Gabe, your sisters are here. Come out and greet them!"

The color left Pete's face. Jesse was asking a dead man to rise from his coffin! He must be crazy! Pete shuddered. He and the rest of the men had spent months following a man who'd turned out to be insane!

"Gabe, come out," Jesse commanded again.

Nothing happened for a moment; then a hand grasped the side of the casket. Pete saw that the hand was pink. Gabe sat up. He looked dazed and swayed slightly. Pete instinctively put his arm around Gabe's shoulders to brace him. "It's all right, Gabe." Jesse's voice was soothing. "Take your time. Those who love you are here to greet you." Gabe took a moment to get his bearings, then gingerly placed his leg over the coffin's edge. He looked at everyone, smiled and swung out of the casket. Legs wobbly, he grasped the casket. His sisters ran to embrace him.

# # #

Artie watched while Pete opened the coffin. When he saw Gabe's hand on the side of the casket, he began shaking uncontrollably. He could hear his heart pounding in his ears. How could a dead man come back to life? When Gabe stood on the grass, Artie ran wide-eyed and screaming from the cemetery.

# # #

Aaron Chapin watched as the coffin lid was opened. He saw Gabe's hand on the side of the casket. When Gabe stood up, Chapin jumped from his chair not feeling the hot coffee searing his leg. "Gwen!" he yelled. "Get me Vole on the phone! I want to know what really happened at that cemetery!"

# # #

Bill and the TV crew crowded around Gabe and his sisters. Bill thrust the microphone in Gabe's face. "Please tell us how you feel."

"I -- I really don't know right now. It's certainly

weird to wake up in a coffin. It feels like I've had a very long sleep. I'm just glad to be back with my sisters." Marta and Marie stood on either side of Gabe, arms locked around him.

"Please," said Marie, "we want to go home now." They began walking toward the vans.

"There you have it, Terry." Bill talked rapidly. "I've never seen anything like it."

"What do you make of it, Bill? Did we see a miracle today?"

"Yes, definitely yes. We're going to follow the Olivers to their house now and see if we can get more of an interview." Bill and the crew packed up and followed the vans.

# # #

Pete rode in silence for a while as the other men talked excitedly with the Olivers about what they'd just seen. He'd been at Jesse's side for many events – healings of hundreds of people, the calming of a storm, feeding of a large group with little food. And now Jesse had raised someone from the dead! Pete was ashamed. He hadn't trusted in Jesse, hadn't believed in him. Finally he placed a hand on Jesse's arm. "I did it again, didn't I?"

"Did what?"

"I doubted you. I'll never do that again," Pete said firmly. "You are the Rescuer. We all saw it today."

"Yes, you are," Marta chimed in. "What can we do to repay you?"

"Follow my teachings and stay with me to the end."

"Always, my Rescuer." Marta said firmly.

Everyone in the van began to chant, "Jesse is the Rescuer!" as they headed toward the Olivers' house.

\# \# \#

There was a crush of reporters at the house. The police had followed behind the van and proceeded to clear everyone out so Marta, Marie and Gabe could have some time together without disturbance.

Pete, Jesse and the rest of the men stayed at the house with the Olivers. Jesse taught them more about the Ways. Pete and the others drank in everything Jesse said and talked long into the night.

CHAPTER TWENTY

Artie fumbled with the key to his room. His hands were shaking uncontrollably. He finally managed to unlock the door. The images of what he'd seen kept flashing through his mind. He couldn't turn them off. A dead man rising from the grave! Impossible! What powers did Jesse possess? Artie had seen Jesse heal people, calm a storm, now raise someone from the dead.

Did Jesse know who he worked for? Would Jesse turn his powers on Artie and punish him by some awful means for working to betray him and his group? Artie was more afraid than he'd ever been in his life. His cell phone started ringing, but he ignored it. He searched his room from top to bottom to make sure no one was there; then moved the dresser in front of the door. He grabbed his suitcase and opened it to pack. He was perspiring heavily so went to the bathroom to rinse his face before loading his suitcase.

He glanced in the mirror. Gabe's face looked back at him. Artie ran groaning back into the bedroom. He decided to watch television to see what the news had to say about the events. Even before he turned the set on, images of Gabe climbing out of the casket flickered across the screen. Artie put his hands to his forehead and began moaning again.

They were all after him! They'd messed with the mirror and the television set! He jumped into bed and, with the covers pulled over his head, lay shivering. He knew Jesse couldn't get to him if he just stayed all covered up.

The cell phone rang incessantly. The constant ringing finally drove him to put one arm gingerly out from under the covers, clutch the phone and bring it to his ear. He covered his head with a pillow to remain safe.

# # #

Aaron Chapin was relieved when he heard the phone pick up. "Vole, is that you?" he growled.

"Yes – yes sir," Artie whispered.

"Speak up, Vole. I can hardly hear you."

"I can't, sir. They might find me."

"Are you in any danger?" Chapin was suddenly alarmed. He didn't want to lose Agent Vole after what he'd seen on television.

"No sir, not right now. I'm in my bed under the covers so I'm perfectly safe."

Chapin held the phone away from his ear and looked at it in disbelief. He decided to change the subject. Maybe if he got Vole to talk about what happened at the cemetery, he'd make more sense. "Agent Vole," he said in his most official tone, "can you tell me exactly what happened at the cemetery this afternoon?"

"Yes, I can. When Jesse went to the graveyard, I thought his mission was ill starred.

But out of the coffin Gabe not
Not likely is he to decompose."
Chapin's free hand clenched into a fist. "That's
really cute, Vole, but I don't need poetry right now. What
I need are observations."
"Okay, how about this. When I saw Gabe's great
gray headstone,
I thought Jesse's mission was blown.
But when Gabe sat up
Looking full ready to sup,
I knew Jesse'd come into his own." Artie giggled.
"Listen here, Vole," Chapin shouted into the phone.
"I need to know how you felt about what you saw and
what action should be taken in regard to this Cartland
fellow."
"All right, I'll tell you. When Jesse commanded
Gabe to rise,
Agent Vole got quite a surprise.
The dead came to life.
Rumors will be rife.
And this event Chapin can't sanitize."
Artie's high-pitched laughter sent chills down Aaron
Chapin's spine. Chapin slammed the phone down, then
dialed another number. "Get over to Agent Vole's hotel
room double quick and pick him up. He's gone loony.
Get him into a sanitarium immediately and don't let him
talk to anybody, understand? Also be sure to pick up his
shaving kit and bring it directly to me."
Chapin paced the floor. Cartland was talking about
a revolution, and he'd lost his undercover agent. What to
do? Suddenly he smiled and looked through some notes.
Of course. Jeb Kerry. Aaron Chapin would have a talk
with him when it was time. He dialed another number.

"Put some surveillance on Jeb Kerry. I want to know every time he takes a breath.

CHAPTER TWENTY-ONE

The phone began ringing early the next morning at the Olivers'. Pete took call after call. When Jesse came to the kitchen for breakfast, Pete waved a handful of notepaper at him. "Look at this, Jesse! These are all offers to speak! We're back in business again!"

Jesse started to talk, but Pete waved for silence. The phone was ringing again. "Hello. … This is Pete Stone, Mr. Cartland's assistant. … Oh? … Why, yes. I think we can arrange that. Give me your phone number so I can get back to you. … Thanks for calling." Pete hung up the phone. He turned to Jesse, a big smile on his face. "You won't believe this! They want us to be in a parade in New Kensington! Now how big- time is that? A city of five million people wants to welcome us with open arms! Wait 'til I tell the guys!"

Jesse spoke quietly as he poured a cup of coffee. "Yes, Mr. Cartland's assistant, you be sure to tell the guys."

Pete paused for a moment. Why wasn't Jesse excited? What was his problem with all the speaking engagements they were getting? Pete shrugged his shoulders, then went to tell the rest of the men the good news.

Pete was bursting with pride as he told the men the good news about all the opportunities Jesse had to speak. He watched their faces as he told them about the parade in New Kensington. Pete grinned as everyone began chattering at once. They all had ideas on how to capitalize on the event.

John raised his hand. "I just had a thought. Who rides in the car with Jesse?"

"I figured Andy and I would – you know – to protect him from the crowd," Pete replied.

"What are the rest of us – chopped liver?" John glared at Pete. "I'm sure Jim and I could protect Jesse as well as you could."

"If you really want crowd protection, then Si and I should be the ones riding with Jesse." Thad looked around the group. "We're a lot bigger than any of the rest of you." Some of the men nodded.

"Maybe I'd like to ride in the car by myself." Everyone turned at the sound of Jesse's voice. He sat down with the men. "You're all really getting in the spirit of this parade, aren't you?" Everyone started talking at once again. Jesse motioned for silence. "Seems you boys have forgotten something I told you after our little plane trip. Remember when I told you we'd travel to a large city where I'd be arrested, tried and sentenced to death? Well, New Kensington's the city."

Pete gasped. His eyes widened. How could he have forgotten that Jesse had predicted his own death? But, wait! "Jesse, you've never been more popular. There's no way anyone would pull anything like that after you raised Gabe from the dead." The rest of the men nodded.

"I agree with Pete," Matt said. "Aaron Chapin's the one who would have to call the shots on any move to arrest you, Jesse. I think he's got too much political savvy to do that right now. He's having enough trouble convincing everybody that the tax hikes for police are justified. He doesn't need to look like the bad guy by going after you."

"We'll see who's right when we get to New Kensington. Before you make any more plans, here's what I'd like to do. I want to schedule one more teaching meeting before we hit the big city. Jeb, can you set that up?"

"Sure, Jesse, I'll get right on it." Jeb smiled. "By the way, has anybody seen Artie?" He usually helps me."

"I don't know," replied Pete, "but he seemed real shook up when Gabe came out of the coffin."

"I think we all were," said Jeb. "I'll check on him later."

# # #

Jeb stopped by Artie's hotel. Artie had checked out earlier, but no one remembered seeing him leave. Jeb wondered for a moment where Artie might be then decided he'd better get busy setting up Jesse's meeting. He selected a small town close to New Kensington and left to make arrangements for Jesse's gathering. Jeb was back in his element! He was whistling as he entered the police station. He found someone who was happy to strike a deal on permit fees, called Pete to tell him where the meeting would be, then headed over to the hall to set up. He made sure plenty of buckets were put out for donations.

Later he watched as people, anxious to see Jesse, poured into the hall. The donation pails filled up at a rate that surprised even Jeb. He decided Matt and Pete were right. Jesse was too popular now. Aaron Chapin wouldn't dare touch him.

Jesse entered the hall. When the people saw him, they jumped to their feet. Their clapping, whistling and yelling echoed through the room. Jesse stood quiet, expressionless, then finally held his hands up to quiet the crowd. "My friends, it's good to see you." Jesse smiled slightly as the throng once again applauded. He stepped closer to the audience. "I want to ask you a question. Have you ever heard about a fireman rushing into a burning building to save someone?" Everyone nodded or said yes. "And what do we say that fireman did? We say he rescued the person in that building, right?" Again everyone agreed. "Sometimes it doesn't go well for the fireman. Sometimes he loses his life. The fireman knows his life is on the line every time he answers an alarm, but he accepts that risk as part of his job."

"There's another Rescuer I want to talk with you about tonight. That Rescuer is mentioned many times in the Old Ways. Do you all recall that?" Some members of the audience looked puzzled while others nodded. "God planned all along to send the Rescuer I'm talking about. He knew you'd need someone to save you, to bring you back to Him. You've wandered far from God, but this Rescuer will save your life so that you may spend it with Him. Think about how much the Rescuer loves you. He's willing to give his life so that you may have a better life." Jesse looked around the crowd. "I see a lot of puzzled looks out there. Do you have any questions?"

An old man raised his hand. "You talk about us having a better life. I remember studying the Old Ways as a kid and learning about the Rescuer. If the Rescuer comes, does that mean we'll have less crime and more money in our pockets?"

"I'm glad you asked that question. This world isn't perfect and never will be. You'll always face problems. However the Rescuer can come into your hearts. He can show you how to love each other and love God. He can bring you all back to God so you can live in harmony with Him for all time."

The old man continued. "Does that mean we'll live forever then?"

Jesse smiled. "I'm talking about the life you'll have with God after you die and leave this world."

The old man shook his head. "So there's no real pay-off right now if this Rescuer does come."

"Yes there is. If you have love in your heart for your fellow man and for God, you'll be surprised at how much easier life is."

People started muttering. Jeb grew nervous. Jesse was getting off on a tangent again. Just when Jeb thought the good times were coming back, Jesse had to go and teach this weird stuff about the Rescuer and having love in your heart, and living with God after you die. Like the old man said, there didn't seem to be a pay-off now.

Jesse motioned for Si and Thad to come to the front of the room. "I've given you a lot to think about so that's all the teaching I'll do this evening. Now let's heal some folks and make your lives better right now."

The crowd settled down. Those who were ailing

were helped to the front, and the healing began.

After the meeting, the men lingered in the hall for a while. "That was a difficult concept you talked about tonight, Jesse." Jeb wanted to see if he had really heard Jesse correctly. "When we were kids and learned about the Rescuer, I think we assumed he'd make a difference in our lives immediately."

"And I will. The teaching was meant to be difficult tonight. Some will never understand what my message is, but you all should. Think about it. If everyone had love and concern for everyone else, what a fantastic place this would be to live! Also think about what may happen to you when you die. Wouldn't you want to spend eternity with God?"

Everyone else agreed with Jesse, but Jeb held back. After he'd found out that Jesse was the Rescuer, he'd assumed he'd have the inside track on a powerful organization he was sure Jesse would set up. Now what would happen? Jeb wished he knew where Artie was. He wanted to know what Artie would think about this evening's meeting.

Jeb decided to keep his thoughts to himself. Back to business. "By the way, Jesse, are there any arrangements I need to make for tomorrow's parade?"

"I'll give you an address. The man will have a nice convertible waiting for me to ride in."

"That's good. A van wouldn't be too impressive. Anything else?"

"No. I think we should all turn in. Next week's going to be very busy."

The rest of the men left for their rooms chatting about the parade. Jeb turned to see Jesse still standing in the hall. He watched as Jesse bowed his head for a moment. Jesse straightened and, without a word, he walked slowly past Jeb, stopped at the door, sighed, then joined the rest of the men.

CHAPTER TWENTY-TWO

Pete rose early the next morning. What a day! Now everyone was going to see how important Jesse's movement was. They'd also see him, Andy and the rest of the men riding along with Jesse. Maybe Mr. Halversen would finally believe they'd all told him the truth when they left the company.

He decided to go to Jesse's room to see if he was ready. He knocked lightly on Jesse's door, not wanting to wake him if he was still sleeping. Jesse opened the door a crack. He was unshaven. His eyes had dark circles beneath them.

"Jesse, you look terrible! What happened? Didn't you get any sleep last night?"

Jesse opened the door wider so Pete could enter his room. "As a matter of fact, no."

"Too excited about the parade, huh?"

"I'm more excited about what's going to happen after the parade."

"There's no way anything will happen to you. For one thing, the crowd's going to be enormous from what I heard. Not even Chapin's police would take on that many people."

"Whatever you say, Pete."

"Are you up for this? Do you want anything to eat?" Pete tried to lead Jesse to a chair.

Jesse waved him off. "I'll be okay, Pete. You don't need to mother hen me. I'll find the strength I need."

"Okay, but I'll take care of everything. You rest. I'll order something from room service."

Pete spent the rest of the morning organizing parade details with the rest of the men. Jeb drove up to their hotel with a vintage convertible. Si and Thad looked over the car as though surveying a fine diamond.

"That's some heap, Jeb. Where'd you get it?" Pete caressed the hood.

"It was the darnedest thing. I went to the address Jesse gave me and rang the doorbell. This old man came out and said 'I suppose you're here for the car.' Then he took me out to the garage, gave me the keys and said there'd be no charge for using it. He told me he gassed it up last week because he knew someone would come for it. Jesse was right again."

Pete smiled then got a queasy feeling in his stomach. Was Jesse also right about what would happen to him in New Kensington? Pete shook his head. No way. They were riding too high.

He went to fetch Jesse. "Your chariot awaits, sir," he grinned and bowed as Jesse answered the door.

Jesse was clean-shaven and dressed in a suit and tie.

Pete was surprised at how rested he looked. "I don't know how you do it, Jesse. You look great now."

"I told you I'd find the strength. Remember that, Pete. Someday you'll need to find that same strength. Now let's get this over with."

They met the rest of the men in the lobby. Jesse put his arm around Thad. "Thad, nothing against you, but I'd like Pete to drive me today."

"Okay, Jesse. Whatever you say. I was hoping I'd get to drive, but this is your day. We'll be right behind you to make sure nothing happens."

"Thanks, my friend. Now let's load up."

Pete and Jesse led the way in the convertible followed by the rest of the men in the vans. They arrived at the start of the parade route. A mass of people stood behind barricades waiting to catch a glimpse of Jesse. Policemen were standing in front of the barriers. Television cameras were strategically located. Pete saw a reporter interviewing someone in the crowd.

The officials sponsoring the parade headed down the route first followed by a local college band, then the convertible with Jesse and Pete. True to his promise, Thad was driving the van right behind Jesse.

As soon as the crowd caught sight of Jesse, they began yelling and clapping. Pete could see people holding up homemade signs reading "Jesse, we love you" and "Jesse's the man!" Some women held up signs saying "Jesse, will you marry me?" People in upper-story windows threw out confetti and streamers.

Pete could see Jesse in the rear view mirror. He was waving to the crowd but was expressionless. "Hey, Jesse, aren't you excited? This is all for you!"

"I'm just the flavor of the month to many of these people. They want a Rescuer who will topple this oppressive government and be their new leader. That's not what I'm here for."

"Can you at least look like you're enjoying this?"

Jesse gave a short laugh. "Okay. For you, Pete, I'll smile."

They continued slowly down the street. The men in the vans had their windows open waving to the crowd. Pete was driving with one hand on the wheel and waving with the other hand. Suddenly a woman with a small child in her arms broke through the barricade. She ran up to the car and thrust her child toward Jesse. The child's face was pale, her limbs sticklike.

"Please, sir, Amy's been sick since she was born. Please heal her." Pete slowed to a stop. Jesse placed his hands on the little girl. Immediately her face turned a healthy pink. The mother raised her child over her head and shouted, "She's healed! Jesse Cartland healed my little girl!"

Pete started down the route again, but people had heard the mother's shouts. The crowds started breaking through the barriers trying to get to Jesse. The police began beating people back with nightsticks. One policeman was yelling for order over a bullhorn. The throngs were still surging toward Jesse's car. Some people fell and were trampled. Others pushed people out of the way in an effort to get to Jesse. Some even picked up rocks and threw them at the police. Another element of the crowd took advantage of the situation and started breaking shop windows and looting stores. The police began firing guns into the air.

"Pete! Stop the car! People are getting hurt!" Pete slammed on the brakes. Thad had to stop abruptly. The van skidded and tapped the back bumper of the convertible. Jesse catapulted himself over the closed convertible door, ran to a policeman and grabbed the bullhorn out of his hands.

"Please, everyone stop! People are getting hurt! Look at what you're doing to each other! This is why you need a revolution…" The policeman grabbed the bullhorn back from Jesse. The rest of what Jesse said was swallowed up in the noise of the crowd.

Seeing Jesse out of the car was all the crowd needed to make one final big surge toward him. Thad jumped out of the van and muscled his way through the melee. He picked Jesse up and threw him in the back seat of the convertible. He ran to the driver's door. Pete sat frozen in the seat.

"Move! We're getting out of here right now!" Thad jumped in as Pete slid over. He put the car in gear and held his hand down on the horn. People were hanging on to the car. He sped up a little, and their hands let go. The crowd parted enough for him to make some headway down the street.   As soon as he found a clear spot in the road, he stomped on the accelerator. The tires screeched as he headed out of town. The vans were close behind.

# # #

Aaron Chapin sat at his desk flipping through television stations with his remote then stopped. There it was – the parade route. Images of crowds behind barricades flickered across the tube. Jesse's resurgence in popularity galled Chapin. Would he ever be done with this upstart? Chapin's world was fashioned exactly as he wanted it. He was in charge. Order was close to being achieved. So what if it cost the taxpayers more money? So what if they had to give up some of their freedoms? At least Aaron could point to crime statistics and say things were much better than they had been last year. Those figures would stand him in good stead when he angled for the National Attorney's job. He didn't need someone coming along stirring up the people by talking about a revolution, especially someone who was as popular as Jesse Cartland.

He pushed an intercom button. "Gwen, make sure this Cartland parade is taped, okay?" He watched as a television commentator replayed a tape of Jesse raising Gabe Oliver from the dead. That was some trick! How did Cartland pull it off? Maybe he'd get a chance to ask him.

Chapin drummed his fingers on the desktop as the parade started. For a while it looked like a normal celebration. He decided to catch up on some paperwork as he watched the parade. His eyes went back and forth from screen to report, then he saw it. He saw a woman carrying a child break through the barricade and run toward Jesse's car. He dropped the report and peered intently at the television set. He saw the riot break out. He heard Jesse call for a revolution, then watched as Thad drove the car away.

He leaned back in his chair, a broad smile on his face. He wanted to enjoy this moment to its fullest. Jesse Cartland had just called for a revolution on national television, and he, Aaron Chapin, had it on tape. Not even Jesse's popularity could save him now.

Chapin straightened in his chair and pushed the

intercom button again. "Gwen, have the boys in media surveillance bring me the tape of Cartland's parade as soon as possible. I also want to hear Vole's audiotapes."

Chapin dialed a number on his phone. "It's time to pick up Kerry. You'll do it discreetly, right? And make sure Mr. Kerry knows he's dealing with powerful people. … No. Bring him to the office at night. The fewer people who know I've talked to him, the better."

Chapin smiled again. This was going to be fun!

CHAPTER TWENTY-THREE

Thad drove until they were well out of the city. No one spoke. The riot was still too fresh in everyone's mind.

Thad slowed the car. "Pete, are the vans all still behind us?"

Pete looked over his shoulder. "Yeah, looks like it."

"There's a podunk motel up ahead on the right. I say we stop there and regroup."

"Agreed." Pete's voice shook. His nerves were raw. He never wanted to see a mob like that again. He was ashamed, too. He'd frozen when Jesse needed him the most.

The men gathered in back of the motel. They decided to check in a few at a time so as not to draw attention to themselves.

Thad threw the car keys at Jeb. "You, Mr. Kerry, have job to do. Please return this convertible to its owner."

"Do I have to do it tonight?'

"Yep. This car's too recognizable. If somebody sees it, they'll know where we are. We need to get rid of it now! You're the only one who knows where the guy lives."

"Okay, okay. I get the message. How will I get back here?"

"Call a cab. I for one am too tired to follow you and bring you back."

"That's going to be expensive, having somebody drive me from the city back out here."

"We'll chip in for your cab fare," said Pete. "I think we're all too tired and too jangled to think straight. Here, take my cell phone, so you can make the call."

Once in his room, Jeb looked at a map for a few moments before he left. He decided it would be safer to take the back road. Jeb drove off, his thoughts in turmoil. He'd been confused after Jesse'd talked about his role as the Rescuer. Jesse didn't appear to have any big plans that would include Jeb. Then they'd gone to the parade. The crowds were enormous. Jeb was excited. He was sure Jesse would see that he had to do something big in order to maintain his popularity. Jeb hadn't foreseen a riot. How would a powerful man like Aaron Chapin who liked order above all else react to the chaos at the parade?

Jeb turned into a narrow dirt road. He arrived at the vehicle owner's house and quietly parked the car. It was late, so he didn't want to disturb the old man. He left the keys in the mailbox, then called for a cab. He went out to the road to wait for his ride and was relieved when he saw headlights coming down the road. He stepped toward the car as it stopped. The door of a sedan opened, and a man stepped out. Jeb's heart started pounding. Where was the cab?

"Sir, if you'll step this way." The man gestured toward the vehicle.

Jeb started backing up. "I think you've made a mistake. I'm waiting for someone else."

"There's no mistake, Mr. Kerry. I have orders to pick you up."

Jeb's heart lurched at the mention of his name. How did these people know him? "But … but I'm waiting for a cab."

"The cab won't be coming any time soon. Now, we really have to be going, Mr. Kerry. We can do this the easy way or the hard way." The man placed his hand on his waist moving his coat away from his body. In the moonlight, Jeb could see the glint of a holstered gun hanging from the man's shoulder.

"Can you at least tell me where we're going?"

"No. Now get in the car. We're in a hurry."

Jeb's hands were perspiring. He lost his grip as he attempted to get in the car. The first man boosted him into the back seat next to another man; then he was sandwiched between the two men. He put his face in his hands as the car started, and the door locks clicked into place. What did these men want? Where were they taking him? Was he going to get out of this alive?

At last they reached their destination. The door locks clicked open. Jeb had thought he'd be glad to leave the car. Now he was afraid. Where was he? Would these men harm him? He was ushered out of the sedan, and the men walked on either side of him, each holding one of his arms in a light grip. Jeb had no doubt those grips would become vises if he tried to run away.

He was placed in a room with a table and a few chairs. The men left. Again Jeb heard the click of a lock. He looked around the room. Only one door. No way to get out. He paced for a while, then sat down at the table. The strain of the car ride and now being locked in this room caught up with him. He was exhausted. He sat with arms folded across his chest gazing down at nothing.

# # #

Chapin and one of his men watched Jeb's pacing through a one-way glass window. "So that's our boy. How was he in the car?"

"Scared."

"Good. We'll give him a little more time, then I'll go in." When Jeb sat down, Chapin observed him carefully for a few moments. "Looks like he's ready." He entered the room carrying a bag.

# # #

Jeb looked up when the door opened and saw the face. Aaron Chapin! Jeb felt the blood in his body congealing. His mind raced as Chapin approached the table. Why did Aaron Chapin want to see him? Was Chapin picking up other men in Jesse's group? What would Chapin do to him?

Chapin sat down across from Jeb and stared at him for a moment. Jeb was impaled by the look. "Hello Mr. Kerry," Chapin said quietly. "Do you know who I am?"

Jeb's mouth was dry. He couldn't speak. He

managed a quick nod.

"Can I get you anything? Some water or coffee perhaps?"

"Wa -- water, please," Jeb croaked.

"Of course." Chapin made a motion toward the one-way glass. "Relax, Mr. Kerry." Chapin's oily tone didn't soothe Jeb. "You have nothing to fear. I just wanted to talk with you about Jesse Cartland."

"Look, if it's about the parade, we had no control over that. That woman just came out of nowhere, then everybody got excited and things got out of hand."

"The parade's only a small part of it, but I'm glad you brought it up." Chapin reached into the bag and withdrew a videotape. "We have Cartland on tape calling for a revolution." He waved the tape in front of Jeb.

"If you've seen the tape, then you know a policeman grabbed the bullhorn from Jesse before he could finish what he was saying."

Chapin's eyes narrowed. "This is only one tape." His tone grew harsher. "We have others where Cartland calls for a revolution."

Jeb wondered where Chapin could have gotten such tapes but was afraid to ask.

"Let me make something perfectly clear to you, Mr. Kerry. We are not, I repeat, are not going to let somebody run around spouting talk about a revolution, even the great Jesse Cartland." Chapin's eyes became slits. "We're going to bring him down."

"Why are you telling me this?" Jeb wished Chapin would quit staring at him.

"Because, much as I hate to admit it, we need a little help from you," Chapin's voice softened again.

Jeb jumped from his seat. "Are you crazy? Jesse's

the Rescuer! He's got awesome powers! I … I'm afraid of what he might do to me if he found out I helped you."

"Sit down, Mr. Kerry. I find your melodramatic reaction tedious. First of all, the Rescuer's nothing more than a myth. I'm sure if we investigated long enough, we'd find Mr. Cartland's miracles are nothing more than the tricks of a charlatan. Secondly, I have power, too. How do you think we found you tonight? We've been watching you for a while now. I know all about your little licensing fee arrangements with the local police."

Deflated, Jeb sat down. "Do you know we could put you in prison for that?" Chapin let his words sink in. "Ever been in prison, Mr. Kerry?" Jeb shook his head. Chapin stood and caressed Jeb's hair. "They'd have a lot of fun with you, Mr. Kerry," Chapin said smiling while his eyes remained cold. "You'd be a delightful package of fresh meat to them."

Jeb jerked his head away from Chapin's touch. He tried not to cry. "What do you want me to do?" he asked defeated.

"As I said, we're going to bring Cartland down, but I want to do it away from any crowds. We don't need another New Kensington riot. I want you to tell us when we can go in and grab him quietly."

"Can I at least think about it?" Jeb was pleading for time. He needed to sort things out.

Chapin slammed his hand down on the table. Jeb jumped. "There's no time to think! I want this done as soon as possible!" Chapin spoke more gently. "By the way, did I mention there's a reward? Come on, Kerry. It's a no-brainer. You work for us and after we capture Cartland, you get enough money to set you up nicely. It's either that or you go to jail for a very long time."

A tear rolled down Jeb's cheek. He thought of all the good things he'd seen Jesse do, but Jesse was going off in a strange direction now – a direction that would leave Jeb out in the cold as far as having an important position. On the other hand, Chapin was breathing down his neck threatening jail time. There was the money, too.

"How much money?"

"Enough to satisfy you. I need an answer, Kerry. Are you going to help us or do you want to go to jail?"

"I'll help," Jeb murmured. He felt a strange coldness in his chest as he and Chapin worked on strategies for Jesse's capture.

CHAPTER TWENTY-FOUR

The agents, again without speaking, drove Jeb back to the motel. They dropped him off far enough away so as not to be seen. His legs leaden, Jeb walked back to his room. It was still dark outside. There was enough time to get some sleep, but Jeb couldn't relax. He kept seeing images of Chapin – a coiled snake ready to strike and destroy anyone who got in his way.

If only he had someone to talk to. Where was Artie when he needed him? Artie! Wait a minute! Was Artie mixed up with Chapin? Jeb remembered that Artie said he knew someone powerful. Artie knew about the metal detectors at that one meeting. Was Artie an agent? Was that how they were able to spy on him and tape what Jesse said? Did Chapin have anything to do with Artie's disappearance?

Jeb had to smile. *You're really getting paranoid now, Jeb. There's no way Artie, inept as he is, would be working for Chapin.*

Growing serious again, Jeb thought about what he

had to do. He'd have to report to Chapin soon with a plan to capture Jesse. Would he be able to pull this off? The thought of prison steeled him. He'd find a way.

The motel offered a small continental breakfast. Jeb wandered into the area first. Since he couldn't sleep, he thought he might as well grab a meal. He was pouring a cup of coffee when Pete approached.

"Morning, Jeb. Get the car back okay?" Pete grabbed a muffin and sat down at a table.

Jeb turned toward him, his face pale, eyes puffy. "Uh, yeah. Everything went fine." It was harder than he thought it would be to face one of the other men in Jesse's group.

"Wow, Jeb! Didn't you get any rest last night?"

"That place was farther away than I realized. Took me a while to get back. Then I was, you know, still upset about the riot." Jeb sat at another table.

"I can understand that. Oh, by the way, can I have my phone back?"

The blood rushed from Jeb's face. Pete's phone! He must have dropped it when the agents picked him up. "I - - I don't have it on me. I'll have to go back to the room." Jeb got up to leave. Jesse entered the room.

"Off so soon, Jeb?"

"Yeah, I need to get Pete's phone."

Jesse blocked Jeb's way as he attempted to leave the room. "Everything go all right with the car last night?"

"Yeah, I just told Pete. Everything went fine." Jeb tried to step around Jesse. Jesse shifted his position.

"Did we give you enough money for cab fare?" Jeb felt Jesse's penetrating gaze.

"Yeah, it was just right as luck would have it." Jeb attempted a smile.

Jesse stepped out of Jeb's way. "Yes, as luck would have it." Jesse looked deep into Jeb's eyes. "Just glad nothing unusual happened."

Jeb scurried back to his room. Did Jesse know what happened to him last night?

As Jeb sat in his room wondering what to tell Pete about his phone, there was a knock at the door. He went to the door and saw Pete's face through the peephole. What now?

"Find my phone?" asked Pete as Jeb opened his door.

"Haven't had a chance to look yet. Do you want to wait a minute while I check?"

"No. Come on. We've got a planning meeting." Jeb tried not to show his relief. A planning meeting! Jeb hoped the group's plan would work to his advantage. He wanted this over with quickly.

After the group gathered, Pete raised his hand. "What do we do now, Jesse. Obviously the parade was a disaster. I know it wasn't your fault, but the media and the police may try to place some blame on us. After all, that part of New Kensington got pretty well trashed."

"I think we need some down time, some time just to get over what happened to us yesterday," suggested Matt. "I also want to check and see if we'll have any legal problems in the aftermath of the riot. After all, Jesse, you had Pete stop the car, and you took some action that led to starting the riot. I realize you had the best of intentions, but it really backfired this time."

"Oh, please," grumbled John, "enough with the lawyer talk. I think we should hold a meeting somewhere so we can get back in people's good graces. Let's face it. People think we're great when we're healing their loved ones. It's just ironic that a healing led to such a disaster yesterday."

Everyone started talking at once about what the best plan of action would be. Jesse sat quietly listening for a few minutes, then stood. "I'll tell you what I'd like to do. I agree with Matt. We need some down time. I'd also like to show you my appreciation for staying with me through the bad times as well as the good times. There's a place that I want to take you for a special meal. Are you up for something like that?"

"You're not planning on feeding us hamburgers, are you, Jesse?" A frown creased Thad's forehead, then he grinned.

"No." Jesse laughed. "This food will be the best and most special you've ever eaten, I promise."

With shouts of "Great!" and "Let's go for it!" the men began talking with Jesse about the outing. Jeb couldn't believe his luck. This meal would present a perfect opportunity. Only thirteen people at a dinner. Surely Chapin and his men could handle that!

The group gathered at the vans. Jesse gestured to Jeb. "Jeb, why don't you ride with me today. I may need you to make some arrangements."

Thad stood by the open driver's door. "Before we take off, I need to know where we're going."

"Don't worry about that. Just turn onto this road. I'll tell you when we get close."

Jeb hopped in the car. *This is not good. Nobody but Jesse knows where we're going. No way to tip off Chapin.*

They drove through the countryside for a while. The rest of the men in the van spent time in idle chatter. Jeb stared out the window memorizing the route they were taking.

Jesse interrupted his thoughts. "You're going to stare a hole through that window, Jeb. What's so interesting?"

"Oh, uh, the country's so beautiful here. I don't want to miss anything." Jeb wished he weren't in the van with Jesse. He wanted to remain as inconspicuous as possible.

"Probably a good thing you're being so attentive. Never know when you might have to find your way home from a place."

Jeb looked at Jesse. Was his remark offhand or did he know something? Jeb turned away and continued staring out the window.

Thad drove on. After a while, Jesse touched his shoulder. "See that man down by that country inn? That's where we're going. Turn in there."

"Roger, Captain," Thad smiled. He pulled to a stop in front of the restaurant. The man came up to the car.

"You the folks we've been expecting?"

Jesse smiled. "We sure are."

"Follow me then. The room's all set up." The man led them to a private dining room on the second floor. A white cloth covered a long dining table in the center of the room. The tableware and chairs had been precisely placed to accommodate thirteen people. A low vase of brightly colored flowers brought a note of cheer to the room. Waitresses began bringing in trays of food and placing them on side tables in preparation for serving.

Jeb looked around. The men he had spent months with were admiring the table and the food they were about to eat. They were laughing and joking with each other, enjoying the moment. The man who had guided them in was apparently the headwaiter. He was directing the rest of the workers. The waitresses were bustling about placing salads on the table and pouring water. Then Jeb looked at Jesse. Jesse was looking at his men, pure love radiating from his brown eyes. Jeb felt guilt stab at his heart, then thought about prison. He took a deep breath. He must go through with this.

The men took their seats. The headwaiter brought the wine for Jesse to sample. He approved the selection then asked the waitresses and waiter to leave. "But sir, this is unusual," the waiter protested. "You need servers."

"That detail will be handled," replied Jesse. "We want to talk in private. Don't worry. You'll still get your tips."

"As you wish, sir." The waiter bowed slightly, then left with the staff.

"You know, Jesse," Pete spoke up, "I'd like to pursue John's idea of holding a meeting so we can get back with the people. He and I could look for ways to do damage control on the New Kensington thing. Maybe each of us could head up teams of locals who are popular in different areas of the country. If we have folks on our side who are well thought of in their home towns, that'll go a long way toward repairing our reputations."

Jesse raised an eyebrow. "And what would your jobs be?"

"As I said, we'd be team leaders. We'd train the folks on what to do and say, then they'd go out and set up the meetings."

"So what you're saying is you'd be sitting in an office somewhere with a title on the door while other people went out to do the work."

"That's a little harsh. I'm thinking out loud right now, but it does seem to me that, since we've obviously had more experience with you than anyone else, we'd be the logical ones to head up any type of operation."

Jesse sighed and shook his head. "You still don't get it, do you?" He rose and went to the side tables. He brought each man a plate laden with the meal's main course.

"What did I just do, Pete?"

"You served us our dinner."

"That's right. I served you. Remember when you went out by yourselves? You each had a great experience in service to others, didn't you?" The men nodded. "The most important thing any of you can ever do is serve your fellow man. You've got to get over thinking about offices and high positions. Serve, and everything else will fall into place."

Pete blushed. "Sorry, Jesse. I forgot," he murmured.

Jesse laid his hand on Pete's shoulder. "I don't think you'll forget again, though, will you?"

Pete shook his head then placed his napkin on his lap. Everyone started talking again and lifted their forks— ready to eat dinner.

Jesse tapped on his wine glass. "Before we eat I have something to say." All heads turned toward him. "Tonight one of you will betray me." Thad dropped his fork. Pete sat open-mouthed, bewildered. Jesse's words bored into Jeb's heart. He felt queasy and almost vomited. Did Jesse know what he was about to do?

Each man studied the faces of the other men at the table, the question plain on everyone's face. Who would want to betray Jesse? And what would someone do that would betray Jesse?

Pete sat staring at his plate. Would he let Jesse down again? Would he do something awful to someone who meant so much to him? He had to know. He went to Jesse's side, tears in his eyes. "Jesse, is it me? Am I going to do something horrible to you?" Jesse gave his arm a reassuring pat.

Each man then got up and went to Jesse with the same question. They each got the same reassuring touch.

The last thing Jeb wanted to do was approach Jesse, but he lined up with the rest and walked to Jesse's side. "Am I going to betray you?" Jesse turned. An immeasurable sadness on his face, he stared at Jeb for a moment then nodded slightly and whispered. "Do what you have to do, but please do it quickly." Jeb ran from the room. Jesse knew what he was up to! He'd have to act right away!

Pete watched as Jeb exited the room. "Why is Jeb leaving?" he asked Jesse. "Did you tell him to do something?"

"In a manner of speaking. Now let me pray over the meal." Jesse blessed the meal, then reached into the basket of bread. He broke the bread into pieces and passed it down the table. "Please eat this bread. This is my body that I give for you." Jesse poured some wine into a glass and started passing it down the table. "Drink some wine from this glass. This is my blood that I shed for you so that you may be brought together with God again."

Pete and Andy looked at each other. "What's he talking about, Pete? Food and wine are his body and blood? I don't understand."

Pete thought for a moment; then something came to

him. "Do you remember that meeting we had where everybody brought a food container in expecting Jesse to feed them?" Andy nodded. "He spoke about giving his flesh and blood at that time, too. Actually this little ceremony makes me feel better. I'll bet Jesse's been talking about his death in the same way. It'll probably be some symbolic teaching, and he won't really die." Andy nodded in agreement.

Jesse spoke again. "I want you to have bread and wine often in this manner so you remember me."

The men ate, drank and talked for a while. Pete noticed that Jesse didn't join in the conversation as much as usual. He looked around the room for Jeb when everyone was about finished eating. *That's odd. He's not back.*

Jesse slid his chair back and stood. "It's time. I want you to be prepared for what will happen later. Tonight you'll all run away. You'll pretend you don't know me."

The men shouted "No way!" and "I'd never do that!"

"It's okay. You'll be scared. You won't see me for a while. Just remember that I will come back to you. Now please come out in back and spend some time with me."

Pete stopped Jesse at the door. "I know I froze yesterday in New Kensington, but I'll never do that again. I won't run away."

"Pete, before the night's over, you'll swear three times that you don't know me."

"Jesse, I'd give my life for you! I'd never say I didn't know you."

#

After Jeb left the dining room, he went downstairs to

look for a phone. The headwaiter took him to the office. Jeb sat down at the desk. "I need to make a private call. Please make sure I'm not disturbed." The waiter nodded and shut the office door.

Jeb dialed a number he had memorized. "Hello, it's me, Kerry. I think you can get Jesse tonight without any problems. … We're out here in a small restaurant eating dinner. Nobody else is around. … Yeah, just the group he always travels with." Jeb gave directions on how to get to the restaurant. "Yeah, I'll stay put. You'd better let me lead you in. I've seen Jesse disappear in a crowd before." Jeb left the office and closed the door quietly behind him. He sat at a table where he could see the stairs.

When he heard the men coming down, he sank back into the shadows. He saw them collecting chairs then going out the back to the restaurant grounds. Even better than the room upstairs, he thought. Chapin's men should be able to arrest Jesse easily in the garden.

# # #

A full moon was out. It shone on the trees and bushes making it easy for the men to find their way about the large lawn. The blinking lights of fireflies illuminated darker portions of the garden. The men placed their chairs on a small path lined with rose bushes. They sat and began chatting again. They stretched and yawned occasionally.

The sound of the crickets was deafening to Jesse. He tried to take in deep breaths, but his chest was tight. He walked over to Pete.

"Pete, can you get John and Jim and come with me? This is going to be a rough night. I could use the company."

"Sure, Jesse. Anything for you."

The four men withdrew a little from the group and sat under a tree. Jesse moved his chair a little apart from the other three men. "I know it's late, but I'd really appreciate it if you could stay awake while I pray."

Jesse bowed his head. Beads of perspiration formed on his brow. His heart beat so that it seemed to want to leap out of his chest. He clasped his hands. They were clammy with cold sweat. "Father, I know this is the time. This is why you sent me here, but I bear such a heavy burden. You ask me to carry the true weight of the world on this fragile body. Must I do this thing? Is there some other way to accomplish what needs to be done?" Jesse continued in prayer for a while then longed for the company of his friends. He stood to speak to Pete, John and Jim, but the wine and heavy meal had done their work. The three men were asleep.

Jesse walked back to the rest of the group. They too had nodded off. Tears flooded Jesse's eyes and rolled down his cheeks. How he wished they could have stayed awake with him! This night of all nights he needed their love and support. He went back to pray again, skin tingling from raw nerves. "I know why I'm here, my Father – to rescue these poor lost people. To bring them back to you. I could not bear to feel separated from you as these people are. I will do your will. My body is weak, though. Please help me." Jesse knelt on the ground, his head in his hands. He felt a warmth gradually envelope his whole being. Strength returned to his body. He raised his eyes to heaven. "Thank you, my Father. I am ready to do your will."

It was then that he heard the footsteps in the grass.

CHAPTER TWENTY-FIVE

Jeb waited by the side of the road in front of the restaurant. He looked in one direction then the other, occasionally standing on tiptoe, watching for the police cars. Finally he spotted them, lights flashing but with no sirens, coming toward him. The adrenaline raced through his body. Even the veins in his face pounded as he watched the relentless approach of Chapin's symbols of power. As he gestured them into the parking lot, the cars' flashing lights and headlights went off. The cruisers glided in darkly, silently – sharks looking for prey.

A policeman stepped out of one of the cars. "You Kerry?" He asked curtly.

"Yes, officer. Looks like you've got the whole police force with you."

"Can't take any chances. You said there were a dozen men out here. We don't know if they're armed or not."

"These guys? No way. How do you want to

proceed?"

"We want to make sure we get the right man, and get out of here quickly with him so there's no trouble."

"I'll lead the way then," Jeb offered. "He'll be the one I shake hands with."

Jeb started off with the police on his heels. Was he doing the right thing? Should he call off the arrest? No! Thoughts of jail and money echoed and re-echoed in his mind.

# # #

Connie and Pete were holding hands and laughing. They'd just finished a picnic and were running through the meadow, Connie's dark hair bouncing about her face, grass crunching beneath their feet. Suddenly she faded from view. The sound of rustling grass became louder.

Pete started. He'd been dreaming. Confused, he looked around at the sound of men's voices. He saw Jeb approaching Jesse, then jumped out of his chair. They were surrounded by a large group of policemen! As he ran toward Jesse, he could see Jesse and Jeb shaking hands. Then several policemen grabbed Jesse and threw him face down on the ground. They roughly placed his arms on his back and handcuffed him.

"Jesse Cartland, you are under arrest for the crime of treason!" The words cut through Pete's brain. This couldn't be happening! It had to be part of the dream! "Jesse! Jeb!" he shouted. "What's going on?"

The other men roused at the sound of Pete's voice. They, too, looked bewildered. Jeb slunk back against a tree. A policeman stepped between Pete and Jesse. "Don't start anything, mister," he warned. "We're here to arrest only Mr. Cartland." The shock and confusion Pete felt exploded into a fist that bloodied the policeman's nose. The officer reached for his nightstick. Other policemen reached for their guns.

"Stop!" They turned. Jesse was standing between two policemen. "Leave him alone, Pete. He's only doing what he has to." The two officers started leading Jesse to a patrol car.

Andy grabbed Pete. "Let's get out of here! We can re-group later."

Pete looked back at Jesse. He could see the policemen ducking Jesse's head as they loaded him into a cruiser. Frightened, Pete ran with the rest of the men.

# # #

The patrol cars all put their blinking lights back on as they sped toward the station house. The passing landscape was a blur to Jesse. He bowed his head briefly, then looked at his surroundings. The grill between his seat and the men in the front, the handcuffs biting into his wrists – yes, he was definitely a prisoner now, but only for a little while.

One of the policemen finally broke the silence. "You know we got a celebrity in the back, Hank?"

"Yeah, I know. Mr. Jesse Cartland. Mr. Cartland thinks it would be a good idea to start a revolution and get rid of us. He doesn't appreciate our work."

"Well, maybe we can show Mr. Cartland a thing or two about appreciation when we get to the station house." The two men laughed. Jesse said nothing.

They finally reached their destination and pulled into an entrance shielded from the press and the public. The two officers walked on either side of him. Their fingers gripped his arms tightly, nails digging into his flesh.

They led him into an interrogation room. As Jesse began to cross the room toward the chair, one policeman stuck his foot out tripping Jesse. Since his hands were still cuffed behind him, Jesse had no way to catch himself. His cheek slammed into the edge of the table. He winced at the sharp pain and the taste of blood in his mouth. He raised his head briefly toward the ceiling. *This is the beginning, Father.*

"You're a mite clumsy there, Mr. Cartland," laughed one of the patrolmen as he helped Jesse up. "Here, let me take those cuffs off and make you comfortable."

Jesse rubbed his wrists as the handcuffs were removed. The policeman shoved him roughly into the chair. Jesse's ribs hit the chair arm hard. He gasped and bent double. *Father; let me feel your strength.*

"Look at that, Hank. Mr. Cartland can't even sit in a chair right. How's he going to lead a revolution?" The two patrolmen laughed, then turned as the door opened.

Aaron Chapin looked from the laughing policemen to Jesse. Jesse's bruised face looked back at Chapin. "You idiots!" Chapin yelled. "The last thing I need is for you men to make Jesse Cartland a victim! Now, get out!"

"Honest, Mr. Chapin, he just tripped," Hank explained as the two patrolmen hurried from the room. Chapin sat across from Jesse, a flame of triumph warming his normally cold eyes. "I do apologize for those men's actions, Mr. Cartland, but you can hardly blame them. After all, you did threaten to put them out of a job." Jesse was silent.

"Nothing to say, Mr. Cartland? Well, I have a few questions to ask you. I'd like some answers." Chapin pulled out a pocket recorder and turned it on. "Did you or did you not on several occasions call for a revolution?"

"I think you already know the answer to that question." Jesse felt searing pain in his face as he spoke.

"But I'd so like to hear your answer." Chapin's tone was soft, but his face was granite hard. Jesse said nothing.

"Are the men you're consorting with involved in a plot to overthrow this government?"

Jesse spoke quickly. "They are innocent men. Please don't harm them." *I must protect my men. They're so frightened and confused now. Father; please be with them.*

"I'll decide what we do with your men. Now I ask you again, did you or did you not call for a revolution?"

"What do you think?"

Chapin slammed his hand on the table. Jesse sat unmoved. Chapin's eyes blazed as he shouted, "I'd stop with the cute responses if I were you, Mr. Cartland. Do you realize the power I have over you? Your life is in my hands."

"And do you realize the power I have?" Jesse spoke quietly. "I am only sitting here because I've allowed you to take control over me. Why don't you ask your agent Vole about my power?"

Chapin's eyes widened for a moment. Cartland knew about Vole! But he mustn't lose control of this interview to Cartland. He jumped out of his chair. "That tears it, mister...."

The door opened. "Matt Levy, attorney for Mr. Cartland." Matt threw his card on the table. "That'll be all the questions for now. What's my client being charged with?"

Chapin glared at Matt. "Treason, Mr. Levy." Chapin tossed Matt's card back at him. "Good luck!" Chapin stomped across the room and slammed the door as he left.

Matt sat down and reached across the table to hold Jesse's hands. "What happened to you, Jesse? You look like you've been hit by a train!"

"They tell me I tripped. By the way, how'd you find me?"

"Jack and I took one of the vans. It wasn't hard to figure out where the cops would take you. If those guys roughed you up, we can charge them with police brutality." Matt pulled a legal pad from his briefcase and began writing.

"Let it go, Matt. We have bigger problems than that. Besides I can understand why the police feel they way they do about me. They don't understand why I'm here."

"Okay, whatever you say, Jesse. I do need to know if you admitted any wrongdoing to Chapin before I entered the room."

"No."

"Good. I can't understand why they came up with a treason charge. It's crazy."

"Chapin said they had evidence that, on several occasions, I called for a revolution."

"When did you ever do that?" Matt frowned and thought for a moment. "Does he mean those times that you called for a revolution of the heart?"

"Probably." Jesse rubbed his face. "Matt, do you think they'd give me an ice pack for this? It's really throbbing."

"Sure, Jesse, but why don't you heal yourself? I know you can do it."

"I need to take on everyone's pain, everyone's hurts;

if my mission is to make any sense."

"I don't understand what that means, and I don't have time to right now. I'll ask about the ice pack in a minute. We need to begin work on a strategy immediately. The charges should be pretty easy to beat. We'll get witnesses to state accurately what you said at the meetings. I'll also line up the best criminal lawyer I can find for you."

Matt continued scribbling notes. Jesse took his hand. "I want you to defend me, Matt."

"Not a good idea, Jesse. I'm a corporate lawyer, not a trial lawyer. You need someone who knows his way around a courtroom. Chapin will undoubtedly try the case himself. We need to find the best pit bull attorney we can to go up against him."

"You know me, Matt. I trust you. I want you. Now do your lawyer thing."

"Okay," Matt shook his head. "I think it's a mistake, but you're the boss. Now I need to ask you a few more questions about what Chapin said."

Several policemen entered the room. Matt looked up. "I'm talking with my client, fellas. I need some privacy."

"Sorry, sir, but we have to move Mr. Cartland. A crowd's gathering and we need to take him to a more secure location." They handcuffed Jesse again and also shackled him.

He shuffled slowly down the hall flanked by the two policemen. Matt followed close behind.

# # #

Pete ran from the garden and jumped in a van with Andy and some of the rest of the men. "Floor it!" he yelled. They peeled out of the parking lot and headed toward the countryside. Pete kept looking out the rear window of the van. "I don't see anybody following us. Guess the cops were telling the truth when they said they were only after Jesse." Pete felt he would never catch his breath. Pictures of what just happened kept flashing through his mind—a slide show of horror. *Jesse's arrested! Why? What's going to happen to me and to the rest of the men now? What about Jesse? Is he okay?*

Andy touched his shoulder. "Pete, do you know what happened back there?"

"No I don't. We were sitting with Jesse keeping him company; then I guess we fell asleep. The next thing I knew Jeb was shaking hands with Jesse; and we were all surrounded by police."

"Jeb!" Andy spat out the name. "I'll bet he had something to do with the police being there. We know he's a crook."

"Hold your horses, little brother. We need to sort out a lot of stuff." Pete looked at the dark countryside, then shouted, "Thad! The headlights aren't on!"

"I know that. I'll turn 'em on now. I didn't want to be too visible to anybody who might be following us." Thad slowed the car and turned on the lights.

"Sorry for yelling. I'm about ready to jump out of my skin."

"What do we do now, Pete?" Andy asked. "We don't have a leader, and we don't know what's going on."

"I heard the cop say something about Jesse being arrested for treason."

"Treason! That's crazy! What did Jesse ever do for them to come up with a charge like that?"

"I don't know, Andy, but I'd like to go to the police station and see what's going on."

"You think that's a good idea?" Thad asked. "You think you'll be safe doing that?"

"They said they were just after Jesse."

"Yeah, like we can trust 'em." Thad gripped the steering wheel tightly, his forearms bulging.

"I still want to be where Jesse is. Why don't the rest of you go back home. We'll meet up later, and I can tell you what the police are doing."

"Do you want some company, brother?"

"No thanks, Andy. If too many of us go we'll attract some unwanted attention. It's better if I go alone."

Thad turned the car around and left Pete off a few blocks from the police station. Pete started walking, his thoughts a whirlpool of panic. *What did Jesse do that was so bad? Are the police after us? What about Connie? Her mother? Are any of us safe?*

Pete saw a crowd gathered in front of the police station. He stood at its edge. A man next to him spoke. "This is something, isn't it?"

"What – what's going on? I saw people standing here and wondered what was happening." Pete kept his head down.

"They arrested that Cartland guy. They say he committed treason." The man peered at Pete for a moment. "Hey, aren't you one of his men? Didn't I see you on television opening a grave?"

"No." Pete started moving away from the man. "You have me mixed up with someone else." Pete could feel his heart skipping beats. Jesse was really arrested for treason! He expected to feel a policeman's hand clamped on his shoulder at any moment. Maybe he shouldn't have come.

Pete shifted to a different side of the crowd. He overheard two women talking. "I always knew there was something fishy about that Cartland. He was too good to be true." The other woman nodded, then caught sight of Pete. She poked her neighbor and pointed at him. "Weren't you driving the parade car for that Cartland guy in New Kensington?"

"No." Pete shied away. "People say I look like him." It was definitely a mistake to be here. He had placed himself, his family and the rest of the men in danger.

Pete tried to leave, but the press vans started rolling in. Pete was caught in the crowd as the crews began setting up cameras and microphones. "Excuse me, mister," one of the assistants pushed Pete aside. "Gotta set up for this story. Should be a big one if Cartland's involved." The assistant stopped for a moment and gazed at Pete. "You look familiar. Aren't you one of Cartland's men?"

"Absolutely not! I know nothing about the man!"

"Okay, okay. Don't get your dander up. Just let me run this cable."

The doors of the police station opened. Policemen started pushing through the crowd making a pathway. Pete was standing at the edge of the cleared walkway when Jesse came out the door. The crowd started yelling and booing Jesse. A patrolman was on either side of him holding his arms tightly. They helped him down the steps. It seemed to Pete that everything was in slow motion as Jesse shuffled toward him in handcuffs, shackles and a bulletproof vest. Reporters moved closer thrusting microphones in Jesse's face, shouting questions. As he neared Pete, Jesse paused for a moment, turned his head and looked at Pete. Pete put his hands to his mouth in horror as he saw Jesse's bruised and swollen face. Then he saw Jesse's eyes full of sadness peering into his soul, and Pete remembered.

He'd told people three times that he didn't know Jesse! His strength and resolve had failed him again! He had denied the Rescuer! He'd denied his friend! Pete tore through the crowd, tears streaming down his cheeks, wanting only to get home and be with Connie.

Pete waved to the driver as the truck drove off. He'd been lucky to be able to hitch a ride home. He'd had the trucker drop him several blocks from his house just in case the police were there. The sun was coming up as Pete trudged toward Connie and the refuge he needed now. He stopped for a moment and looked toward his house. Good! No police activity around it.

When he reached his front yard, Pete paused again. *Seems like an eternity since I left this house to travel with Jesse. We started out wanting to make people's lives better. What happened?*

Pete thought about all the miracles he'd seen Jesse perform, about the people he and Andy had helped when they went out by themselves. Now his life had turned upside down. Jesse'd been arrested, and they were all on the run. He needed to see Connie, to hold her in his arms. Maybe she could help him make sense of this insanity.

He opened the back door quietly. He realized he was hungry and decided to make a snack before he woke Connie. He began rummaging through the refrigerator.

"Stop right there!" Pete turned; startled. Connie was standing in the doorway with one of his golf clubs raised, ready to swing.

Pete lifted his arms. "Connie, it's me! It's okay!"

Connie dropped the club and ran into his arms. "I heard a noise … I didn't know…." She started crying. They stood there, husband and wife clinging to each other, sobbing together, locked in love and needing each other.

Finally Connie's tears abated. Still sniffling, her voice shook as she spoke. "I was so scared last night. I was watching television, and I saw Jesse coming out of the police station. I didn't know whether they'd arrested you or not. I didn't know where you were."

Pete led her to the kitchen table and told her what had happened in the garden and at the police station. He cried again when he told her about denying Jesse. She patted his arm. "Don't beat yourself up, Pete. You were confused and scared. I'm sure Jesse would understand."

"But you didn't see the way he looked at me. He was so sad." The words choked Pete. He went to the sink for a drink of water.

"What are you going to do now?"

"I'm going to get out of here pretty fast. I don't want you to be in danger."

"Do you have to go right away?"

"Yeah, I do. It's best that way. I couldn't bear it if anything happened to you because I stayed around. Do you have any extra money?"

Connie nodded and ran for her purse. Pete dialed Andy's cell phone. They decided to meet with the rest of the men to work out a plan.

Pete packed a few things, then kissed Connie and headed toward the door. "We're going to decide where to hole up while all this craziness is going on. I'll get word to you about where we are."

Andy's car drove up, and Pete jumped in.

Connie was still staring out the window long after the car was gone, tears running down her cheeks.

# # #

Jeb straightened his tie as he entered Aaron Chapin's office. He was glad this would be the last time he'd have to deal with the man. He patted the plane tickets in his breast pocket. He'd make a quick trip to the airport, hop on a plane and get as far away from Chapin as possible after this meeting.

The receptionist motioned for Jeb to sit down. As he waited, the events of the previous evening flashed through his mind. The quiet of the garden as he and the police entered; then the look of deep pain and betrayal he saw in Jesse's eyes as he shook hands with him. Everything seemed to speed up after that. Police were shouting and throwing Jesse to the ground. Men he'd worked with for months were screaming and running away. Jeb gave a quick shake of his head trying to empty his brain of painful images. He'd done what he had to do—nothing more.

A buzzer sounded on the receptionist's desk. She ushered Jeb into Chapin's office.

Chapin looked up from his paperwork. "Ah, Jeb," he rose smiling and extended his hand.

"Please, sit down."

Jeb sat perched on the edge of the chair, afraid to relax into it.

"I'm very pleased with the way the operation went last night. We nabbed Cartland, and nobody got hurt."

Chapin sat again at his desk. "Now, what can I do for you?"

"I -- I…" Jeb croaked.

"Need some water, Mr. Kerry?" Chapin poured Jeb some water from a pitcher behind his desk.

Jeb could see Chapin's amusement at his discomfort. He took a long swallow of the liquid, then, looking at the water glass, spoke again. "I came for the money you promised me."

"Of course, the money. Frankly, I thought you'd be here when the office first opened." Chapin opened a desk drawer and withdrew a thick envelope. "Here you are, in cash, no less. Untraceable."

Jeb couldn't resist counting the money. He thumbed through the bills, then recounted them. "There's only five hundred dollars here! What gives?" Jeb felt white-hot anger rising in him. Nobody, not even Chapin, could put him through what he went through last night and give him only five hundred dollars!

"Not enough for you, Jeb? Oh, that's right. I forgot to tell you the other part of the deal. I need you to testify at Cartland's trial. You'll get the rest of the money after that."

The air whooshed from Jeb. He felt like he'd been hit in the stomach with a sledgehammer. It took a few moments for him to recover enough to speak. "What do you mean testify? You never said anything about me appearing in court."

"Yes, you're right about that. I've decided, after looking at the evidence and talking with Cartland, that I'd have a stronger case if one of Cartland's own followers stood up in court and said he heard Cartland calling for a revolution. You're that follower, Jeb." Chapin gave a dry laugh.

Jeb could feel the plane tickets against his chest. He wanted to run, to go anywhere just as long as it was far away from here. He didn't want to have to face Jesse in court. "What if I refuse? I've already done everything you asked."

"Remember jail, Jeb? Remember the package of fresh meat?" Chapin's words were razors cutting on Jeb's nerves. "Oh, and by the way, don't worry about catching that plane. We've already cancelled your reservation."

Jeb slumped back in his seat, defeated. "Okay, when do you want me to be there?"

"We're pushing the judge on the trial date. We want it as soon as possible. I don't want to give anybody time to rally large groups to Cartland's defense. One of my staff will contact you and coach you on your testimony." Chapin turned back to the papers on his desk.

Jeb sat, stunned. He had no friends, nobody to rely on except Chapin. How he wished he could find Artie!

Chapin looked up from a folder. "That'll be all for now, Kerry. I have a lot of work to do to get ready for this trial." Chapin motioned for him to leave.

Jeb left the office, not seeing or hearing anything. Would Jesse sit in court and look at him with those same pained, betrayed eyes that he saw in the garden? Would the other men be there to see him testify against Jesse, against their work? Jeb leaned his head on the cold metal frame of the elevator. *What will become of me? What have I done?*

CHAPTER TWENTY-SIX

The sound of the clanking metal door echoed through the jail. Matt stepped into Jesse's cell, briefcase gripped in one hand. Jesse was sitting on his cot, head bowed. Matt sat down beside him, and after a moment, Jesse raised his eyes.

"Sorry I couldn't meet you in an interview room, Jesse. Security is really tight. I'd like to see you get out of this cell, but it doesn't look like that's possible right now."

"That's the least of my problems." Jesse gave a short laugh.

"I've got some bad news and some bad news. It seems Chapin's moving this trial along at light speed. We'll be going to court very soon. I tried to get the judge to extend the trial date, but he wouldn't play ball."

"What's the other cheery news?"

"I can't find anyone to testify for our side. All our men went into hiding, and I haven't been able to find them yet. Other people who saw you speak are fearful of

Chapin. They won't admit they were ever at one of our meetings, so we can't get them to testify."

"What options do we have left?"

"If I can't find anyone else, the only thing I can do is put you on the stand. Normally I wouldn't do that, but the jury has to hear what you said in New Kensington after you called for a revolution. Chapin's men have shared the tape with me, and, as it stands, the tape's damaging for our side. I can see your lips moving, though, after the cop pulled the bullhorn away from you. What did you say?"

"What do you think I said?"

"If it's like the other times, I'd say you called for a revolution of the heart."

"That's what I said."

"That's great!" Matt felt hopeful for the first time since Jesse's arrest. "All you have to do is get up on the stand and state that! The jury would understand that you weren't trying to overthrow the government. You were trying to change people."

"I won't testify, Matt."

"What! Why not?" Matt was stunned. "You realize you'll get the death penalty if you're found guilty, don't you?"

"I'm well aware of consequences you can't even begin to imagine."

Matt thought for a moment. It wasn't in his nature to lose a case even if his client wouldn't co-operate. What could he do to help Jesse? His face brightened. "I know! Jack and I can testify as to what we heard at the meetings! We wouldn't be the strongest witnesses in the world, but our testimony would cast doubt in the jury's minds."

Jesse placed his hand on Matt's. "Matt, I know

you're trying to do your job, but the best way you can help me right now is to be my friend. Don't testify. Don't have Jack testify either. Just sit beside me at the trial, and let me feel you care for me. There's only one way this trial can end. Please accept that fact and know that I accept it."

"But, Jesse...."

Jesse held up his hand for silence. "I'll dismiss you as my lawyer and defend myself if you don't do as I say."

Matt stared at the floor, beaten. "Okay," he sighed. "I'll do as you ask. I don't want to, but I will. I don't want you to go through this by yourself."

Matt rose to leave the cell; then turned to face Jesse. "Your mind's made up?"

"My mind's made up." Jesse spoke firmly.

Matt shook his head, then motioned for the guard.

Jesse's voice was clear, even on the small tape recorder. Chapin re-wound the tape and played it again. Jesse was calling for a revolution of the heart. He sounded harmless on the audiotapes, but Chapin knew he wasn't. The interview for National Attorney was coming up. He must have an unblemished record. Cartland mustn't be allowed to disrupt things again, but what to do? Aaron went to the tape-editing machine, inserted the audiotapes and spliced them at strategic points. As he finished, there was a knock on his door.

"Ah, Ben, come on in." Chapin motioned for his assistant, Ben Daniels, to have a seat. "Are you ready for this case?"

Daniels, thin with auburn hair, sat in front of

Chapin's desk. "Yes, sir. I've seen the videotape where Cartland calls for a revolution. I need to hear the audiotapes. The sound guys said you had them."

"I certainly do. Here goes." Chapin inserted a tape in the recorder and pushed a button. Jesse's voice called for a revolution. "That satisfy you, Ben?"

"Sure does. Sounds like we have a good case against Cartland."

"Got anybody who'll testify that's what was said at the meetings?"

"We can't find anybody closely connected with this case who will testify. They're all scared and hiding out. We do have some people who could be persuaded, though. The problem is we'd have to do them some favors in return, so that option's out."

"No, it isn't. Go ahead and do the favors as long as they aren't too big and can't be traced back to me."

Daniels frowned. "Are you sure about this? I'd really be sticking my neck out. If anyone ever found out... My career...."

"Do it, Daniels! We've got to stop Cartland!" Chapin's tone left no room for argument. "How's Vole doing? Would he be able to testify?"

Daniels rolled his eyes. "Artie's still the rhyme-of-the day guy out at the sanitarium. He's starting to drive them crazy."

Chapin chuckled briefly then became serious again. "Too bad. He'd make a fine witness. We do have Kerry, though, and whoever else you can dig up. Guess that'll have to do. Anything else?"

"We haven't been able to find any of Cartland's men except his lawyers, of course. The rest could turn up to testify at the last minute and put holes in our case."

"Does Levy know where they are?"

"He says he doesn't, but who knows?"

"Who knows indeed." Chapin crossed his arms and looked, unseeing, toward the files on his desk. After a few moments, he straightened. "I think we'll have to make sure these rats stay in their nests. Get out some warrants and start searching these men's homes. Tell their relatives they're wanted for questioning."

"Do we have any cause for taking this action?"

"We certainly do. Isn't the word 'revolution' enough for you?" Daniels faced the full power of Chapin's flinty gaze. "Cartland is threatening to tear down everything I've built up, everything I've accomplished to bring order. I won't have it!" Chapin's coffee cup shook as he slammed his fist on the desk. "Now let's put a little fear into these men's families! Get the warrants!"

Connie was propped up in bed, trying to read a book, but not concentrating—her thoughts a jumble. Where was Pete? Was he all right? Why hadn't he called yet? She heard cars pulling up in front and looked at her watch. Who would be out at this hour? It was well into curfew. Her heart leaped. Maybe it was Pete!

She sat on the edge of the bed, listening. All of a sudden, there was pounding at the door. "Police! Open up!"

Connie grabbed for her robe. "I—I'm coming! Just a minute!" she shouted. The robe floated behind her as she ran down the hall.

"Police! Open up immediately!"

Connie opened the door a crack. "What's going on?

Why are you here?" She squinted as she looked into a flashlight.

"We have a warrant to search your property and take Peter Stone into custody for questioning. Stand aside." Several policemen pushed past Connie and started searching the house.

Connie sank down on the couch in the living room. She wanted to cry, to scream; but she wouldn't show any weakness in front of these men who were violating her home.

One of the policemen approached her while the others searched. "Do you know the whereabouts of Mr. Stone, ma'am?"

"No, I don't." She stared back at the policeman and spoke firmly. "I haven't seen or heard from him in several days. I have no idea where he is. Why do you want to question him?"

"I can't tell you that. I can only say it's a very serious matter--a very serious crime."

Connie blanched. *What serious crime is Pete involved in? Where is he? Please be safe, my darling Pete!*

The police finished ransacking the house. The officer in charge spoke to Connie as he was leaving. "If you hear from Mr. Stone, notify us immediately."

Connie said nothing. She slammed the door behind them. She turned and looked at her home. The police had pulled seat cushions from furniture, opened drawers and dumped the contents, thrown things from closets. Connie stood frozen, not knowing where to start at putting things in order.

The phone began ringing. Maybe it was Pete! Connie searched frantically through the mess. *Please don't hang up! Please keep ringing! Ah, there it is!* She grabbed the receiver. "Hello!" she was breathing heavily.

"Connie?" Pete asked.

At the sound of his voice, Connie began crying. "Pete..."

"Connie, what's wrong!" Connie held the phone from her ear as Pete shouted.

"The police were just here. They searched through everything. They said they wanted to question you!" The events of the evening caught up with Connie, and she began trembling.

"Question me? Why? What would they want with me?"

"They wouldn't tell me. They said something about a serious matter--a serious crime. Is it in connection with Jesse?"

"They said in the garden they were there to arrest only Jesse. This doesn't make any sense."

"Unless they changed their minds."

"Are you all right now, Connie?"

"Yes, I'm starting to settle down."

"I called to tell you where I am. Got a pencil?"

"No, Pete! Don't tell me where you are! For all we know they have this line tapped. I want to be truthful if I have to tell them again that I don't know where you're located."

"Do you want me to come home?"

"Absolutely not! You may be in terrible danger!"

Pete's voice was tender. "Are you gonna be okay?"

"Yes, Pete," Connie said, calming. "I want you to stay safe. Now I think we'd better hang up in case they're tracing this call."

"I love you, Connie."

"I love you, too, Pete." Connie quickly hung up the phone. She placed the cushions back on the couch and sat down. She looked at the rest of the living room. The lamp was overturned, books were strewn on the floor, cabinets were open—their contents trailing across the floor. Suddenly she clenched her fists as the tears came again. She gave a muffled scream and began beating the cushions. Her life was like her house—once in perfect order, now in chaos. She spent the rest of the night huddled under a blanket on the sofa. She greeted the dawn with swollen, red eyes, the same questions reverberating through her mind. Would Pete ever be safe again? Would their lives ever be normal again?

# # #

After Pete told the other men what had happened at his house, they decided to call their families. They learned the police had raided their relatives' homes. All their families were frightened.

"What do we do now, big brother?" asked Andy.

"We try to find out what this is all about. Meanwhile we tell no one where we are, and we don't make any stupid moves."

CHAPTER TWENTY-SEVEN

Pete slept fitfully after talking with Connie. He awoke early the next morning. Andy was already up and in the bathroom. Pete spoke through the door. "Think I'll go get a paper."

"Be careful." Andy's muffled voice replied.

Pete put on a cap and jacket and left the shabby motel room. Thad had found this hideout for them, and rest of the men had checked in over a period of several hours so as not to attract attention.

He found the morning paper at the front desk. Headlines about Jesse's capture, and pictures of Jesse, Pete and the rest of the men blazoned across the front page. Pete pulled his cap down further over his face as he picked up the paper.

Back in the room, he was poring over the story when Andy stepped out of the bathroom. "Listen to this, Andy! They're having the trial almost right away! I'm glad Jesse's got Matt and Jack with him. I hope they can help him beat the charge." Pete threw the paper across the room. "Treason! It's so ridiculous!"

"Ridiculous or not, if Chapin's behind this, you can bet he's got a strong case. I still have the same question I had last night. What do we do now?"

"Let's call everybody to our room and see if we can come up with some ideas."

Pete picked up the paper and began studying it again as Andy called the other men's rooms. They began to gather, continental breakfasts in hand, and ate as Pete brought them up to date.

"It says here the trial date is firm, and Jeb will be the chief witness."

Everyone groaned at the mention of Jeb's name. "I'd like to punch that guy's lights out!" Thad hit his open palm with his fist.

Pete looked at the group. "What do you think about going down to the courthouse and showing support for Jesse. I realize we're in danger ourselves, but I don't want him to have to go through this alone. I know he's got Matt and Jack, but maybe seeing us would help him."

John raised his hand. "Is the trial going to be televised?"

"Yes."

"It seems to me that we'd be better off to stay put and watch the proceedings from here. What if they nabbed us at the courthouse and made one of us testify against Jesse? How would we feel then?" The rest of the men nodded their heads in agreement. "Also, we can't minimize the danger we're all in. Even our families could be arrested. We don't know what Chapin's going to do next."

"So that's the plan, then?" Pete looked at each man. "We just sit here and watch TV?"

"What would you have us do?" John spread out his hands in a helpless gesture.

"I don't know. I want to go to Jesse to say I'm sorry for letting him down again. I want to see Connie and hold her in my arms. I want to tell her everything'll be okay." Pete sagged onto the bed, head down. " I want to lead a normal life." Andy put an arm around his shoulder. All were quiet for a moment, then Pete straightened. "John's probably right. We'll stay here and watch the trial. We need to know the verdict before we can make any other plans. Sound good?"

The men voiced their assent. Pete took in a long breath and blew it out. "Let's be careful, then, guys. Be aware of your surroundings at all times. We may have to move out of here at a moment's notice if we think we've been spotted. Now let's pray for Jesse, Matt and Jack."

All bowed their heads.

# # #

Matt entered Jesse's cell carrying a garment bag. "Here you go, Jesse. I got this for you so you'd look presentable in court."

Jesse looked up. The bruise on his face had faded to a yellowish color. "Thanks, Matt. How're things going?"

"Chapin's come up with some real prize witnesses. Jack's checking them out. One of them has a questionable background, so I may be able to break her. As you know, the most damaging parts of Chapin's case are the parade videotape and Jeb testifying for their side."

Jesse nodded. "Whatever happens, don't beat yourself up, Matt. Please believe me when I tell you the right verdict will come in."

"Wish I had your confidence. Are you ready for tomorrow?"

Jesse nodded; then Matt continued to talk with him about aspects of their case.

# # #

Matt walked into the courtroom. The rich brown color of the wood paneling, the elevated judge's bench, the huge bronze regional seal on the wall behind it, even the jury box inspired him. He experienced the same emotion he'd felt, when as a younger man, he'd first seen a courtroom and decided to become a lawyer--anticipation that justice would be done.

As people started coming in, Matt leaned over the defense table, taking a few deep breaths to calm his nerves. Jack came in, handed his brother a folder; then took his seat. All the other players in this game of life and death quickly assembled. Chapin strode in surrounded by his legal team. The guards ushered Jesse in; the jury filed in, then the judge.

"All rise!" the bailiff commanded. The words blared in Matt's ears. This was it—the clarion call! *Jesse's life is at stake. I've got to come through for him!*

Pete turned on the TV set as the men gathered in his room. He saw the judge enter the courtroom from his chambers; then another camera showed the defense table. Pete looked at his friends seated before the judge. Unbelievable! Jesse on trial for treason. "Jesse looks pretty good… wait a minute! What's that mark on his face?"

Andy peered at the screen. "Looks like a bruise to me. Wonder how that happened?"

"Matt's fiddling with his pencil. Looks nervous," observed John. "I hope the jury doesn't pick up on that." John looked around the room. "You know what, fellas? I don't think we should all be in the same room. If the cops come, we'll be sitting ducks. Why don't some of you come to my room to watch this?"

"John's right," agreed Pete. "I wish we could all stick together, but I guess that wouldn't be wise."

As some of the men filed out, Pete called after them, "Let's meet at the pizza place later. We can use that back room to talk about what we saw today."

# # #

"Zach!" Marika called. "It's starting! The judge is coming in!" Zach came into Marika's living room holding a cup of coffee. Marika sat down in an easy chair. "I still can't believe what's happened, can you?"

Zach shook his head. "No. I thought when Jesse brought Gabe back to life, and they threw that big parade in New Kensington for him; he'd be right back on top. Now look at him." The camera showed Jesse seated at the defense table. "On trial for his life. I still don't believe it."

When Marika saw Jesse, she removed a handkerchief from her pocket and dabbed at her eyes. Clutching her handkerchief, she whispered, "Please don't let anything happen to him."

"I'll hear opening statements now." The judge turned toward Chapin's table. "Counsel for the prosecution, are you ready to begin?"

"Yes, your honor." Chapin rose and buttoned his jacket. He strode toward the jury, back straight, eyes unblinking. "Ladies and gentlemen of the jury, we will prove beyond a reasonable doubt that Jesse Cartland is guilty of the crime of treason. We will present witnesses and taped evidence that will prove that Mr. Cartland called for a revolution. One of his own men will testify to that fact. I have no doubt, ladies and gentlemen, that when all the evidence is presented; you will find that man," Chapin pointed at Jesse, "guilty of treason." Chapin marched back to his seat, a soldier for justice.

"Counsel for the defense; your opening statement."

"Thank you, your honor." Matt took a swallow of water, then rose and looked at the jury. "Ladies and gentlemen, we intend to prove that Mr. Cartland was not calling for a revolution in the traditional sense of the word. He was merely calling for people to change their lives for the better." Matt took his seat again; wishing Jesse had given him more to work with.

Judge Parsons nodded at Chapin's table. "Call your first witness, Mr. Chapin."

"Miss Ellen Greene to the stand!"

A slender young woman wearing a low-cut blouse and tight skirt entered the courtroom. Chapin looked at her attire, then glared at Daniels. Daniels looked away; suddenly busy taking notes. The witness moved to the stand and was sworn in.

Chapin approached the stand and smiled at the witness. "Miss Greene, do you know the defendant?"

"Can't say as I really know him. I did go to one of his meetings."

"But you know who he is, don't you?"

"Of course. Everybody knows that's Jesse Cartland." Miss Greene pointed toward Jesse.

"When did you go to this meeting?"

Miss Greene gave a date.

"And why did you go to this meeting?"

"I heard a lot of talk about Jesse Cartland—you

know, how he healed people and fed people. I wanted to see for myself."

"What did you see, Miss Greene?"

"Well, Mr. Cartland, he talked for a while about some stuff I didn't understand; then he said we had hard lives and we should get involved in a revolution."

"Let me play a tape for you, Miss Greene." Chapin went to his table and turned on the tape player. Everyone could hear Jesse's voice saying, "Then you must have a revolution…" Chapin turned off the recorder; then approached the witness again. "Is that what you heard Mr. Cartland say?"

"It sure is." Miss Greene gave a slight nod of her head, accentuating her testimony. "That's what Jesse Cartland said."

"Thank you, Miss Greene."

Judge Parsons looked at Matt. "Your witness, Counselor."

Matt picked up Jack's folder from the table and approached the witness. "You say you heard Mr. Cartland call for a revolution."

"Yes, sir. He sure did." Miss Greene nodded more emphatically.

"And he said nothing after the word 'revolution' like maybe the words 'of the heart'?"

"No, sir, he didn't."

"Would you tell me again the date you went to Mr. Cartland's meeting?"

Miss Greene fidgeted in her seat as she repeated the date.

"Miss Greene, would you say you have good hearing?"

"Yes, I would."

"I would agree. I'd say you have excellent hearing, Miss Greene, to hear Jesse Cartland speaking when you were on a cruise ship on the date in question." Matt took some papers from the folder and waved them at Miss Greene, then the jury.

Mouth open and eyes wide, Miss Greene stared first at the jury then at Chapin.

The courtroom observers murmured to each other. The judge banged his gavel and called for order.

"Your honor, I'd like to place Miss Greene's itinerary into evidence as exhibit four." Matt handed the papers to the judge with a slight flourish, then turned back to Miss Greene.

"How did you manage to be in two places at once, Miss Greene?"

"Well, you see… It's like this…" Miss Greene looked to Daniels for help. He began scribbling again. Miss Greene turned red and cleared her throat. She began to cough.

"Can I have some water, Judge?" Miss Greene pleaded. The bailiff handed her a glass of water. She took a long swallow and composed herself. "Now I remember. Silly me." She tried to laugh but it came out a nervous giggle. "I gave my sister that ticket at the last minute. She went in my place."

"And why did you do that?"

"Because I really wanted to see Mr. Cartland."

"Your testimony is that you wanted to see Jesse Cartland so badly that you gave up a cruise ticket to do it?"

"That's right."

"Nothing further." Matt returned to his seat.

"Any re-direct, Mr. Chapin?" The judge asked.

"Yes, your honor." Chapin rose, approached Miss Greene, smiling again.

"You're absolutely sure that your sister took the trip on the day in question?"

"I'm positive."

"And she'd testify to that fact?"

"Yes, she would."

"Thank you, Miss Greene. That's all the questions I have for you."

"Any re-cross, Mr. Levy?"

"No, your honor."

"Then the witness is excused."

Miss Greene scurried from the courtroom.

"Call your next witness, Mr. Chapin," the judge directed.

"Excuse me, your honor. May we have a short recess? I need to confer with my assistant." Chapin sounded relaxed, but gripped his pen tightly.

"Twenty minutes, Mr. Chapin." The judge banged his gavel.

#

Chapin tramped down the hall carrying a legal pad. He entered a conference room, Ben Daniels close behind. Chapin slammed the door and threw the pad across the room.

"What was that in there? Where did you get that witness? She looked like a whore! And such weak testimony!" Chapin batted his eyes and spoke in a high voice. "Why, yes, I gave up a cruise just to see Jesse Cartland." Chapin nailed Daniels with a cold stare. "Think anybody'll buy that?"

Daniels was strung out. He'd been working twenty-hour days helping Chapin prepare for trial. He knew how important the case was to Chapin. He also knew he was walking a tightrope with his own career. The legal pad hitting the wall was the firing pin for his own anger. "You asked me to find witnesses to testify about Cartland calling for a revolution. Guess what! Everybody's afraid to testify! They're afraid if they cross you in any way they'll rot in jail! I did the best I could!"

Chapin stared at Daniels for a moment, then bent to pick up his pad. "I'm sorry, Ben," Chapin spoke quietly. "I didn't realize you were under such pressure. Before we continue, though, I have to know if there are going to be any surprises from any of the rest of the witnesses."

"I don't think so. Levy won't be able to trace the other witnesses, and Kerry's well prepared. I've been very careful on that score."

Chapin patted Daniels' arm. "Okay. Let's go back in and take care of Cartland."

Daniels followed Aaron Chapin back to court wondering if they should be taking care of Cartland.

# # #

Zach and Marika laughed at the expression on Ellen Greene's face when Matt questioned her about the cruise. Marika could feel her knotted stomach relaxing.

"I'd say Jesse's home free if that's the type of witness who's going to testify against him," said Zach.

"I agree." Marika nodded her head. "Uh, oh, trial's starting again. This should be fun!"

# # #

Matt, Jesse and Jack huddled during the recess. "Good job, Matt," Jack congratulated his brother.

"Not so fast, Jack. That one was easy. I'm worried about the rest of the witnesses. Did you find anything on them?"

"Nothing. It's like they appeared out of thin air." Jack tapped his pencil on his legal pad. "I wish the rest of the guys would contact us. We could use their statements about what they heard Jesse say. If we don't have them, Jeb's testimony will really hurt our case."

"Remember what I told you in the cell, Matt?" Jack and Matt turned toward Jesse as he spoke. "I said the right verdict would come in. Don't beat yourselves up."

"Okay, Jesse. We'll certainly need one of your miracles for this trial." Matt turned and looked up the courtroom aisle. "Here come Chapin and Daniels. Time to gear up for battle again."

Chapin called several more witnesses. Their stories were the same as Miss Greene's. They'd gone to one of Jesse's meetings and heard him call for a revolution. All denied they heard Jesse say anything else to clarify what type of revolution he was calling for.

The judge looked at the clock. "Do you have any more witnesses, Mr. Chapin?"

"Yes, your honor, just one more."

"I suggest then that, since it's growing late, we pick up the proceedings tomorrow at nine o'clock." The judge banged his gavel. "Court is adjourned."

As Jesse was led back to his cell, Matt and Jack conferred. "I'm going out to try to find the guys again," Jack started up the aisle.

Matt loaded his briefcase. "And I'll work on some

angles to put holes in Jeb's testimony. Good luck on finding the men."

# # #

Pete, John and Andy were the first to gather at the pizza parlor. They moved the tables around in the back room so they couldn't be seen from the door. "That first witness was a pip, wasn't she?" Pete giggled.

"Yeah." John joined in the laughter. "I thought Matt had it made after he got done with her. Didn't seem like he made a dent in the other witnesses, though."

Andy put in his order then sat down. "I'm worried about Jesse. Are you sure we shouldn't go and offer to testify? After all, we do know he called for a revolution of the heart."

"No way!" John exclaimed. "Did you see the look on Chapin's face when he was questioning those witnesses? He's out for blood. I believe he'd do anything, and I mean anything, to win this case. Look at how he's already intimidated our families!"

Pete stared at his soda stirring it with his straw. "John's right. I'm worried about Connie. She's all by herself. She won't let me contact her for fear they'll trace my whereabouts. Besides Chapin would probably twist our testimony. We might end up making things worse for Jesse. I guess we should stay put."

The rest of the men gradually entered the room. Pete ate quietly not joining in the others' conversation. *Am I doing the right thing or am I just a coward? Am I letting Jesse down again? No, John's right. We should stay hidden until the trial's over.*

#

Matt looked hopefully at his brother as Jack came down the courtroom aisle. "Sorry," said Jack. "I couldn't find 'em. There's so many places those men could be. I gave it my best shot."

"I'm sure you did." Matt clasped Jack's shoulder briefly then began pulling things from his briefcase. "I think I'm ready for Jeb. I've got some questions ready that'll put holes in his credibility. Just wish his ex-boss hadn't disappeared. I'm sure we could have used his testimony."

The court came to life as Chapin and his men, Jesse, the jury and the judge came into the room.

"Call your next witness, Mr. Chapin."

"Jeb Kerry to the stand!"

#

Jeb paced in the hallway. *Keep your cool, buddy. Just one more miserable day and you're home free. Chapin'll give you the rest of the money, then you can go anywhere you want and start life over.*

The door to the courtroom opened, and the officer motioned for Jeb to enter. Jeb put on his suit coat and entered the courtroom. His legs were shaking. He looked neither to the left or right. He was focused only on reaching the witness chair as soon as possible.

Jeb settled himself on the stand. He met Jesse's eyes and saw sadness and disappointment in them. He quickly looked away.

Chapin approached the stand, eyes glittering like a predator, ready for the kill.   "Mr. Kerry, how well do you know the defendant, Mr. Cartland?”

“I traveled with him for months. I acted as his accountant.” Jeb went on to describe his travels with Jesse and his duties.

“Mr. Kerry, I ask you to listen to these audiotapes, then I’ll show you a videotape.” Chapin played the two audiotapes. Again the jury heard Jesse talk about a revolution. Chapin inserted the videotape into the player. The jury saw Jesse with a bullhorn in his hand at the New Kensington parade saying people needed a revolution.

“Now, Mr. Kerry, I ask you—did you hear and see Jesse Cartland make these statements calling for a revolution?”

Jeb paused. His brain cells amplified Chapin’s words. They echoed and re-echoed loudly in his mind. Jeb knew his answer could literally kill Jesse.

“Mr. Kerry, please answer the question,” demanded Chapin.

“Yes.” Jeb coughed and cleared his throat. “Yes, I did hear and see Mr. Cartland making those statements.”

The crowd in the courtroom started buzzing. The judge called for order.

“No further questions. Your witness,” Chapin barked at Matt.

Jeb gripped the chair arms as Matt approached him. They had traveled together for months, but he knew Matt now considered him the enemy and would try to destroy him. Would he be able to stand up to Matt’s questioning?

“Mr. Kerry, do you know me?”

“Yes, you and I traveled together with Mr. Cartland.”

“What did you do before you began traveling with Mr. Cartland?”

“I was an accountant with the Bradbury firm.”

"Why did you leave Bradbury's?"

"I told them I wanted to travel with Mr. Cartland."

"Were there any irregularities when you left Bradbury's?"

"What do you mean by irregularities?" Matt thrust his face close to Jeb's. "Any problems with the books you were keeping?
Any money missing? Is that why you left? Remember, you're under oath."

Jeb paused. Did Matt know why he was anxious to leave his job and travel with Jesse? He decided to call Matt's bluff.

"My employers wanted to cut back," Jeb's voice was steady. "It worked out that I wanted to leave at the same time."

Matt turned back to his table. "How convenient!" He faced Jeb again. "You say you were the accountant with the group. Please explain once more what your duties were."

"I'd collect the money at the meetings. The donations people gave us covered our expenses. I'd also go to the local police stations and pay the permit fees for the meetings we held in each town."

"These permit fees—what were they for?"

"To cover expenses for local police presence in case anything happened."

"But usually nothing happened, did it?"

"No. Things were usually quiet."

"So the police had no reason to think a heavy presence would be required, did they?"

"Objection!" Chapin half-rose "Mr. Kerry couldn't know what the police thought."

"Sustained. Next question."

"These fees you spoke of—were they set fees?"

"Each locale had its own fee schedule."

"And did you negotiate that fee schedule sometimes?"

Jeb took in a quick breath. Matt knew about his fee arrangements! *Stay steady, Jeb. Stay focused. Don't let your voice shake.* "My job was to go to each police station to pay the local fees."

"That's not what I asked you. Did you negotiate fees sometimes? In other words, did you and someone at the local station rake off part of the fee?"

"I went to each police station and paid the fees required of me."

Matt pushed further. "Did you pocket any of the money?"

"Asked and answered, your honor," Chapin snapped from his table.

"Move along, Mr. Levy," the judge prompted.

"You've seen and heard the tapes, Mr. Kerry. Did Mr. Cartland add any words after the word 'revolution'?"

"I don't know what you mean. I heard Jesse say 'revolution'."

"Did he say 'of the heart' after the word 'revolution'?"

Jeb was perspiring, but knew he didn't dare wipe his face. He could see the jury from the corner of his eye. He knew they were weighing every nuance of his testimony. In order to save himself from prison, he had to make these people believe him. Jeb spoke quietly, but distinctly. "I heard and saw Mr. Cartland make the statements on those tapes."

Matt thrust his face into Jeb's. "Jeb, you know what Jesse said! You know what he was really talking about!

Now tell the court! Tell them he said 'a revolution of the heart'!"

"Your honor, I object." Chapin stood, protective of his witness. "Counsel's badgering the witness and also testifying for him."

"Sustained. Settle down, Mr. Levy!"

Jack half-rose, but Matt waved him back into his seat. "Mr. Kerry," Matt's voice was softer, "I'm sure you're aware there's a penalty for perjury. Now tell me what Mr. Cartland said after the word 'revolution'!"

Jeb looked down at his hands. "I can only tell you that what Mr. Cartland said on those tapes was exactly what   I   saw   and   heard."

"Look me in the eye, and tell me that!" Matt snapped.

"Your honor…." Chapin drawled.

"I told you to settle down, Mr. Levy!" Judge Parsons chided Matt. "Do you have any more questions for this witness?"

"No." Matt went back to the table and sat down heavily.

"Re-direct, Mr. Chapin?"

"Yes. Mr. Levy tried to paint a picture of meetings that were calm. Isn't it true, Mr. Kerry, that sometimes the meetings did require police intervention?"

"Yes, several times we had angry crowds."

"So the police were definitely required." Chapin turned to face the jury. "And we all know what happened in New Kensington."

Matt leaped to his feet. "Objection! Now opposing counsel's testifying!"

"Settle down, both of you!" Judge Parsons gave a stern look to both lawyers. "Any more re-direct?" Chapin shook his head. Parsons turned to Matt. "Any re-cross?"

"No, your honor."

"Then the witness is excused."

Jeb left the witness stand. As he drew alongside the defense table, he once again gazed into Jesse's eyes. Brown pools of sadness looked back at him. Jeb felt a stab of guilt. He left the courtroom quickly.

"Call your next witness, Mr. Chapin."

"The prosecution rests, your honor."

Judge Parsons leaned back in his seat and turned to Matt. "All right, Mr. Levy, it's your turn. Call your first witness."

Matt turned toward Jack and whispered, "Do you think you could find the men if we had one more day?"

"I don't know, but it's worth a try. We don't have a chance without them."

Matt rose. "Your honor, could we please have one more day to locate our witnesses?"

Chapin pushed back his chair. "Your honor, Mr. Levy has had as much time as I to prepare his case," he droned.

"You're right, Mr. Chapin. Mr. Levy, you need to get on with your defense."

"Please, your honor. We've had trouble finding our witnesses. A man's life hangs in the balance. I'm only asking for one more day."

"All right, Mr. Levy. Due to the seriousness of the charge, I'll grant your request. However, you must be ready with your defense by ten o'clock tomorrow morning.

"Thank you, your honor."

Chapin rose and gathered his papers, shaking his head in disgust. He wanted this trial finished and Jesse

Cartland behind bars.

As the officer led Jesse away, Jack called out, "I'll do my best, Jesse. I'll find them."

"Is there any place you haven't looked?" asked Matt.

"Frankly, none that I can think of, but I'll turn this town upside down tonight."

"I'll look, too. Let's split up the possibilities."

Matt scoured the motels and hotels until dawn. He kept in contact with Jack by cell phone, but neither of them had any luck finding Pete and the other men. Matt headed back to his room for a little shuteye before the trial started again. Jack wanted to follow up one more lead and promised to meet Matt at the courtroom.

# # #

Matt, red-eyed and tired, walked with slumped shoulders to the defense table. Jack wasn't there yet. Maybe that was a good thing.

Jesse, looking surprisingly fresh, was led in by the guard. He patted Matt's arm but said nothing.

Chapin and Judge Parsons entered. Parsons turned to Matt. "Mr. Levy, are you ready to begin your defense?"

Matt rose. "Your honor, if you'll be patient, I'm waiting…" Matt heard the door open. He turned his head. Jack stood at the open door, lips tight, shaking his head. Matt held up his hand. "Your honor, one moment, please."

Jack came down the aisle as the courtroom observers began to chatter. "I'm sorry, Matt. My hunch didn't pan out." Jack sat down at the table, defeated.

Parsons banged his gavel for order. "Mr. Levy, will you please begin your defense!"

Matt looked down at the pen twisting in his hands. His tone was muffled. "I have no witnesses, your honor. The defense rests."

Judge Parsons jerked upright in his chair. "What? No witnesses! Well, I, ah, I guess we'll be ready to hear closing arguments tomorrow. Court's adjourned!"

The banging gavel echoed and re-echoed in Matt's head. It was a death knell. The trial was all but over, and he'd failed Jesse miserably. He hadn't been able to crack Jeb the way he'd wanted to. Matt sat dejected for a moment then brightened. His miserable defense might be Jesse's best hope!

"Jack," he called to his brother, "let's go back to the office. I have an idea to discuss with you."

Matt patted Jesse's hand as the guards came for him. "Jesse, I think it'll be okay. Jack and I are going to work on a strategy."

"I'm not worried at all," Jesse called over his shoulder as he was led away.

Marika jumped up after the judge lowered his gavel. "Zach, we've got to get to Matt immediately! All he needs is for someone to testify that Jesse did say 'revolution of the heart'." I heard Jesse say that at a meeting. He wasn't calling for a revolution the way we think of it. He was calling for inner change." Marika ran to get her coat.

Zach grabbed her arm as she raced toward the door. "Wait a minute! Are you sure this is a wise move? Jesse's men must have heard the same thing, and I don't see any of them rushing into the courtroom. Testifying could be dangerous for you!"

Marika pulled from Zach's grasp. "I don't care! Jesse gave me my life back. I can't do any less for him now!"

"All right. If you're that determined, I'll go with you." They jumped in the car and headed toward the jail.

They arrived at the jail and learned that Matt wasn't there. "He's probably at his office, Marika. Why don't we head over there?"

"Okay. Do you think we could see Jesse before we leave, though? I'd like for him to know there's a chance he'll win."

"I'll see what I can do." Zach was told visiting hours were over. He pulled out his cell phone and made a few calls. Soon he and Marika were seated on one side of a glass screen. Jesse was led in from his cell and sat, smiling, on the other side of the screen. They each picked up phones and held them to their ears.

"It was good of you to come."

"Jesse, I've got great news…" Marika paused. "What happened to your face?"

Jesse waved a hand. "It's not important. What's your news?"

Marika grinned broadly as she spoke. "Jesse, I can help you! I know you were talking about a revolution of the heart. I heard you! I can testify for you! When they hear me, the jury will understand what you were really saying!"

When Jesse frowned, Marika was surprised. Her testimony could free him to do his work! Why wasn't he happy?

Jesse held his hand up and touched the glass. Marika did the same. "My dear faithful friend." His warm tone soothed her. "I can't allow you to do that. I won't be able to complete my mission if you testify."

"What? I don't understand! I just want to help you! Please let me!" Her eyes filled with tears.

"No, Marika. I've already told Matt the right verdict will come in, so don't worry about that. I'm more grateful than you'll ever know that you and Zach came here today, but I want you to promise that you won't contact Matt about testifying."

"But, Jesse…."

Jesse motioned for the guard. His voice was metallic in her ear. "Don't contact Matt! You must do this for me." He left the room.

Marika turned to Zach. "I don't understand. Why won't he let me help him?" She collapsed weeping onto the table. Zach put his arm around her and tried futilely to comfort her.

# # #

Jeb waited until he saw Chapin enter his office building, then rode in a separate elevator to Chapin's headquarters. The receptionist had gone home for the day, so he knocked on Chapin's door. Chapin looked surprised for a moment when he saw Jeb, then laughed dryly.

"I underestimated you, Jeb. Even I didn't think you'd come for the rest of the money so soon."

"I want to get out of town as quickly as possible. Do you have the money here?"

"Of course." Chapin crossed to his desk. "You don't think I'd let anybody see the two of us together at a bank, do you?"

"And what about the charges against me regarding the permit fees? Are they taken care of?"

"What charges?" Chapin's unctuous tone did nothing to soothe Jeb. "I don't know what you're talking about." Chapin pulled open his desk drawer. Jeb craned his neck for a view of the money. "Look, as far as anyone knows, there was no hanky-panky with the permit fees. Believe me, the local police are just as glad as you are to forget about that.
There are a few cops out looking for work, though." Chapin rummaged in his drawer for a few more seconds. "Ah, here it is." He withdrew an envelope and handed it to Jeb.

Jeb sat in a chair across the desk from Chapin. "You don't mind if I count it, do you? I got quite a surprise the last time."

"Go right ahead. I do have to get ready for my closing argument, though, so make it fast."

Jeb counted the bills, stared at them in disbelief, then recounted them. He jumped to his feet and threw the money on Chapin's desk. "What are you trying to pull? There's only five hundred dollars here again! You said you'd give me enough money so I'd be comfortable!"

Chapin gave Jeb a steady gaze as he eased open one of his desk drawers. "I know a lot of people who could be comfortable on a thousand dollars. And don't forget, you're not going to jail. You'll be way ahead financially earning a living instead of rotting in a cell." Chapin cackled as he withdrew his hand from the desk drawer. Jeb gaped as he saw a handgun pointed at him. "Now pick up that money and get out!" Chapin snarled. "I've got work to do!"

Jeb scooped up the money and left hurriedly. His

part in the trial was over. He had to get away as soon as possible. He had to try to forget that last look Jesse gave him.

#

It galled Matt to watch Chapin strut into court the next morning. Chapin smirked at Matt and Jack as he took his seat.

Jack whispered in Matt's ear. "Guess he's already declared himself the winner."

"Unfortunately, he is. Jesse's tied our hands. He won't testify, and he won't let us testify. I've never felt so helpless in my life. We'll probably have to use the ace in the hole we talked about."

Just then the guards led Jesse in. After he was seated, Matt grasped his hand. "Jesse, are you sure you won't change your mind? I can still tell the judge we have some witnesses."

Jesse's tone was firm. "No, Matt. You must trust me. The right thing will happen."

"Okay. I hope you know what you're doing."

"Matt," Jesse looked determined. "I've known for a long time what I'm doing."

The judge entered and called for the prosecution's closing argument. Chapin rose and seemed to grow taller as he approached the jury, carrying the tapes.

"Ladies and gentlemen of the jury, for several days now, you've heard witnesses testify that they heard Jesse Cartland call for a revolution." He waved the tapes at the jury. "You've heard and seen yourselves that Mr. Cartland called for a revolution." Chapin stepped closer to the jury box. "You've heard Jeb Kerry, Mr. Cartland's own assistant testify that he heard Mr. Cartland call for a revolution. Ladies and gentlemen, I submit to you that you have no choice but to find Mr. Cartland guilty of treason!"

Judge Parsons indicated it was Matt's turn. Matt rose and stood by his table. "Ladies and gentlemen, the word 'revolution' can have many meetings. As Mr. Chapin indicated, it can refer to a government overthrow, but it can also mean a gentler kind of turning or change. When Mr. Cartland used the word, he meant for people to have a change of heart--to love their fellowmen. He was not calling for a change of government. Mr. Cartland, therefore, should be found innocent of the charge of treason." Matt sat down, not wanting to look at the jury. His face was red with shame. He'd failed miserably at Jesse's defense.

The judge instructed the jury; then they were ushered out to deliberate. Matt and Jack went to a conference room to wait.

"How long do you think they'll take?" Jack asked.

"Hard to say. Of course, I haven't had any experience with juries, so I don't know if waiting a long time or a short time is good for our side."

"Do you suppose they'd give us some coffee?" Jack went to look for a coffeepot.

They were sipping the strong brew when a court officer ducked his head in the door. "Jury's back," he announced.

Matt looked at his watch, then at Jack. "Twenty minutes. It only took them twenty minutes."

They stood up, ready to go back to the courtroom. Matt wished he knew if a quick verdict was a good sign.

CHAPTER TWENTY-EIGHT

Matt and Jack started down the hall. Matt's heart was racing. *What would the verdict be?* His breath was coming fast. Suddenly the corridor started spinning. He grabbed at the wall for support.

"Matt! What's wrong?" Jack put an arm around his brother.

"I think I'm hyperventilating." Matt panted as he hung on to Jack.

"Breathe slower, Matt. Slower." Jack helped Matt to a bench.

Matt's breathing gradually became more regular. "It's just that I wanted to do a good job for Jesse, and I didn't. I let him down."

"I know what you mean." They sat for a moment longer thinking about the disastrous trial; then Jack stood. "Let's go see what the jury has to say."

As they settled themselves at the defense table, Jesse

was led in. Chapin and Daniels were already seated. Chapin was impatiently tapping his pencil on the table. He smiled when the jury filed into their box.

"All rise!" Judge Parsons entered the court and took his seat on the bench, then everyone else sat down. The courtroom was crowded, but very quiet as the judge looked toward the jury box. "Mr. Foreperson, do you have a verdict."

The foreman rose. "Yes, we do, your honor."

The bailiff handed the judge the piece of paper containing Jesse's fate. He looked at it then passed it to the clerk. "Will the defense please rise?" Matt rested his fingertips on the edge of the table to steady himself. He glanced at Jesse out of the corner of his eye. *Jesse's amazing! He looks serene!*

"Madame Clerk, please read the verdict."

It seemed to take forever for the clerk to unfold the paper and begin reading. "We, the jury in the above entitled action, find Jesse Cartland guilty of the crime of treason."

The judge looked at the jury. "So say you all, Mr. Foreperson?"

"So say we all, Judge."

"Your honor."

"Yes, Mr. Levy?"

"I'd like to have the jury polled." Matt wanted everyone on the jury to have to say in public that they'd found Jesse guilty.

As each juror affirmed the verdict, Matt's heart grew heavier. Each affirmation was a stab in his chest.

"Very well." Judge Parsons turned to Jesse. "Mr. Cartland, you have been found guilty of treason. That crime is punishable by a mandatory death sentence. We'll meet at ten o'clock tomorrow morning to decide how that sentence will be carried out."

Judge Parsons looked at Matt. "Did you hear me, Counselor?"

Matt started. He'd heard nothing after the jury was polled. His friend and teacher was facing death. That couldn't happen! His plan for appeal must work!

Jack answered for Matt. "Ten o'clock is fine, your honor."

"Bailiff, please remove the prisoner. Court's adjourned." Parsons banged down his gavel.

The reporters dashed out to file their stories. Jesse Cartland was guilty!

Matt reached out to Jesse as the bailiff led him away. "Jesse, I'm sorry. Don't worry, though. I'll come by this afternoon. I have an idea for an appeal."

#

Marika busied herself in the kitchen making a cup of tea. "Do you want something to drink?" she called to Zach.

"No, thanks." Zach was in the living room watching the jury go out to deliberate Jesse's fate.

"Wonder how long they'll take?" Marika settled herself on the couch, placing her cup on the coffee table. She fluffed the pillows, trying to keep busy.

"No telling. I hate to say it, but Matt really looked lame at the end. I still can't believe he had no defense at all."

"We don't know everything. Remember, Jesse wouldn't let me testify. Maybe Jesse tied Matt's hands."

"That's possible," Zach agreed.

They continued to talk for a bit then Zach rose to turn off the television set. "Think I'll take a walk." He reached for the dial, then paused. "I don't believe this!"

"What?" Marika looked up from her tea.

"The jury's coming back in already! It hasn't even been half an hour!"

Marika's heart beat faster. "Is that good or bad?"

"We'll soon know." They watched as the courtroom ritual played out.

Marika sat, barely breathing, as the clerk unfolded the paper. *Please, please let him be found innocent!*

The clerk read the verdict. "No! No!" Marika screamed. "This is so wrong! Zach..." She jumped up, crying and screaming. Zach put both arms around her, steering her back to the couch. They sat arms wrapped around each other, rocking back and forth as Marika cried uncontrollably.

#

Pete watched the verdict by himself. The other men had gone out for some fresh air, figuring the jury would take a while to reach its verdict.

He heard the clerk pronounce Jesse guilty, then flipped off the TV set. He looked into the mirror hanging above the television set. *How does it feel to be a gutless wonder, Pete?* He should have gone to the trial. Connie would have understood. He could have found some way to protect her. <u>I failed Jesse again!</u> Pete looked at himself in disgust.

Andy came back to the room to find Pete sitting on the bed, expressionless, tears flowing down his cheeks.

Jeb walked quickly down the street. Each step

carried him closer to his room, closer to being able to leave this town, closer to starting over. As he passed an appliance store, the television set in the window caught his eye. The set was tuned to a news station. The letters streaming across the bottom of the picture read "Jury back in Cartland case".

Jeb watched as the jury filed in. The camera shifted to the defense table. Jesse's face filled the screen. A small boy standing beside Jeb was also looking at the picture.

"Mister, do you think that man's going to be okay?" The boy pointed toward the TV set.

"I don't know, son. Why?"

"He fixed my arm a few months ago. I was born with it all crooked, and Mr. Cartland straightened it right up." The boy thrust out his arm, showing Jeb its perfection. "I sure hope nothing happens to him."

Jeb couldn't meet the boy's eyes. He looked back at the television screen. He saw the clerk read the verdict. He felt his heart thump as the judge pronounced the mandatory death sentence.

The boy started crying. "Isn't there anything we can do, mister?" His innocent eyes pleaded with Jeb. "Mr. Cartland's a good man. He can't die!"

He looked at the boy—evidence of Jesse's goodness and knew he spoke the truth. Jesse was a good man. Jesse shouldn't have been sentenced to death, but he, Jeb, had helped make sure Jesse would die.

Jeb looked down the street, saw the store, and started walking toward it. There was something he'd have to buy before he took the longest trip of his life.

# # #

Jeb carefully smoothed a spot on his bed and sat down, arms in his lap; a bag at his side. He thought about the boy—so grateful to Jesse, so worried about him. Then Jeb thought about himself. He remembered all the times he'd lied to people; all the times he'd cheated people just to have a little extra cash in his pocket.

When Jesse'd come into his life, things had changed. He relived all the time they'd spent together, all the times he'd seen Jesse help people. He felt the thrill again when he thought about how Tom Gems and he had gone out by themselves and brought hope to folks they didn't know.

Now he was in a box with no escape. He'd deceived everyone. He had no friends left. Worst of all, he kept seeing Jesse's eyes. Eyes that were once so warm, so loving, looked so betrayed in court. Jesse'd looked like a wounded animal, and Jeb knew he'd done the wounding. There was nothing left to do. Jeb opened the bag and withdrew the gun. He looked at it for a moment, then cocked it and placed it in his mouth.

The barrel tasted sweet. *Forgive me, Jesse.*

He pulled the trigger.

# # #

Matt tried to force some lunch down before he met with Jesse. He knew it was important to keep his strength up, but his stomach was churning. The words "guilty" and "death sentence" were hammers repeatedly hitting him in the belly. At least they had a chance for an appeal. Jesse would be glad.

After finally downing a soda, he headed to the jail. He spread out papers on the table as he waited for Jesse.

He looked up and smiled as Jesse entered, escorted by a guard.

"Good afternoon, Counselor." Jesse smiled back. "What did you mean when you said you had an idea for an appeal?"

"Jesse, we can claim you had incompetent and inadequate representation at your trial. You know Jack and I didn't even put on a defense. You saw how surprised the judge was when I didn't call any witnesses. On these grounds I'm sure we could get you a new trial with a far better lawyer than I—a lawyer with a lot of trial experience." Matt was relieved. He'd given Jesse a way out.

"My dear, dear friend," Jesse grew serious. "It's still not too late to teach you something."

"What do you mean? Aren't you excited about getting another chance?"

"Remember when I told you the right verdict would be pronounced?" Matt nodded. "Well, it was."

"I don't understand. You're not listening to what I'm trying to tell you!" Matt was puzzled. Why didn't Jesse want to talk about an appeal?

"Do you also remember when all of you men agreed that I was the Rescuer?"

"How can I forget? Raising Gabe from the dead was the most amazing thing I've ever seen."

"What does the word 'rescue' mean?"

"It means 'to save'. Jesse, why are you going through all this?" Matt was growing impatient. Why talk about what a word means at a time like this?

"Because my job, as the Rescuer, is to die so all people may be saved, forgiven and brought back to God."

Matt was alarmed. "You can't mean you want to die!

Jesse, please listen to me about the appeal!" Matt reached across the table to grasp Jesse's hands. The guard stepped forward. Matt drew his arms back.

"Matt, try to understand. I came here to do a job. That job is almost finished. I want to complete my mission and return to my Father."

"Your father? I thought he was dead."

Jesse gestured toward the ceiling. A light of understanding shone through Matt's eyes. "Oh! I see!" Matt could only sit silently as he finally comprehended Jesse's purpose. *Jesse told us he had to die. If he's the Rescuer, that means he'll go back to the Father after his death! This is the right verdict!*

After a time he got up. "I'll be with you tomorrow, Jesse," Matt's voice was husky. "And I'll be with you the rest of the way. I'll make this as easy as I can for you." Matt's voice broke as he left the room.

\# \# \#

Judge Parsons glared at the buzzing intercom then punched the button hard. "What? … Oh, all right. Send him in." Parsons scowled. *What does Chapin want? Why does he have to interrupt me while I'm trying to prepare for tomorrow?* Parsons forced a smile as Chapin entered his office.

"Hello, Aaron. You surprise me. I thought you'd be out celebrating. The Cartland victory was a walk in the park for you."

Chapin took a seat in front of the judge's desk. "That's what worries me. I'm afraid they'll appeal and stretch this thing out."

"You must agree that Cartland didn't get much of a

defense.”

“Maybe. Maybe not. I’d just like to be rid of him. He’s a trouble-maker.”

“Why did you stop by?”

“We both know that treason carries the death penalty. I want to know what the options are on carrying out that sentence?”

“Interesting that you should ask that question. I’ve been looking through some law books. In this region you have the choice of firing squad or death by lethal injection.”

“Firing squad!”

Judge Parsons smiled. “Unreal, isn’t it? It’s an old penalty that’s been on the books for years.”

“You’re not considering that option, are you?”

“Let’s stop beating around the bush, Aaron. What do you want?”

“I want Cartland put to death as quickly and quietly as possible. I don’t want any of his followers getting up in arms and starting something.”

“Ah, yes. Order must be maintained at all costs.” Chapin fixed Parsons with a flinty stare. Parsons ignored the look. “I take it you’re emphasizing ‘quickly’?”

Chapin’s face softened. “Yes, if you can arrange it.”

“For once we’re in agreement. Of course everything will depend on what Cartland’s lawyers do tomorrow, but I’m inclined to agree we need to put an end to this whole affair as soon as possible.”

Chapin shook Parsons’ hand and rose to leave. His cell phone rang. “What? … I can’t hear you. I’m going out in the hall. Wait a minute.” He whispered “Sorry, Judge,” and left the office.

Chapin found a quiet spot in the hall. “Now I can

hear you. What did you say? … You're not serious! … Meet me in my office immediately! Use the back door!" Chapin sprinted down the hall; phone still clutched in his hand.

# # #

Chapin heard a light tap at the private door to his office. He let the agent in then looked both ways down the hall.

"Don't worry. I made sure nobody saw me." The man took a seat.

Chapin sat on the edge of the desk. "Repeat what you told me on the phone. I want to make sure I heard you correctly."

"Jeb Kerry was found in his room with his brains blown out. Apparently he committed suicide."

"That's just great. Who else knows about this?"

"The police, of course, and the woman who reported the gunshot. She's one of the other tenants in the building."

"The police are easy. What about the woman? Did she actually see Kerry's body?"

"I don't think so."

"Did anyone else hear the shot?"

"I don't think so."

Chapin jumped to his feet. "I don't want to hear any more 'I don't think sos'. The next time you come in here, you'd better know the answers to those questions." Chapin thrust his face close to his undercover worker's. "I want this thing kept quiet for a while. I particularly don't want Cartland's lawyers finding out about it. Understand?"

"Whatever you say, Mr. Chapin."

Chapin stepped toward the private door. "Now go take care of it."

The operative slipped out the door.

Chapin started to do some paperwork then threw his pen on the desk. *My chief witness is dead! What do I do if the Levys find out about Kerry?*

# # #

Matt walked into the courtroom. The bronze seal on the wall now mocked him. He wanted no part of a system that was putting his friend, his Rescuer, to death. All he could do was cling to what Jesse'd told him yesterday—that his death was necessary.

The familiar ceremony took place as Jesse, then the judge entered.

The judge seated himself, then looked toward Matt. "Counselor, do you have anything you wish to bring before the court before I pass sentence?"

Matt rose, but looked at the papers before him on the table. "No, your honor."

The judge opened his mouth, closed it, paused, then spoke. "No appeals, Mr. Levy?"

Matt raised his eyes and faced the judge. "My client does not wish to appeal, your honor."

Chapin stared at Matt, wide-eyed, then turned back toward the judge, a triumphant smile on his face.

"I, uh, I see." Judge Parsons shuffled some papers, then cleared his throat. "Will the defendant please rise then."?

As the three men rose, Jesse was the pillar supporting Matt and Jack.

"Jesse Cartland, you have been found guilty of the crime of treason. It is therefore the sentence of this court that you be put to death by lethal injection three days hence. You will be held in the regional prison until such time as your sentence is carried out. Bailiff, arrange for the prisoner's transfer. Court is adjourned."

As the gavel banged down, reporters ran for the phones. Jesse Cartland would die in three days!

"Jesse," Matt called after his friend, "I'll be out to see you as soon as possible." Jesse nodded as he was led away.

Matt sat down heavily. "Jack, can you believe it? Three days! Three days and they're going to execute Jesse!"

"I know, Matt. This has to be Chapin's doing. He obviously wants Jesse out of the way quickly, but why so fast?"

Matt began gathering up his things. "I don't know. Who knows why Chapin does anything? We'd better be going. We need to make this as easy as possible for Jesse."

He looked at Jack, tears forming in his eyes. "Trouble is, I don't know how to do that." Matt broke down and sobbed.

Chapin, the triumphant prosecutor, walked to the microphones placed on the courthouse steps. Cameramen angled for good shots. Reporters started screaming questions at him. Chapin held up his hand. "I'll make a brief statement, then I must get back to my office. Today you saw justice done. A jury of his peers found Jesse Cartland guilty of treason. He was sentenced to death—a proper punishment for his heinous crime. Let this serve as a warning for anyone else out there who might act

against this government. We will come after you."
Chapin left for his office, a gaggle of reporters trailing
behind him trying to get interviews.

As they left, Matt and Jack waved off the reporters.
They were too heavy-hearted to talk with anyone.

# # #

Pete and some of the men met in his room to watch
Jesse's sentencing hearing. The rest had gone to John's
room. They saw Judge Parsons sentence Jesse to death by
lethal injection.

Pete left the room in disgust when Chapin's face
filled the TV screen. He took a walk to clear his head,
then returned. All the men had gathered in his room.

"You should have stayed for Chapin's statement,"
said Andy.

"Why? I didn't feel like watching the great Aaron
Chapin crow about his latest victory."

"Sit down and listen, Pete," John motioned to a spot
on the bed. "Chapin talked about coming after anyone
else who might act against the government. He may have
plans to round us up and charge us with treason."

"We don't know that for sure, though, do we?"

"No, but I don't want to see you go off half-cocked
and get into serious trouble."

Pete jumped up and faced the group. "Are you afraid
of Chapin?" They looked at each other, then sheepishly
nodded.

Pete banged his fist on the dresser. "I'm tired of
running scared! I've made up my mind. I'm going to be
with my friend when he dies, no matter what Chapin
does! I'm not going to let him go through this alone!"

"What about Connie?" Andy asked. "Aren't you concerned for her safety?"

"Of course. I'll take care of Connie," Pete snapped.

"Relax, Pete. I'm on your side. John's right. We don't want to see you do something hasty and get yourself in trouble."

"You mean you don't want me to do something that might get you in trouble."

"That's not fair, Pete." John stood facing Pete, hands on hips. "We all have families to think about."

"Think about this! I've let Jesse down too many times. I'm not going to now. I have to be with him when he dies. I want him to know he has a friend who cares about him."

John stepped closer to Pete. "We all care about Jesse! Are you saying we don't?"

"I'm saying that I can't live with myself if I don't do this thing."

Pete and John glared at each other. Thad stepped between them, "Let's cool off now, guys. Pete, are you set on going out to the prison?" Pete nodded. "Okay, then let's do some planning. First of all, how will you even get in the place?"

"I thought about that while I was walking. I know they allow observers, and Zach seems to be well connected. Maybe he can make some calls."

"Sounds good. You may not believe this, Pete, but we're concerned for your safety. Would you at least try to disguise yourself?"

Pete thought a moment. "That's a good idea. Yeah, I can do that."

"Okay, then you can carry all our prayers out there to Jesse when you go. We'll help you get ready."

Pete grabbed the phone. "I'll call Zach right now."

Zach was worried about Marika. She hadn't slept all night. She'd been wandering through the house weeping and talking about what Jesse meant to her. He decided to call the doctor and get a sedative for her. As he reached for the phone, it rang. "Hello. …
Oh, hi, Pete. You know this isn't the greatest time … You what? … Yes, I can arrange it, if that's what you want. … I'll get back to you."

"Who was that?" Marika entered the room. Her eyes were red from crying, and her face was pale.

"Nothing, Marika, don't worry about it. Here, sit down."

"I heard you mention Pete's name. Is he the one who called?"

"I told you it was nothing. Now, if you don't mind, I'd like to call the doctor so he can give you something to help you sleep."

"You're treating me like a child, and I'm getting annoyed. What was the phone call about?"

Zach sighed. "Okay, it was Pete. I didn't think you'd want to hear what he called about."

"Let me judge for myself. Just tell me what he said."

Zach glanced out the window for a moment then looked back at Marika. "He wants to be with Jesse when they execute him."

A silent "oh" came from Marika's lips. She stood rigid, thought for a moment, then spoke. "I want to go, too."

"No, Marika, no. You're not up to it."

"Yes, I am, Zach. I know why Pete wants to go. He wants Jesse to know someone's there who loves him. I want him to know I'm there and I love him, too."

"Are you sure?"

"Yes!"

"All right. I'll arrange it. I don't want you to go alone, though. I'll come along."

"Thanks. I'd appreciate that."

"Think I'd better arrange something else, too."

"What's that?"

"I've been thinking about what happens after … you know, after two days from now. I have a family mausoleum. I'll see that Jesse's buried there. The building is locked. His body would be safe from prying eyes and tampering."

Marika began crying again. Zach called the doctor.

CHAPTER TWENTY-NINE

The guard came to Jesse's cell carrying shackles and handcuffs. "Okay, Cartland. Let's get ready for your last ride. You know the drill."

Jesse stood with his hands behind his back facing away from the guard. The guard put on the handcuffs tightly so they cut into Jesse's wrists. He winced in pain.

"Is that too tight?" the guard laughed. "I don't want you to lose your new bracelets so I think we'll keep it that way." The guard put the shackles around Jesse's ankles then turned him around rapidly. Jesse got tangled in the shackles and fell hard to his knees.

He gasped then looked up at the guard. "My friend, you may not believe it, but I came to help you, too."

"Yeah, sure. You called for a revolution. You said we were oppressing people."

"I believe you are just as much victims of this system as anyone else. I came, in part, to show you a better way to live." Jesse spoke softly.

The guard was puzzled. "Now you're going to die, and there's nothing you can do about it. Why aren't you upset?"

"Let's say it's part of my job."

Shaking his head, the guard helped Jesse up, loosened his handcuffs; then led him toward the back door.

"Coast clear?" he called to the guard at the door.

"Yeah. All the reporters are chasing Chapin around town. We can transport Cartland."

They escorted Jesse to the van. A guard was waiting inside. The van pulled out of the driveway and headed for the regional prison.

The guard, looking bored with his assignment, said nothing. Jesse looked out the window, trying to take in all the countryside as they drove toward their destination. His Father had made a beautiful world. He savored this last chance to enjoy the bright sunshine and lush green fields before enduring the pain he knew lay ahead.

At last they arrived at the prison. The gates swung open. Several guards were waiting to receive Jesse. He saw their faces hard with hate staring in the window at him. He bowed his head. *Father, you and I both know these people don't understand why I'm here. Please be patient with them, and help them grasp what my purpose is.*

The doors opened and several guards grabbed Jesse, pulling him from the van. They started shoving him roughly toward the door. Jesse tripped again. A guard came out the door and caught Jesse. "I'll take it from here, boys. You go on back to your duties."

Once inside the door, the guard stopped and pulled out a key. "Let's get those leg irons off so you can walk better, Mr. Cartland." The guard unlocked the shackles.

"Now we'll get you processed." He gently led Jesse through the formalities, then took him to his cell.

Jesse turned after being led into the cell. "Who are you?"

"Name's Spencer, Mr. Cartland. You healed my niece some months back. She was confined to a wheelchair for quite some time, now she's out running track. I'll always be grateful to you for that."

"Will I see you again?"

"Yes, sir, you sure will. I asked for this duty. I guess you realize you're not the most popular guy with some of the folks around here." Spencer laughed. "Thought I'd better be the one to take care of you while you're here. Now try to relax. A meal will be coming in a bit."

Jesse eyed his surroundings. Not much to look at—a cot, a toilet and a sink. He smiled, thinking his heavenly home. Such a contrast! Then he thought about his life. The joy of being able to heal people of their afflictions, of being able to plant love in people's hearts brought a warm feeling to him. But there were also the other times when he could see hate in men's eyes. When he was run out of his hometown. When he was arrested. He realized his life was much like others with its ups and downs. His death would be different, though.

Spencer interrupted his thoughts. "Your lawyer's here, Mr. Cartland.

The door clanked shut behind Matt. "How are you doing, Jesse?"

"Better now that you're here. It's nice to see a friendly face."

"Are they treating you all right? Because if they're not...."

Jesse smiled and put up a hand. "Everything's okay.

I have a very nice guard who's looking after me."

"Good. I thought it would be wise to go over procedures with you so you'll know what to expect."

"You mean when they execute me?"

"Yeah." Matt looked down and cleared his throat, then looked back at Jesse. "The event will occur at midnight. That gives the governor and me plenty of time to stop things in case new evidence comes to light."

"It won't, so continue."

"You'll be led into a room containing what looks like a surgical table. They'll strap you down and, at the appointed time, they'll administer a sedative so you'll go to sleep. You won't be aware of anything else, Jesse. You won't feel any pain, nothing."

"What will actually kill me?"

"They'll give you a muscle paralyzer, then some potassium. The potassium will stop your heart, and that'll be it." Matt looked down again, clenching his jaw.

"Anything else?"

"There will be observers. Some reporters will be there. Jack and I will be there as your attorneys, of course. As I understand it, Marika also wants to come to lend support. Zach's bringing her and someone else. They wouldn't give me the other person's name."

"I know who it is. It's going to be tough on all of you to see this." Jesse grasped Matt's chin so that Matt was looking him in the eye. "You all must remember that something wonderful will happen when I die. Keep that thought close to your heart."

"I'll try, Jesse, but I keep hoping we'll find a way to prevent your death." Matt pulled away. "I gotta go now." He motioned for the guard and took a handkerchief from his pocket as he left the cell.

Spencer brought Jesse a meal. Jesse ate then fell exhausted onto his cot.

He woke the next morning, the sun shining in his eyes. He sat up trying to orient himself, then realized where he was. He lifted his head up to the barred window and looked out. It was a beautiful day. He smiled at the contrast—the bright blue sky outside, the gray cell inside. *Father, just a little while and I will be with you. Help me bear this last little bit.* Spencer brought his breakfast.

As he was eating, someone in one of the other cells yelled out, "Yo! You down there! The new boy! Did I hear someone say you were Jesse Cartland?"

"Yes, you did. I am Jesse Cartland."

"Hey, guys, guess what? We got us a celebrity."

The other inmates started whistling and yelling. A second inmate yelled, "Pipe down! Spencer'll come, and we'll all be in trouble."

After the noise died down, the first inmate said, "I don't understand. If you're so big at performing miracles, why don't you just bust out of here?"

"I need to be here now," Jesse replied.

"Well, I sure don't need to be. If you don't want to leave, why don't you spring me?" The first inmate howled with laughter.

"Leave him be." The second inmate spoke sharply. "My sister saw one of his meetings. She told me about him. He's never done anything but try to help people. Can you say the same thing?"

"Why, I'm pure as the driven snow and totally innocent, just like everybody else on this cell block." Everyone started laughing.

"Mister Cartland," said the second inmate, "if you could think kindly of me even for a minute, it sure would be a comfort to me."

"Friend," replied Jesse, "you'll soon find out that I'll do more than that for you."

# # #

The few days passed slowly for Jesse. He was anxious to complete his mission and be in the presence of his Father again. He spent hours in prayer for his friends, asking that they wouldn't feel lost when he died. He thought of his family and his childhood. He thought of his travels with Pete and the other men.

He pictured all the healings he'd performed, all the crowds he'd talked to. Hopeful faces of those whose lives he'd touched, like a fast-forwarded film, sped through his mind. He also thought of his death and what it would mean to the world he was in now.

# # #

The night of the execution, Pete met Marika and Zach in the parking lot. He wore a cap over his dyed-black hair. The stubble on his face hid his fair complexion.

"Pete?" Marika asked.

Pete held a finger to his lips. Zach gave him a fake ID card, then they headed toward the door. As they got closer, Marika swayed. Zach caught her.

"Are you sure you want to go through with this?"

"Absolutely. Put your arm around me, and I'll be fine." Zach supported Marika as they entered the prison.

They were ushered into the appropriate room. Reporters were already in another observation room. They waited to see Jesse.

# # #

Spencer stood in front of Jesse's cell. "It's time, Mr. Cartland."

Jesse turned his back, expecting to be cuffed and shackled. Spencer merely opened the cell door and led him out. "I don't think we'll need the hardware," he said.

Jesse nodded his thanks.

They walked to the chamber. As Matt had said, it contained a table.

Spencer came to his side. "Please, sir, climb up on the table now."

Jesse lay down with arms outstretched. His wrists were strapped down on the armrests, ankles strapped down on the table. The technician inserted needles in both his arms, then left the room.

Matt, Aaron Chapin, the warden and a physician were in an anteroom along with the execution team. Phones were hanging on the wall in case a call came through to stop the procedure.

Chapin studied some apparatus also attached to the wall. "You guys still using this old machine to administer the drugs?"

One of the men spoke. "Yep. No need to change. We hardly ever have any death penalty cases that reach this stage."

The warden signaled for the curtain to be drawn back.

Marika gasped when she saw Jesse, then tried to smile to cheer him. "Marika, he can't see you. It's a one-way glass," Zach explained.

The warden told Jesse he could make a statement.

Jesse turned his head toward the window where Pete,

Marika and Zach sat. "My friends, something wonderful will happen in three days." His voice resounded in the chamber.

Pete was bewildered. What did Jesse mean? He wanted desperately to accept what Jesse said, but what wonderful thing could possibly happen in three days? He wanted another chance to prove himself to Jesse, but he could see the room and the instrument of ultimate punishment. He'd have no more chances to show Jesse how much he believed in him.

The hand on the clock hit twelve. The warden gave the sign, and the technician began administering the sedative. Jesse prayed *My Lord and my God*! Then he knew only blackness.

Matt watched as the clock hand hit twelve. He saw the warden signal the execution team and was glad when Jesse went into a peaceful sleep. Then the phone rang. Everyone jumped. The warden yelled for the technician to stop as he picked up the phone. He listened, banged it against his hand a few times then listened again.

"No one there. Are either of you lawyers expecting a call from the governor." Both shook their heads. "Then check this phone out, Spencer." He nodded at the man standing at the device. "Continue."

The man finished administering the sedative. "I'm ready for the second drug now. This will paralyze his muscles."

"Can't you wait just a few minutes?" asked Matt. "The governor's office might be trying to get through."

The warden nodded.

The phone rang again. The warden banged the receiver against his palm. "Spencer, what's going on? There's no one on the line."

"They're fixing it now, sir. Just a glitch in the line."

After a few moments, they received word that the phone was repaired. "We'll wait a few minutes, then continue," said the warden.

"I'm so glad Jesse's asleep," said Matt. "I'd hate for him to have to hear that phone ring, then find out the governor's not on the other end."

"Administering the second drug now," said the technician.

Jesse's muscles rippled. Suddenly he began convulsing. The doctor ran through the door to Jesse's side.

"What's going on?" Pete yelled. "I thought Jesse was just going to sleep!" Zach and Marika sat frozen with horror as their friend's body strained against the straps. The ankle and wrist restraints bit into Jesse's flesh as the seizures continued. His mouth contorted into a horrible grimace.

Chapin yelled into the chamber. "Doctor, what's happening?"

"The machine must have gotten out of sequence with all the interruptions."

The technician was frantically pushing buttons. "He's not getting the paralyzer. He's getting the potassium."

"Fix it! Now!"

"There's nothing I can do."

Jesse continued twisting on the table in ghastly contortions of death. Matt looked away from Jesse's tortured body. Zach caught Marika as she slumped over in a faint. Pete banged on the window with his fists. "Stop it! Stop it! This is inhuman!"

Jesse finally relaxed. The doctor listened to his chest with a stethoscope, then looked at the warden and nodded.

"He's dead?" the warden asked.

"Yes."

Chapin charged the man at the machine. "That'll be the last prisoner you execute. I'll see that you're dismissed for incompetence."

"Back off, Chapin," growled the warden. "You heard him. The machine malfunctioned."

"Yes, and it malfunctioned with a roomful of reporters watching. I can hardly wait to see the headlines tomorrow."

The warden turned to leave the room. "Are you coming? I have to announce the time of death officially."

"All right. But make it plain there will be no questions at this time."

"Let me in!" Someone pounded at the door. Matt recognized Jack's voice and ran to open the door.

"Am I in time?" Jack paused for breath. "Is Jesse still alive?" Then Jack saw the still form on the table. "Oh, no! No! This can't be!"

Jack turned to Matt, a look of deep distress on his face. "Matt, why didn't anybody pick up the phone? I called a couple of times from the cell phone while I was driving."

"The phone did ring twice, but the warden said there was no one on the line."

Jack started toward the warden, furious. "What did you do to the phone?"

"Honest, mister," the warden backed away, "I didn't hear anybody on the other end of the line. It's my job to stop executions if there's any reason at all to do so."

Matt grabbed Jack's arm. "He's right, Jack. He stopped the proceedings every time the phone rang. Why were you calling?"

"I decided to do some last minute digging to see if I could come up with anything at all that might stop Jesse's execution. Guess what I found out?" He turned to Chapin, a venomous look on his face. "Jeb Kerry committed suicide a few days ago!"

"What?" Matt took a giant step toward Chapin, grabbed him by the lapels and threw him against the wall. He pressed his face close to Chapin's. "Did you know about this?"

For once, Chapin was frightened and unable to speak.

"Tell me the truth, you piece of slime!" Matt tightened his grip.

Chapin, choking in Matt's grasp, nodded. Matt loosened his grip. Chapin slid to the floor. Matt stood over him. "You knew you were in trouble because your star witness was dead, so you said nothing. As far as I'm concerned, you're guilty of murder, Aaron Chapin."

Matt and Jack turned back to Jesse's body as the attendant prepared it for transport.

Pete heard the shouting from the anteroom. He heard Jack say that Jeb Kerry was dead. He'd just seen his friend die a terrible death. Now to find out it might have been prevented! It was too much for him. He headed toward the door.

Zach looked up from attending to Marika. "Where are you going?"

"I'm going to punch Chapin's lights out for starters, then I'll improvise as I work my way down his body."

Zach jumped up and put himself between Pete and the door. "Don't do this, Pete. Chapin still has power. He'll trump up a charge against you, and you'll end up like Jesse. Go back to the rest of the men. Tell them what you've seen. They'll need a leader now more than ever."

Pete knew Zach was right. He looked back at Jesse before he left. He saw red marks from the restraints on Jesse's ankles and wrists—indelible imprints of a criminal on the body of a perfectly innocent man.

# # #

The warden stood in front of a microphone in the press area ready to make his announcement. Some of the reporters were still shaken after witnessing Jesse's death, but they sat with pads ready to take notes. Cameramen were focusing on the warden's image in their viewfinders.

"At twelve a.m." the warden intoned, "the procedure was initiated on Mr. Jesse Cartland. At 12:20 a.m., Mr. Cartland was pronounced dead." The warden stepped from the microphone.

"What went wrong during the execution?" one of the reporters shouted.

The warden leaned his head back toward the mike. "No questions will be taken at this time." He left hurriedly, reporters continuing to shout out questions after him.

Dogs started barking in the distance. The reporters heard a dull rumbling sound. They looked at each other. What was it? The floor began shaking. Everyone screamed and ran for cover.

The metal cell doors clanked. Prisoners dived under their cots. The warden and Chapin stood beneath a doorway bracing themselves against the frame. The walls creaked around them. They could hear dishes in the nearby kitchen crashing to the floor. Finally the shaking stopped.

"Quite a coincidence, isn't it?" the warden's voice shook. "An earthquake right after I announced Cartland's death."

"You don't think the two are connected, do you?"

"I can't help but wonder. I read stories about what Cartland did. What if he really was the Rescuer?"

Chapin snorted. "I don't believe in any 'Rescuer'." He paused for a moment, looking at the warden. "However, if he was, we'll be remembered for all time for making one of the biggest mistakes any two men ever made."

# # #

Spencer'd been knocked flat by the earthquake. He got up, dusted himself off and smiled. Jesse was the Rescuer!

CHAPTER THIRTY

Chapin returned to his office. It was still dark outside. He needed time to think, to sort things out, before his office got busy. He'd just seen a man die a horrible death—a death he knew he was partly responsible for. There was nothing he could do about that now, but what about the earthquake? Was it a coincidence or not that the earth shook after Cartland died? Chapin's hand trembled slightly as he poured himself a cup of coffee. He kept remembering the warden's question. What if Cartland was the Rescuer? Chapin shook his head to clear it. Ridiculous! The Rescuer was a myth. Chapin sat in his chair, eyes closed. He leaned back enjoying the aroma of the fresh-brewed coffee, trying to relax. Suddenly he sat bolt upright. He dialed a number.

"This is Chapin. Do we know what they're going to do with Cartland's body? ... Really? ... Okay, after the body's placed there, I want you to put guards in front of the mausoleum. Nobody gets near Cartland's body, understand?"

What did Cartland mean when he said something wonderful would happen in three days? Jesse's followers might be up to some funny business like removing his body from the grave to make it look like he came back to life as another one of his miracles. Chapin would see that they didn't succeed.

Chapin pulled a pad and pencil out of his desk drawer. *Might as well get busy on some damage control ideas.* The press would be all over him later today.

#

Marika sat motionless in her room with curtains drawn. It was morning. She was still wearing the clothes she'd worn to Jesse's execution. There was a light tap at the door. Zach's voice called to her.

"Marika, may I come in? I have some breakfast for you." Zach opened the door and carried in a tray containing cereal and juice. Marika still didn't move.

Zach laid the tray on the nightstand. "Marika, I'm worried about you. Please try to eat something." Zach poured some milk on the cereal. "Would you like me to feed you?"

"Don't be ridiculous. Get out of the room and leave me alone. I don't feel like eating."

"Can I at least open the curtains and let some light in?"

"Don't you dare touch those curtains! There is no light any more! Jesse's dead!" Marika began sobbing. "Please, get out!"

Zach left the room shaking his head. He called the doctor.

The doctor came and examined Marika, then talked with Zach. "I'll give you some medicine for her, but don't leave the bottle in her room. She's very depressed and may try to commit suicide by taking an overdose. Watch her closely. In fact I'd recommend that you get a private nurse for her."

"I'll do that, doctor. Thank you." Zach saw the doctor to the door.

As the doctor left, he said, "She's lucky to have a friend like you."

"We both just lost the best friend we'll ever have. I'm trying to help her through the rough spots."

Zach was overwhelmed. He'd have to arrange for Marika's care and also for Jesse's burial. Eyes red from lack of sleep; he watched the birds flying from tree to tree in the morning sunlight, singing their songs, as if the world were the same. A tear fell from his eye. Nothing would ever be the same. He wiped his cheek and got on the phone.

Later he tapped on Marika's door again. A young woman followed him into the room. "Marika, this is Miss Marsh. She'll be helping you out for a while."

Marika looked from Zach to Miss Marsh. "You mean she'll have custody of me for a while."

"I'm here to help, Mrs. Madsen." Miss Marsh stepped forward.

Zach waved her back. "I also wanted to tell you that I've made the arrangements for Jesse. He'll be placed quietly in the mausoleum. There will be no ceremony. I don't want the press crawling all over the cemetery yelling and trying to take pictures."

"That's the first thing you've said that makes me feel better."

"Unfortunately Aaron Chapin insists on putting guards in front of the tomb. I don't know what he thinks might happen."

"I can't talk about this any more, Zach. Please leave. And you, Miss Marsh or Marshmallow or whatever your name is, you can do what you like."

For a few days, Marika would neither eat nor take her medicine. Zach was getting very worried. The nurse could do nothing with her. He decided to call the doctor again after breakfast. He was banging about the kitchen scrambling some eggs when he heard a voice.

"That smells delicious."

Zach turned, surprised. "Marika! What are you doing out of your room?"

"Is that any way to greet me? I thought you'd be pleased to see me out of my dark hole." Marika was bathed, dressed and made up.

"I am, believe me. What made you come out?"

"I was thinking about Jesse. He found me in a dark room and gave me hope. He brought me out into the light. I thought staying in the light was the least I could do for him."

"You're right. Is there anything you'd like to do today?"

"Yes. I'd like to go to Jesse's grave."

"Do you think that's wise? You've been so upset."

"I need to do this, Zach. I'll be fine."

"Okay, let me bring the car around, and I'll take you."

"No, Zach. I want to go alone. I don't even want Marshmallow tagging along."

Zach smiled at the name; then asked, "Are you sure you're up to it?"

"Positive. I'll eat something then be on my way."

"Be careful of Chapin's guards."

Marika parked the car and walked toward the mausoleum. She wanted to be near Jesse again even if it was only to touch the door of the tomb. The earth rumbled and shook. Another earthquake! Marika grabbed at a tree for support. The tremor soon stopped. Marika waited for her frayed nerves to settle then finished the walk to her destination.

The guards were nowhere to be seen. The quake had opened the tomb door. Marika went inside and looked around. Where was Jesse's body? It wasn't where Zach had said it would be. She searched the stone room frantically. There was no place to hide a body. Where could Jesse be? She started crying. Chapin probably took Jesse. He'd cheated her out of even the small comfort of being close to Jesse's remains. Marika left the tomb and leaned against the door, still weeping.

"Ma'am, why are you crying?"

Marika looked in the direction of the voice. A man stood before her. *Good, he's probably a caretaker. Maybe he knows where Jesse is.*

"Please, sir, can you tell me where they took Jesse Cartland's body?" This man was her one hope. *Please know where Jesse is!*

The man spoke gently, "Marika."

His voice caressed her ears. She thrilled to the sound of it. She knew that gentle tone, but it couldn't be! Then she saw his warm brown eyes, his tender smile. It was! It was Jesse! Jesse was alive! He was standing before her!

She sank to her knees, her face radiant with joy, her arms outstretched. "My Rescuer!" Her heart was so full of gladness she felt it would burst. Jesse's smile broadened as she stretched out her arms toward him. She wanted to touch him, to make absolutely sure he was really alive again.

Suddenly she felt strange. Every cell in her body began to quiver. What was happening? Jesse was drifting away. He was getting smaller. Then she realized she was in the vortex again. "Stop! Wait! Jesse!" She could see buildings, then cities, then continents, then she was back in the mist with Father.

"Father, why did you take me away? Please, I want to go back."

"What do you think of my son, Christine?"

"He's wonderful. He healed me and helped me understand that, even if bad things happen, your son is there to help."

"You've learned your lesson well, little one. Now you're ready to go back to your life."

"No, please, Father. I don't want to leave my new life. I want to find out what happened to Jesse and the other men."

"Patience, little one. You need to go back and finish your life. You have much to offer now."

"You're right, of course, Father. I'll go back and do your work, but will I ever find out what happened to Jesse and the others?"

"Yes, Christine. Someday you'll return, and I'll finish the story for you." Another presence floated into the mist. "Ah, there's Carello. Please take Christine back now."

Carello guided Christine back through the red cloud. She heard a voice calling.

"Nurse! Nurse; come quick! She's opening her eyes."

Christine blinked a few times, then focused on a face looking down on her. It was Carol, the Telecare worker.

"Christine, do you know who I am?" Carol asked.

"Of course, you're Carol."

"Thank heavens." Carol took her hand. "You gave us quite a scare, young lady. I came to the house to check on you, and there you were, half hanging out of bed. I called the ambulance right away, and the doctors did the rest."

The nurse came in to check on Christine. "I've called your doctor. He'll be here in a while." She took Christine's blood pressure and fussed with her pillow. Christine smiled when she saw the nurse's name badge. Her last name was Marsh.

"Marshmallow, you don't need to coddle me. I'll call you when I need you." Carol and the nurse looked at each other, worried. "It's all right, ladies. I'm in my right mind. Carol, I want you to do me a favor. Is there a Bible in the nightstand?"

Carol opened the drawer. "Why, yes there is."

"Please read me the passage where Mary Magdalene goes to Jesus' tomb and finds him alive." Carol flipped through the pages, then paused. Christine saw the questioning look on her face. "Yes, Carol, I really do want you to read to me from the Bible," Christine smiled. "I want to hear about a friend."

Carol settled herself in the chair. "Now on the first day of the week Mary Magdalene came to the tomb early…" As Carol read, Christine thought about Jesse and the other people she had met on her adventure. She thought about the wonder of Jesse's words and works.

She smiled and looked out the window at the bright, new world she would work in. She looked forward to many adventures in this world. And she looked forward to the day she would return to hear the rest of Jesse's story. *Thank you, Father.*

THE END